D0302037

Jeff Lindsay is the author of the acclaimed Dexter novels, now adapted into an award-winning TV series. In addition, Jeff's plays have been performed on the stage in New York and London. Outside of his writing, Jeff is a musician and karate enthusiast. He lives in Cape Coral, Florida, with his family.

DEARLY DEVOTED DEXTER

JEFF LINDSAY

An Orion paperback

First published in Great Britain in 2005
by Orion
This paperback edition published in 2006
by Orion Books Ltd,
Orion House, 5 Upper St Martin's Lane,
London WC2H 9EA

An Hachette Livre UK company

A CIP catalogue record for this book is
available from the British Library.

ISBN 978-0-7528-7788-4

Printed and bound in Great Britain by
Clays Ltd, St Ives plc

The Orion Publishing Group's policy is to use papers that
are natural, renewable and recyclable products and
made from wood grown in sustainable forests. The logging
and manufacturing processes are expected to conform to
the environmental regulations of the country of origin.

www.orionbooks.co.uk

For Tommie and Gus,
who have certainly waited long enough

ACKNOWLEDGMENTS

Nothing is remotely possible without Hilary.

I would also like to thank Julio, the Broccolis, Deacon and Einstein and, as always, Bear, Pook, and Tinky.

Additionally, I am indebted to Jason Kaufman for his steady and wise guiding hand, and to Nick Ellison, who has made all the difference.

CHAPTER 1

IT'S THAT MOON AGAIN, SLUNG SO FAT AND LOW in the tropical night, calling out across a curdled sky and into the quivering ears of that dear old voice in the shadows, the Dark Passenger, nestled snug in the backseat of the Dodge K-car of Dexter's hypothetical soul.

That rascal moon, that loudmouthed leering Lucifer, calling down across the empty sky to the dark hearts of the night monsters below, calling them away to their joyful playgrounds. Calling, in fact, to that monster right there, behind the oleander, tiger-striped with moonlight through the leaves, his senses all on high as he waits for just the right moment to leap from the shadows. It is Dexter in the dark, listening to the terrible whispered suggestions that come pouring down breathlessly into my shadowed hiding place.

My dear dark other self urges me to pounce – now – sink my moonlit fangs into the oh-so-vulnerable flesh on the far side of the hedge. But the time is not right and so I wait, watching cautiously as my unsuspecting victim creeps past, eyes wide, knowing that something is watching but not knowing that I am *here*, only three steely feet away in the hedge. I could so easily slide out like the knife blade I am, and work my wonderful magic – but I wait, suspected but unseen.

One long stealthy moment tiptoes into another and still I wait for just the right time; the leap, the outstretched hand, the cold glee as I see the terror spread across the face of my victim –

But no. Something is not right.

And now it is Dexter's turn to feel the queasy prickling of eyes on his back, the flutter of fear as I become more certain that something is now hunting *me*. Some other night stalker is feeling the sharp interior drool as he watches *me* from somewhere nearby – and I do not like this thought.

And like a small clap of thunder the gleeful hand comes down out of nowhere and onto *me* blindingly fast, and I glimpse the gleaming teeth of a nine-year-old neighbor boy. 'Gotcha! One, two, three on Dexter!' And with the savage speed of the very young the rest of them are there, giggling wildly and shouting at me as I stand in the bushes humiliated. It is over. Six-year-old Cody stares at me, disappointed, as though Dexter the Night God has let down his high priest. Astor, his nine-year-old sister, joins in the hooting of the kids before they skitter off into the dark once more, to new and more complicated hiding places, leaving me so very alone in my shame.

Dexter did not kick the can. And now Dexter is *It*. Again.

You may wonder, how can this be? How can Dexter's night hunt be reduced to this? Always before there has been some frightful twisted predator awaiting the special attention of frightful twisted Dexter – and here I am, stalking an empty Chef Boyardee ravioli can that is guilty of nothing worse than bland sauce. Here I am, frittering away precious time losing a game I have not played since I was ten. Even worse, I am IT.

'One. Two. Three – ' I call out, ever the fair and honest gamesman.

How can this be? How can Dexter the Demon feel the weight of that moon and not be off among the entrails, slicing the life from someone who needs very badly to feel the edge of Dexter's keen judgment? How is it possible on this kind of night for the Cold Avenger to refuse to take the Dark Passenger out for a spin?

'Four. Five. Six.'

Harry, my wise foster father, had taught me the careful balance of Need and Knife. He had taken a boy in whom he saw the unstoppable need to kill – no changing that – and Harry had molded him into a man who only killed the killers; Dexter the no-bloodhound, who hid behind a human-seeming face and tracked down the truly naughty serial killers who killed without code. And I would have been one of them, if not for the Harry Plan. *There are plenty of people who deserve it, Dexter*, my wonderful foster-cop-father had said.

'Seven. Eight. Nine.'

He had taught me how to find these special playmates, how to be sure they deserved a social call from me and my Dark Passenger. And even better, he taught me how to get away with it, as only a cop could teach. He had helped me to build a plausible hidey-hole of a life, and drummed into me that I must fit in, always, be relentlessly normal in all things.

And so I had learned how to dress neatly and smile and brush my teeth. I had become a perfect fake human, saying the stupid and pointless things that humans say to each other all day long. No one suspected what crouched behind my perfect imitation smile. No one except my foster sister, Deborah, of course, but she was coming to accept the real me. After all, I could have been much worse. I could have been a vicious raving monster who killed and killed and left towers of rotting flesh in my wake. Instead, here I was on the side of truth, justice, and the American way. Still a monster, of course, but I cleaned up nicely afterward, and I was OUR monster, dressed in red, white, and blue 100 percent synthetic virtue. And on those nights when the moon is loudest I find the others, those who prey on the innocent and do not play by the rules, and I make them go away in small, carefully wrapped pieces.

This elegant formula had worked well through years of happy inhumanity. In between playdates I maintained my perfectly average lifestyle from a persistently ordinary apartment. I was never late to work, I made the right jokes with co-workers, and I was useful and unobtrusive in all things, just as Harry had taught me. My life as an android was neat, balanced, and had real redeeming social value.

Until now. Somehow, here I was on a just-right night playing kick the can with a flock of children, instead of playing Slice the Slasher with a carefully chosen friend. And in a little while, when the game was over, I would take Cody and Astor into their mother, Rita's, house, and she would bring me a can of beer, tuck the kids into bed, and sit beside me on the couch.

How could this be? Was the Dark Passenger slipping into early retirement? Had Dexter mellowed?

Had I somehow turned the corner of the long dark hall and come out on the wrong end as Dexter Domestic? Would I ever again place that one drop of blood on the neat glass slide, as I always did – my trophy from the hunt?

'Ten! Ready or not, here I come!'

Yes, indeed. Here I came.

But to what?

It started, of course, with Sergeant Doakes. Every superhero must have an archenemy, and he was mine. I had done absolutely nothing to him, and yet he had chosen to hound me, harry me from my good work. Me and my shadow. And the irony of it: me, a hardworking blood-spatter-pattern analyst for the very same police force that employed him – we were on the same team. Was it fair for him to pursue me like this, merely because every now and then I did a little bit of moonlighting?

I knew Sergeant Doakes far better than I really wanted to, much more than just from our professional connection. I had made it my business to find out about him for one simple reason: he had never liked me, in spite of the fact that I take great pride in being charming and cheerful on a world-class level. But it almost seemed like Doakes could tell it was all fake; all my handmade heartiness bounced off him like June bugs off a windshield.

This naturally made me curious. I mean, really; what kind of person could possibly dislike me? And so I had studied him just a little, and I found out. The kind of person who could possibly dislike Debonair Dexter was forty-eight, African American, and held the department's record for the bench press. According to the casual gossip I had picked up, he was an army vet, and since coming to the department had been involved in several fatal shootings, all of which Internal Affairs had judged to be righteous.

But more important than all this, I had discovered first hand that somewhere behind the deep anger that always burned in his eyes there lurked an echo of a chuckle from my own Dark Passenger. It was just a tiny little chime of a very small bell, but I was sure. Doakes was sharing space with something, just like I was. Not the same thing, but something very similar, a panther to my tiger. Doakes was a cop, but he was also a cold killer. I had no real proof of this, but I was as sure as I could be without seeing him crush a jaywalker's larynx.

A reasonable being might think that he and I could find some common ground; have a cup of coffee and compare our Passengers, exchange trade talk and chitchat about dismemberment techniques. But no: Doakes wanted me dead. And I found it difficult to share his point of view.

Doakes had been working with Detective LaGuerta at the time of her somewhat suspicious death, and since then his feelings toward me had grown to be a bit more active than simple loathing. Doakes was convinced that I'd had something to do with LaGuerta's death. This was totally untrue and completely unfair. All I had done was watch – where's the harm in that? Of course I had helped the real killer escape, but what could you expect? What kind of person would turn in his own brother? Especially when he did such neat work.

Well, live and let live, I always say. Or quite often, anyway. Sergeant Doakes could think what he wanted to think, and that was fine with me. There are still very few laws against thinking, although I'm sure they're working hard on that in Washington. No, whatever suspicions the good sergeant had about me, he was welcome to them. But now that he had decided to act on his impure thoughts my life was a shambles. Dexter Derailed was fast becoming Dexter Demented.

And why? How had this whole nasty mess begun? All I had done was try to be myself.

CHAPTER 2

THERE ARE NIGHTS EVERY NOW AND THEN WHEN the Dark Passenger really must get out to play. It's like walking a dog. You can ignore the barking and scratching at the door for only so long, and then you must take the beast outside.

Not too long after Detective LaGuerta's funeral, there came a time when it seemed reasonable to listen to the whispers from the backseat and start to plan a small adventure.

I had located a perfect playmate, a very plausible real estate salesman named MacGregor. He was a happy, cheerful man who loved selling houses to families with children. Especially young boys – MacGregor was extremely fond of boys between the ages of five and seven. He had been lethally fond of five that I was sure of, and quite likely several more. He was clever and careful, and without a visit from Dark Scout Dexter he would probably stay lucky for a long time. It's hard to blame the police, at least this once. After all, when a young child goes missing, very few people would say, 'Aha! Who sold his family their house?'

But of course, very few people are Dexter. This is generally a good thing, but in this case it came in handy to be me. Four months after reading a story in the paper about a missing boy, I read a similar story.

The boys were the same age; details like that always ring a small bell and send a Mister Rogers whisper trickling through my brain: 'Hello, neighbor.'

And so I dug up the first story and compared. I noticed that in both cases the paper milked the grief of the families by mentioning that they had recently moved into new homes; I heard a small chuckle from the shadows, and I looked a little closer.

It really was quite subtle. Detective Dexter had to dig quite a bit, because at first there didn't seem to be any connection. The families in question were in different neighborhoods, which ruled out a great many possibilities. They went to different churches, different schools, and used different moving companies. But when the Dark Passenger laughs, somebody is usually doing something funny. And I finally found the connection; both houses had been listed with the same real estate agency, a small outfit in South Miami, with only one agent, a cheerful and friendly man named Randy MacGregor.

I dug a little more. MacGregor was divorced and lived alone in a small concrete-block house off Old Cutler Road in South Miami. He kept a twenty-six-foot cabin cruiser at Matheson Hammock Marina, which was relatively close to his house. The boat would also be an extremely convenient playpen, a way to get his little chums off alone on the bounding main where he would not be seen or heard while he explored, a real Columbus of pain. And for that matter, it would provide a splendid way to dispose of the messy leftovers; just a few miles out from Miami, the Gulf Stream provided a nearly bottomless dumping ground. No wonder the boys' bodies were never found.

The technique made such good sense that I wondered why I hadn't thought of it to recycle my own leftovers. Silly me; I only used my little boat for fishing and riding around the bay. And here MacGregor had come up with a whole new way to enjoy an evening on the water. It was a very neat idea, and it instantly moved MacGregor right to the top of my list. Call me unreasonable, even illogical since I generally have very little use for humans, but for some reason I care about kids. And when I find someone who preys on children it is very much as if they have slipped the Dark Maître d' twenty dollars to move to the front of the line. I would happily unclip the velvet rope and bring MacGregor right in – assuming he was doing what it looked like he was doing. Of course, I had to be absolutely certain. I had always tried to avoid slicing up the wrong person, and it would be a shame to start now, even with a real estate salesman. It occurred to me that the best way to make sure would be to visit the boat in question.

Happily for me, the very next day it was raining, as it generally rains every day in July. But this had the look of an all-day storm, which made it just what the Dexter ordered. I left my job at the Miami-Dade police forensics lab early and cut over to LeJeune, taking it all the way to Old Cutler Road. I turned left into Matheson Hammock; as I'd hoped, it seemed deserted. But about one hundred yards ahead I knew there was a guard booth, where someone would be waiting eagerly to take four dollars from me for the great privilege of entering the park. It seemed like a good idea not to make an appearance at the guard booth. Of course saving the four dollars was very important, but even more so was that on a rainy day in the middle of the week I might be just a little bit conspicuous, which is something I like to avoid, particularly in the course of my hobby.

On the left side of the road was a small parking lot that served the picnic area. An old coral-rock picnic shelter stood beside a lake on the right. I parked my car and pulled on a bright yellow foul-weather jacket. It made me feel very nautical, just the thing to wear for breaking into a homicidal pedophile's boat. It also made me highly visible, but I was not terribly worried about that. I would take the bicycle path that ran parallel to the road. It was screened in by mangroves, and in the unlikely event that the guard stuck his head out of the booth and into the rain, he would see nothing but a bright yellow blur jogging by. Just a determined runner out for his afternoon trot, come rain or shine.

And trot I did, moving about a quarter of a mile down the path. As I had hoped, there was no sign of life at the guard booth and I jogged to the large parking lot by the water. The last row of docks off to the right was home to a cluster of boats slightly smaller than the big sports fishermen and millionaires' toys tied up closer to the road. MacGregor's modest twenty-six footer, the *Osprey*, was near the end.

The marina was deserted and I went blithely through the gate in the chain-link fence, past a sign that said ONLY BOAT OWNERS PERMITTED ON DOCKS. I tried to feel guilty about violating such an important command, but it was beyond me. The lower half of the sign said NO FISHING OFF DOCKS OR IN MARINA AREA, and I promised myself that I would avoid fishing at all costs, which made me feel better about breaking the other rule.

The *Osprey* was five or six years old and showed only a few signs of wear from the Florida weather. The deck and rails were scrubbed clean and I was careful not to leave scuff marks as I climbed aboard. For some reason the locks on boats are never very complicated. Perhaps sailors are more honest than landlubbers. In any case, it took only a few seconds for me to pick the lock and slip inside the *Osprey*. The cabin did not have the musty smell of baked mildew that so many boats get when they are sealed up even for a few hours in the subtropical sun. Instead there was a faint tang of Pine-Sol in the air, as though someone had scrubbed so thoroughly that no germs or odors could hope to survive.

There was a small table, a galley, and one of those little TV/VCR units on a railed shelf with a stack of movies beside it: *Spider-Man*, *Brother Bear*, *Finding Nemo*. I wondered how many boys MacGregor had sent over the side to find Nemo. I dearly hoped that soon Nemo would find him. I stepped to the galley area and began to open drawers. One was filled with candy, the next with plastic action figures. And the third was absolutely crammed with rolls of duct tape.

Duct tape is a wonderful thing, and as I know very well, it can be used for many remarkable and useful things. But I did think that having ten rolls of it stuffed in a drawer on your boat was a bit excessive. Unless, of course, you were using it for some specific purpose that required a great deal of it. Perhaps a science project involving multiple young boys? Just a hunch, of course, based on the way I use it – not on young boys, of course, but on upstanding citizens like, for instance . . . MacGregor. His guilt had started to seem very likely, and the Dark Passenger flicked his dry lizard tongue with anticipation.

I went down the steps into the small forward area the salesman probably called the stateroom. It wasn't a terribly elegant bed, just a thin foam-rubber pad on a raised shelf. I touched the mattress and it crackled under the fabric; a rubber casing. I rolled the mattress to one side. There were four ring bolts screwed into the shelf, one on each corner. I lifted the hatch beneath the mattress.

One might reasonably expect to find a certain amount of chain on a boat. But the accompanying handcuffs did not strike me as being quite so nautical. Of course, there might be a very good explanation. It was possible that MacGregor used them on quarrelsome fish.

Under the chain and handcuffs there were five anchors. That could very well be a good idea on a yacht that was meant to cruise around the world, but it seemed a bit much for a small weekend boat. What on earth could they be for? If I was taking my little boat out into the deep water with a series of small bodies I wished to dispose of cleanly and completely, what would I do with so many anchors? And, of course, when you put it that way, it seemed obvious that the next time MacGregor went cruising with a little friend he would come back with only four anchors under the bunk.

I was certainly gathering enough small details to make a very interesting picture. Still life without children. But so far I had not found anything that could not be explained away as massive coincidence, and I needed to be absolutely sure. I had to have one overwhelmingly conclusive piece of evidence, something so completely unambiguous that it would satisfy the Harry Code.

I found it in a drawer to the right of the bunk.

There were three small drawers built into the bulkhead of the boat. The interior of the bottom one seemed to be a few inches shorter than the other two. It was possible that it was supposed to be, that it was shortened by the curve of the hull. But I have studied humans for many years now, and this has made me deeply suspicious. I pulled the drawer all the way out and, sure enough, there was a small secret compartment on the back end of the drawer. And inside the secret compartment –

Since I am not actually a real human being, my emotional responses are generally limited to what I have learned to fake. So I did not feel shock, outrage, anger, or even bitter resolve. They're very difficult emotions to do convincingly, and there was no audience to do them for, so why bother? But I did feel a slow cold wind from the Dark Backseat sweep up my spine and blow dry leaves over the floor of my lizard brain.

I could identify five different naked boys in the stack of photographs, arranged in a variety of poses, as if MacGregor was still searching for a defining style. And yes indeed, he really was a spendthrift with his duct tape. In one of the pictures, the boy looked like he was in a silver-gray cocoon, with only certain areas exposed. What MacGregor left exposed told me a great deal about him. As I had suspected, he was not the kind of man most parents would wish for a scout-master.

The photos were good quality, taken from many different angles. One series in particular stood out. A pale, flabby naked man in a black hood stood beside the tightly taped boy, almost like a trophy shot. From the shape and coloring of the body I was quite sure the man was MacGregor, even though the hood covered his face. And as I flipped through the pictures I had two very interesting thoughts. The first was, Aha! Meaning, of course, that there was absolutely no doubt about what MacGregor had been doing, and he was now the lucky Grand Prize Winner in the Dark Passenger's Clearinghouse Sweepstakes.

And the second thought, somewhat more troubling, was this: Who was taking the pictures?

There were too many different angles for the pictures to have been taken automatically. And as I flipped through them a second time I noticed, in two shots that had been snapped from above, the pointy toe of what looked like a red cowboy boot.

MacGregor had an accomplice. The word sounded so very Court TV, but there it was and I could not think of a better way to say it. He had not done all this alone. Someone had gone along and, if nothing else, had watched and taken pictures.

I blush to admit that I have some modest knowledge and talent in the area of semiregular mayhem, but I had never before run into anything like this. Trophy shots, yes – after all, I had my little box of slides, each with single drop of blood on them, to commemorate every one of my adventures. Perfectly normal to keep some kind of souvenir.

15

But to have a second person present, watching and taking pictures, turned a very private act into a kind of performance. It was absolutely indecent – the man was a pervert. If only I had been capable of moral outrage, I am quite sure I would have been full of it. As it was, though, I found myself more eager than ever to get viscerally acquainted with MacGregor.

It was stiflingly hot on the boat, and my wonderfully chic foul-weather suit was not helping. I felt like a bright yellow tea bag. I picked several of the clearest pictures and put them in my pocket. I returned the rest to their compartment, tidied the bunk, and went back up into the main cabin. As far as I could tell from peeking out the window – or did I have to call it a porthole? – there was no one lurking about and observing me in a furtive manner. I slipped out the door, making sure it locked behind me, and strolled off through the rain.

From the many movies I have seen over the years, I knew very well that walking in the rain is the correct setting for reflecting on human perfidy, and so I did just that. Oh that wicked MacGregor and his shutterbug friend. How could they be such vile wretches. That sounded about right, and it was all I could come up with; I hoped it was enough to satisfy the formula. Because it was far more fun to reflect on my own perfidy, and how I might feed it by arranging a playdate with MacGregor. I could feel a rising tide of dark delight flooding in from the deepest dungeons of Castle Dexter and building up at the spillways. And soon it would pour out on MacGregor.

There was no longer any room for doubt, of course. Harry himself would acknowledge that the photographs were more than enough proof, and an eager chuckle from the Dark Backseat sanctified the project. MacGregor and I would go exploring together. And then the special bonus of finding his friend in the cowboy boots – he would have to follow MacGregor as soon as possible, of course; no rest for the wicked. It was like a two-for-the-price-of-one sale, absolutely irresistible.

Filled with my happy thoughts, I didn't even notice the rain as I strode manfully and rapidly back to my car. I had a great deal to do.

CHAPTER 3

IT IS ALWAYS A BAD IDEA TO FOLLOW A REGULAR routine, particularly if you are a homicidal pedophile who has come to the attention of Dexter the Avenger. Happily for me, no one had ever given MacGregor this vital bit of information, and so it was quite easy for me to find him leaving his office at 6:30 PM, as he did every day. He came out the back door, locked it, and climbed into his big Ford SUV; a perfect vehicle for hauling people around to look at houses, or for carrying bundled-up little boys down to the dock. He pulled out into the traffic and I followed him home to his modest concrete-block house on S.W. 80th Street.

There was quite a bit of traffic going by the house. I turned onto a small side street half a block away and parked unobtrusively where I had a good view. There was a tall, thick hedge running down the far side of MacGregor's lot that would keep the neighbors from seeing anything that went on in his yard. I sat in my car and pretended to look at a map for about ten minutes, just long enough to scheme and be sure that he wasn't going anywhere. When he came out of his house and began to putter around the yard, shirtless and wearing a pair of battered madras shorts, I knew how I would do it. I headed for home to get ready.

In spite of the fact that I normally have a robust and healthy appetite, I always find it difficult to eat before one of my little adventures. My interior associate quivers with rising anticipation, the moon burbles louder and louder in my veins as the night slides over the city, and thoughts of food begin to seem so very ordinary.

And so instead of enjoying a leisurely high-protein dinner, I paced my apartment, eager to begin but still cool enough to wait, letting Daytime Dexter melt quietly into the background and feeling the intoxicating surge of power as the Dark Passenger slowly took the wheel and checked the controls. It was always an exhilarating sensation to allow myself to be pulled into the backseat and let the Passenger drive. Shadows seem to grow sharper edges and the darkness fades into a lively gray that brings everything into much sharper focus. Small sounds become loud and distinct, my skin tingles, my breath roars in and out, and even the air comes alive with smells that were certainly not noticeable during the boring and normal day. I was never more alive than when the Dark Passenger was driving.

I forced myself to sit in my easy chair and I held myself in, feeling the Need roll over me and leave behind a high tide of readiness. Each breath felt like a blast of cold air sweeping through me and pumping me up bigger and brighter until I was like an enormous invincible beacon of steel ready to slash through the now-dark city. And then my chair became a stupid little thing, a hiding place for mice, and only the night was big enough.

And it was time.

Out we went, into the bright night, the moonlight hammering at me and the dead-roses breath of the

Miami night blowing across my skin, and in almost no time at all I was there, in the shadows cast by MacGregor's hedge, watching and waiting and listening, just for now, to the caution that curled around my wrist and whispered *patience*. It seemed pathetic that he could not see something that gleamed as brightly as I did, and the thought gave me another surge of strength. I pulled on my white silk mask and I was ready to begin.

Slowly, invisibly, I moved from the darkness of the hedge and placed a child's plastic piano keyboard beneath his window, putting it under a gladiolus bush so it would not be seen immediately. It was bright red and blue, less than a foot long, and only had eight keys, but it would repeat the same four melodies endlessly until the battery died. I switched it on and stepped back into my place in the hedge.

'Jingle Bells' played, and then 'Old MacDonald.' For some reason, a key phrase was missing in each song, but the little toy piped on and into 'London Bridge' in the same cheerfully lunatic tone.

It was enough to make anyone crazy, but it probably had an extra effect on someone like MacGregor who lived for children. At any rate, I certainly hoped so. I had quite deliberately chosen the little keyboard to lure him out, and I sincerely hoped, in fact, that he would think he had been found out – and that a toy had come from Hell to punish him. After all, why shouldn't I enjoy what I do?

It seemed to work. We were only on the third repetition of 'London Bridge' when he came stumbling out of his house with a look of wide-eyed panic. He stood there for a moment, gaping around, his receding reddish hair looking like it had gone through a storm and his pale belly hanging slightly over the waist of his dingy pajama bottoms. He did not look terribly dangerous to me, but of course I was not a five-year-old boy.

After a moment, in which he stood with his mouth open, and scratched himself, and looked like he was modeling for a statue of the Greek god of Stupidity, MacGregor located the source of the sound – 'Jingle Bells' again by now. He stepped over and bent slightly to touch the little plastic keyboard and did not even have the time to be surprised before I had a noose of fifty-pound-test fishing line pulled tight around his throat. He straightened and thought he might struggle for a moment. I pulled tighter and he changed his mind.

'Stop fighting,' we said in our cold and commanding Passenger voice. 'You'll live longer.' And he heard his future in the words and thought he might change it, so I pulled hard on his leash and held it like that until his face turned dark and he dropped to his knees.

Just before he passed out completely I eased the pressure. 'Now do as you're told,' we said. He didn't say anything; he just choked in a few large and painful breaths, so I tweaked the line a touch. 'Understand?' we said, and he nodded so I let him breathe.

He did not try to fight anymore as I frog-marched him into the house for his car keys and then back out into his big SUV. I climbed into the seat behind him, holding the leash in a very tight grip and allowing him only enough breath to stay alive, for now.

'Start the car,' we told him, and he paused.

'What do you want?' he said in a voice that was rough with new-made gravel.

'Everything,' we said. 'Start the car.'

'I have money,' he said.

I pulled hard on his cord. 'Buy me a little boy,' we said. I held it tight for a few seconds, too tight for him to breathe and just long enough to let him know that *we* were in charge, *we* knew what he had done, and *we* would let him breathe only at our pleasure from now on, and when I loosened the line again he had nothing to say.

He drove as we told him to, back up S.W. 80th Street to Old Cutler Road and then south. There was almost no traffic this far out, not at this time of night, and we turned into a new development that had been going up on the far side of Snapper Creek. Construction had halted due to the owner's conviction for money laundering, and we would not be disturbed. We guided MacGregor through a half-built guard booth, around a small traffic circle, east toward the water, and to a halt beside a small trailer, the temporary office of the site, now left to teen thrill seekers and others, like me, who only wanted a little privacy.

We sat for just a moment, enjoying the view – moon over the water, with pedophile in noose in the foreground, very beautiful.

I got out and pulled MacGregor out after me, pulled him hard so that he fell to his knees and clawed at the line around his neck. For a moment I watched him choking and drooling in the dirt, his face turning dark again and his eyes going red. Then I pulled him to his feet and pushed him up the three wooden steps and into the trailer. By the time he had recovered enough to know what was going on, I had him tied to the top of a desk, hands and feet secured with duct tape.

MacGregor tried to speak and just coughed instead. I waited; now there was plenty of time. 'Please,' he said finally, in a voice like sand on glass, 'I'll give you whatever you want.'

'Yes, you will,' we said, and saw the sound of it cut into him, and even though he couldn't see it through my white silk mask we smiled. I took out the photos I had taken from his boat and showed them to him.

He stopped moving completely and his mouth hung open. 'Where did you get those?' he said, sounding rather petulant for someone who was about to be cut into small pieces.

'Tell me who took these pictures.'

'Why should I?' he said.

I used a pair of tin snips and cut off the first two fingers of his left hand. He thrashed and screamed and the blood came, which always makes me angry, so I shoved a tennis ball into his mouth and cut off the first two fingers of his right hand. 'No reason,' I said, and I waited for him to slow down just a little bit.

When he finally did, he rolled an eye to me and his face was filled with that understanding that comes when you have gone beyond pain into knowing that the rest of this was forever. I took the tennis ball out of his mouth.

'Who took the pictures?'

He smiled. 'I hope one of them was yours,' he said, which made the next ninety minutes a lot more rewarding.

CHAPTER 4

NORMALLY I FEEL PLEASANTLY MELLOW FOR several days after one of my Nights Out, but the very next morning after MacGregor's hasty exit I was still all aquiver with eagerness. I wanted very badly to find the photographer in the red cowboy boots and make a clean sweep of it. I am a tidy monster, and I do like to finish whatever I begin, and to know that someone was out there clumping around in those ridiculous shoes, carrying a camera that had seen far too much, made me anxious to follow those footprints and wrap up my two-part project.

Perhaps I had been too hasty with MacGregor; I should have given him a little more time and encouragement, and he would have told me everything. But it had seemed like something I could easily find by myself – when the Dark Passenger is driving, I am quite sure I can do anything. So far I have not been wrong, but it had put me in a bit of an awkward spot this time, and I had to find Mr. Boots on my own.

I knew from my earlier research that MacGregor did not have a social life beyond his occasional evening cruises. He belonged to a couple of business organizations, which was to be expected from a realtor, but I had not discovered anyone in particular that he seemed to pal around with. I also knew he had no criminal record, so there was no file to pull and search for known associates. The court records on his divorce simply listed 'irreconcilable differences' and left the rest to my imagination.

And there I was stuck; MacGregor had been a classic loner, and in all my careful study of him I had never seen an indication that he had any friends, companions, dates, mates, or cronies. No poker night with the boys – no boys at all, except for the young ones. No church group, no Elks, no neighborhood bar, no weekly square-dancing society – which might have explained the boots – no nothing, except the photographs with those stupid pointed red toes sticking out.

So who was Cowboy Bob, and how did I find him?

There was really only one place I could go for an answer, and that would have to be soon, before someone noticed that MacGregor was missing. In the distance I heard thunder rumble, and I glanced at the wall clock with surprise. Sure enough, it was 2:15, time for the daily afternoon storm. I had moped all the way through my lunch hour, very unlike me.

Still, the storm would once again give me a little cover, and I could stop for something to eat on the way back. So with my immediate future neatly and pleasantly planned, I headed out to the parking lot, got into my car, and drove south.

The rain had started by the time I got to Matheson Hammock, and so once again I pulled on my sporty yellow foul-weather gear and jogged down the path to MacGregor's boat.

I picked the lock again quite easily and slipped inside the cabin. During my first visit to the boat, I had been looking for signs that MacGregor was a pedophile. Now I was trying to find something a little bit more subtle, some small clue to the identity of MacGregor's photographer friend.

Since I had to start somewhere, I went back down to the sleeping area. I opened the drawer with the false bottom and flipped through the pictures again. This time I checked the back as well as the front. Digital photography has made sleuthing a great deal more difficult, and there were no marks of any kind on the pictures and no empty film packets with traceable serial numbers, either. Any clod in the world could simply download the pictures to his hard drive and print them out at will, even someone with such hideous taste in footgear. It didn't seem fair: Weren't computers supposed to makes things easier?

I closed the drawer and searched through the rest of the area, but there was nothing that I hadn't seen before. Somewhat discouraged, I went back upstairs to the main cabin. There were several drawers there, too, and I flipped through them. Videotapes, action figures, the duct tape – all things I had already noticed, and none of them would tell me anything. I pulled the stack of duct tape out, thinking, perhaps, that there was no sense in letting it go to waste. Idly, I turned over the bottom roll.

And there it was.

It really is better to be lucky than to be good. In a million years I could not have hoped for something this good. Stuck to the bottom of the duct-tape roll was a small scrap of paper, and written on the paper was, 'Reiker,' and under that a telephone number.

Of course there was no guarantee that Reiker was

the Red Ranger, or even that he was a human being. It could well be the name of a marine plumbing contractor. But in any case, it was far more of a starting place than I'd had, and I needed to get off the boat before the storm stopped. I stuck the paper inside my pocket, buttoned up my rain slicker, and snuck off the boat and onto the footpath again.

Perhaps I was feeling so happily mellow from the after-effects of my evening out with MacGregor, but as I drove home I found myself humming a catchy little Philip Glass tune from *1000 Airplanes on the Roof*. The key to a happy life is to have accomplishments to be proud of and purpose to look forward to, and at the moment I had both. How wonderful it was to be me.

My good mood lasted only as far as the traffic circle where Old Cutler blends into LeJeune, and then a routine glance in my rearview mirror froze the music on my lips.

Behind me, practically nosing into my backseat, was a maroon Ford Taurus. It looked very much like the sort of car the Miami-Dade Police Department maintained in large numbers for the use of plainclothes personnel.

I did not see how this could possibly be a good thing. A patrol car might follow for no real reason, but someone in a motor-pool car would have some kind of purpose, and it looked like that purpose was to make me aware I was being followed. If so, it was working perfectly. I could not see through the glare of the windshield to know who was driving the other car, but it suddenly seemed very important to know just how long the car had been following me, who was driving, and how much the driver had seen.

I turned down a small side street, pulled over, and parked, and the Taurus parked right behind me. For a moment, nothing happened; we both sat there in our cars, waiting. Was I going to be arrested? If someone had followed me from the marina, it could be a very bad thing for Dashing Dexter. Sooner or later, MacGregor's absence would be noticed, and even the most routine investigation would reveal his boat. Someone would go to see if it was there, and then the fact that Dexter had been there in the middle of the day might seem very significant.

It's little things like this that make for successful police work. Cops look for these funny coincidences, and when they find them they can get very serious with the person who is in too many interesting places by mere happenstance. Even if that person has a police ID and an amazingly charming fake smile.

There really seemed nothing for me to do except bluff my way through: find out who was following me and why, and then convince them it was a silly way to waste time. I put on my very best Official Greeting face, got out of my car, and stepped briskly up to the Taurus. The window rolled down and the always angry face of Sergeant Doakes looked out at me, like an idol for some wicked god, carved from a piece of dark wood.

'Why you leaving work in the middle of the day so much lately?' he asked me. His voice had no real expression in it but still managed to give the impression that whatever I said would be a lie and he would like to hurt me for it.

'Why, Sergeant Doakes!' I said cheerfully. 'What an amazing coincidence. What are you doing here?'

'You got something to do more important than your job?' he said. He really seemed uninterested in maintaining any sort of flow in the conversation, so I shrugged. When faced with people who have very limited conversational skills and no apparent desire to cultivate any, it's always easier simply to go along.

'I, um – I had some personal things to take care of,' I said. Very weak, I agree, but Doakes displayed an unnerving habit of asking the most awkward questions, and with such an understated viciousness, that I found it hard enough not to stutter, let alone come up with something clever.

He looked at me for several endless seconds, the way a starving pit bull looks at raw meat. 'Personal things,' he said without blinking. It sounded even stupider when he repeated it.

'That's right,' I said.

'Your dentist is over in the Gables,' he said.

'Well – '

'Your doctor, too, over on Alameda. Got no lawyer, sister still at work,' he said. 'What kind of *personal things* did I leave out?'

'Actually, um, I, I – ' I said, and I was amazed to hear myself stammer, but nothing else came out, and Doakes just looked at me as though he was begging me to make a run for it so he could practice his wing shot.

'Funny,' he said at last, 'I got *personal things* to do out here, too.'

'Really?' I said, relieved to find that my mouth was once again capable of forming human speech. 'And what would that be, Sergeant?'

It was the first time I had ever seen him smile, and I

have to say that I would have greatly preferred it if he had simply jumped out of the car and bitten me. 'I'm watching YOU,' he said. He gave me a moment to admire the high gloss of his teeth, and then the window rolled up and he vanished behind the tinted glass like the Cheshire cat.

CHAPTER 5

GIVEN ENOUGH TIME, I AM SURE I COULD COME UP with an entire list of things more unpleasant than having Sergeant Doakes turn into my own personal shadow. But as I stood there in my high-fashion foul-weather gear and thought of Reiker and his red boots slipping away from me, it seemed bad enough, and I was not inspired to think of anything worse. I simply climbed into my car, started the engine, and drove through the rain to my apartment. Ordinarily, the homicidal antics of the other drivers would have comforted me, made me feel right at home, but for some reason the maroon Taurus following so close behind took away the glow.

I knew Sergeant Doakes well enough to know that this was not simply a rainy-day whim on his part. If he was watching me, he would keep watching me until he caught me doing something naughty. Or until he was unable to watch me anymore. Naturally enough, I could readily think of a few intriguing ways to make sure he lost interest. But they were all so permanent, and while I did not actually have a conscience, I did have a very clear set of rules that worked somewhat the same way.

I had known that sooner or later Sergeant Doakes would do something or other to discourage my hobby, and I had thought long and hard about what to do when he did. The best I had come up with, alas, was wait and see.

'Excuse me?' you might say, and you have every right. 'Can we truly ignore the obvious answer here?' After all, Doakes might be strong and lethal, but the Dark Passenger was much more so, and no one could stand against him when he took the wheel. Perhaps just this once . . .

No, said the small soft voice in my ear.

Hello, Harry. Why not? And as I asked, I thought back to the time he had told me.

There are rules, Dexter, Harry had said.

Rules, Dad?

It was my sixteenth birthday. There was never much of a party, since I had not learned yet to be wonderfully charming and chummy, and if I was not avoiding my drooling contemporaries then they were generally avoiding me. I lived my adolescence like a sheepdog moving through a flock of dirty, very stupid sheep. Since then, I had learned a great deal. For example, I was not that far off at sixteen – people really are hopeless! – but it just doesn't do to let on.

So my sixteenth birthday was a rather restrained affair. Doris, my foster mom, had recently died of cancer. But my foster sister, Deborah, made me a cake and Harry gave me a new fishing rod. I blew out the candles, we ate the cake, and then Harry took me into the backyard of our modest Coconut Grove house. He sat at the redwood picnic table that he had built by the brick barbecue oven and motioned me to sit, too.

'Well, Dex,' he said. 'Sixteen. You're almost a man.'

I wasn't sure what that was supposed to mean –

me? a man? as in human? – and I did not know what sort of response was expected of me. But I did know that it was usually best not to make clever remarks with Harry, so I just nodded. And Harry gave me a blue-eyed X-ray. 'Are you interested in girls at all?' he asked me.

'Um – in what way?' I said.

'Kissing. Making out. You know. Sex.'

My head whirled at the thought as though a cold dark foot were kicking at the inside of my forehead. 'Not, uh, no. I, um,' I said, silver-tongued even then. 'Not like that.'

Harry nodded as if that made sense. 'Not boys, though,' he said, and I just shook my head. Harry looked at the table, then back at the house. 'When I turned sixteen my father took me to a whore.' He shook his head and a very small smile flickered across his face. 'It took me ten years to get over that.' I could think of absolutely nothing to say to that. The idea of sex was completely alien to me, and to think of *paying* for it, especially for your child, and when that child was *Harry* – well really. It was all too much. I looked at Harry with something close to panic and he smiled.

'No,' said Harry. 'I wasn't going to offer. I expect you'll get more use out of that fishing rod.' He shook his head slowly and looked away, far out over the picnic table, across the yard, down the street. 'Or a fillet knife.'

'Yes,' I said, trying not to sound too eager.

'No,' he said again, 'we both know what you want. But you're not ready.'

Since the first time Harry had talked to me about what I was, on a memorable camping trip a couple of years ago, we had been getting me ready. Getting me, in Harry's words, *squared away*. As a muttonheaded young artificial human I was eager to get started on my happy career, but Harry held me back, because Harry always knew.

'I can be careful,' I said.

'But not perfect,' he said. 'There are rules, Dexter. There have to be. That's what separates you from the other ones.'

'Blend in,' I said. 'Clean up, don't take chances, um . . .'

Harry shook his head. 'More important. You have to be sure before you start that this person really deserves it. I can't tell you the number of times I knew somebody was guilty and I had to let them go. To have the bastard look at you and smirk, and you know and he knows, but you have to hold the door for him and let him go – ' He clenched his jaw and tapped a fist on the picnic table. 'You won't have to. BUT . . . you have to be sure. Dead sure, Dexter. And even if you're absolutely positive – ' He held his hand up in the air, palm facing me. 'Get some proof. It doesn't have to hold up in court, thank God.' He gave a small and bitter laugh. 'You'd never get anywhere. But you need proof, Dexter. That's the most important thing.' He tapped the table with his knuckle. 'You have to have proof. And even then – '

He stopped, an uncharacteristic Harry pause, and I waited, knowing something difficult was coming. 'Sometimes even then, you let them go. No matter how much they deserve it. If they're too . . . *conspicuous*, for example. If it would raise too much attention, let it go.'

*

Well, there it was. As always, Harry had the answer for me. Whenever I was unsure, I could hear Harry whispering in my ear. I was sure, but I had no proof that Doakes was anything except a very angry and suspicious cop, and chopping up a cop was certainly the sort of thing the city got indignant about. After the recent untimely demise of Detective LaGuerta, the police hierarchy would almost certainly be a little sensitive about a second cop going out in the same way.

No matter how necessary it seemed, Doakes was out of bounds for me. I could look out the window at the maroon Taurus nosed under a tree, but I could do nothing about it except wish for some other solution to spontaneously arise – for example, a piano falling on his head. Sadly enough, I was left hoping for luck.

But there was no luck tonight for poor Disappointed Dexter, and lately there had been a tragic lack of falling pianos in the Miami area. So here I was in my little hovel, pacing the floor with frustration, and every time I casually peeked out the window, there was the Taurus parked across the way. The memory of what I had been so happily contemplating only an hour ago pounded in my head. *Can Dexter come out and play?* Alas, no, dear Dark Passenger. Dexter is in time-out.

There was, however, one constructive thing I could do, even cooped up in my apartment. I took the crumpled piece of paper from MacGregor's boat out of my pocket and smoothed it out, which left my fingers sticky from the leftover gunk off the roll of duct tape to which the paper had been stuck. 'Reiker,' and a phone number. More than enough to feed to one of the reverse directories I could access from my computer, and in just a few minutes I had done so.

The number belonged to a cell phone, which was registered to a Mr. Steve Reiker of Tigertail Avenue in Coconut Grove. A little bit of cross-checking revealed that Mr. Reiker was a professional photographer. Of course, it could have been a coincidence. I am sure that there are many people named Reiker around the world who are photographers. I looked in the Yellow Pages and found that this particular Reiker had a specialty. He had a quarter-page ad that said, 'Remember Them as They Are Now.'

Reiker specialized in pictures of children.

The coincidence theory might have to go.

The Dark Passenger stirred and gave a small chuckle of anticipation, and I found myself planning a trip over to Tigertail for a quick look around. In fact, it wasn't terribly far away. I could drive over now, and –

And let Sergeant Doakes follow along playing Pin the Tail on the Dexter. Splendid idea, old chum. That would save Doakes a great deal of boring investigative work when Reiker finally disappeared some day. He could cut through all the dull routine and just come get me.

And at this rate, when would Reiker disappear? It was terribly frustrating to have a worthwhile goal in sight, and yet to be held in check like this. But after several hours Doakes was still parked across the street and I was still here. What to do? On the plus side, it seemed obvious that Doakes had not seen enough to take any action beyond following me. But leading the way in the very large minus column, if he continued to follow me I would be forced to stay in character as the mild-mannered forensic lab rat, carefully avoiding anything more lethal than rush hour on the Palmetto Expressway. That would never do. I felt a certain pressure, not just from the Passenger but from the clock. Before too much time passed I needed to find some proof that Reiker was the photographer who took MacGregor's pictures, and if he was, have a sharp and pointed chat with him. If he realized MacGregor had gone the way of all flesh he would most likely run for the hills. And if my associates at police headquarters realized it, things could get very uncomfortable for Dashing Dexter.

But Doakes had apparently settled in for a long stay, and at the moment there was nothing I could do about it. It was terribly frustrating to think of Reiker walking around instead of thrashing against the duct tape. Homicidus interruptus. A soft moan and a gnashing of mental teeth came from the Dark Passenger, and I knew just how he felt, but there seemed to be very little I could do except pace back and forth. And even that wasn't very helpful: if I kept it up I would wear a hole in the carpet and then I would never get back my security deposit on the apartment.

My instinct was to do something that would throw Doakes off the track – but he was no ordinary bloodhound. I could think of only one thing that might take the scent out of his quivering, eager snout. It was just barely possible that I could wear him down, play the waiting game, be relentlessly normal for so long that he would have to give it up and return to his real job of catching all the truly horrible residents on the underside of our fair city. Why even now they were out there double parking, littering, and threatening to vote Democratic in the next election. How could he waste time on little old Dexter and his harmless hobby?

All right then: I would be unstintingly ordinary until it made his teeth hurt. It might take weeks rather than days, but I would do it. I would live fully the synthetic life I had created in order to appear human. And since humans are generally ruled by sex, I would start with a visit to my girlfriend Rita.

It's an odd term, 'girlfriend,' particularly for grown persons. And in practice an even odder concept. Generally speaking, in adults it described a woman, not a girl, who was willing to provide sex, not friendship. In fact, from what I had observed it was quite possible for one to actively dislike one's girlfriend, although of course true hatred is reserved for marriage. I had so far been unable to determine what women expect in return from a boyfriend, but apparently I had it as far as Rita was concerned. It certainly wasn't sex, which to me seemed about as interesting as calculating foreign trade deficits.

Luckily, Rita also was uninterested in sex, for the most part. She was the product of a disastrous early marriage to a man whose idea of a good time turned out to be smoking crack and beating her. Later he branched out into infecting her with several intriguing diseases. But when he battered the kids one night Rita's marvelous country-song loyalty ruptured, and she flung the swine out of her life and, happily, into prison.

As a result of all this turmoil, she had been looking for a gentleman who might be interested in companionship and conversation, someone who did not need to indulge the crude animal urges of base passion. A man, in other words, who would value her for her finer qualities and not her willingness to indulge in naked acrobatics. Ecce, Dexter. For almost two years she had been my ideal disguise, a key ingredient of Dexter as the world at large knew him. And in return I had not beaten her, had not infected her with anything, had not forced my animal lust on her, and she actually seemed to enjoy my company.

And as a bonus, I had become quite fond of her children, Astor and Cody. Strange, perhaps, but nonetheless true, I assure you. If everyone else in the world were to mysteriously disappear, I would feel irritated about it only because there would be no one to make me doughnuts. But children are interesting to me and, in fact, I like them. Rita's two kids had been through a traumatic early childhood, and maybe because I had, too, I felt a special attachment to them, an interest that went beyond maintaining my disguise with Rita.

Aside from the bonus of her children, Rita herself was quite presentable. She had short and neat blond hair, a trim and athletic body, and she seldom said things that were outright stupid. I could go in public with her and know that we looked like an appropriately matched human pair, which was really the whole point. People even said we were an attractive couple, although I was never sure what that meant. I suppose Rita found me attractive somehow, although her track record with men didn't make that too flattering. Still, it's always nice to be around somebody who thinks I am wonderful. It confirms my low opinion of people.

I looked at the clock on my desk. Five thirty-two:

within the next fifteen minutes Rita would be home from her job at Fairchild Title Agency, where she did something very complicated involving fractions of percentage points. By the time I got to her house, she should be there.

With a cheerful synthetic smile I headed out the door, waved to Doakes, and drove over to Rita's modest South Miami house. The traffic wasn't too bad, which is to say that there were no fatal accidents or shootings, and in just under twenty minutes I parked my car in front of Rita's bungalow. Sergeant Doakes cruised past to the end of the street and, as I knocked on the front door, he parked across the way.

The door swung open and Rita peered out at me. 'Oh!' she said. 'Dexter.'

'In person,' I said. 'I was in the neighborhood and wondered if you were home yet.'

'Well, I – I just walked in the door. I must look like a mess . . . Um – come on in. Would you like a beer?'

Beer; what a thought. I never touch the stuff – and yet, it was so amazingly normal, so perfectly visit-the-girlfriend-after-work, even Doakes had to be impressed. It was just the right touch. 'I would love a beer,' I said, and I followed her into the relative cool of the living room.

'Have a seat,' she said. 'I'm just going to freshen up a little.' She smiled at me. 'The kids are out back, but I'm sure they'll be all over you when they find out you're here.' And she swished off down the hall, returning a moment later with a can of beer. 'I'll be right back,' she said, and went away to her bedroom at the back of the house.

I sat on the sofa and looked at the beer in my hand.

I am not a drinker – really, drinking is not a recommended habit for predators. It slows the reflexes, dulls the perceptions, and knits up the raveled sleeve of care, which always sounded to me like a very bad thing. But here I was, a demon on vacation, attempting the ultimate sacrifice by giving up my powers and becoming human – and so a beer was just the thing for Dipsophobic Dexter.

I took a sip. The taste was bitter and thin, just as I would be if I had to keep the Dark Passenger buckled into his seat belt for very long. Still, I suppose beer is an acquired taste. I took another sip. I could feel it gurgle all the way down and splash into my stomach, and it occurred to me that with all the excitement and frustration of the day I hadn't eaten lunch. But what the hell – it was just a light beer; or as the can proudly proclaimed: LITE BEER. I suppose we should be very grateful they hadn't thought of a cuter way to spell beer.

I took a big sip. It wasn't that bad when you got used to it. By golly, it really WAS relaxing. I, at any rate, felt more relaxed with each swig. Another refreshing sip – I couldn't remember that it had tasted this good when I'd tried it in college. Of course, I was just a boy then, not the manly mature hardworking upright citizen I was now. I tilted the can, but nothing came out.

Well – somehow the can was empty. And yet I was still thirsty. Could this unpleasant situation really be tolerated? I thought not. Absolutely intolerable. In fact, I did not plan to tolerate it. I stood up and proceeded to the kitchen in a firm and unyielding manner. There were several more cans of lite beer in the refrigerator and I took one back to the couch.

I sat. I opened the beer. I took a sip. Much better. Damn that Doakes anyway. Maybe I should take him a beer. It might relax him, get him to loosen up and call the whole thing off. After all, we were on the same side, weren't we?

I sipped. Rita came back wearing a pair of denim shorts and a white tank top with a tiny satin bow at the neckline. I had to admit, she looked very nice. I could really pick a disguise. 'Well,' she said as she slid onto the couch next to me, 'it's nice to see you, out of the blue like this.'

'It certainly must be,' I said.

She cocked her head to one side and looked at me funny. 'Did you have a hard day at work?'

'An awful day,' I said, and took a sip. 'Had to let a bad guy go. Very bad guy.'

'Oh.' She frowned. 'Why did – I mean, couldn't you just . . .'

'I wanted to just,' I said. 'But I couldn't.' I raised the beer can to her. 'Politics.' I took a sip.

Rita shook her head. 'I still can't get used to the idea that, that – I mean, from the outside it seems so cut-and-dried. You find the bad guy, you put him away. But politics? I mean, with – what did he do?'

'He helped to kill some kids,' I said.

'Oh,' she said, and looked shocked. 'My God, there must be something you can do.'

I smiled at her. By gum, she had seen it right away. What a gal. Didn't I say I could pick 'em? 'You have put your finger right on it,' I said, and I took her hand to look at that finger. 'There is something I can do. And very well, too.' I patted her hand, spilling only a little bit of beer. 'I knew you'd understand.'

She looked confused. 'Oh,' she said. 'What kind of –
I mean – What will you do?'

I took a sip. Why shouldn't I tell her? I could see she
already got the idea. Why not? I opened my mouth,
but before I could whisper even one syllable about the
Dark Passenger and my harmless hobby, Cody and
Astor came racing into the room, stopped dead when
they saw me, and stood there looking from me to their
mother.

'Hi Dexter,' Astor said. She nudged her brother.

'Hi,' he said softly. He was not a big talker. In
fact, he never said much of anything. Poor kid. The
whole thing with his father had really messed him
up. 'Are you drunk?' he asked me. It was a big speech
for him.

'Cody!' Rita said. I waved her off bravely and faced
him.

'Drunk?' I said. 'Me?'

He nodded. 'Yeah.'

'Certainly not,' I said firmly, giving him my very
best dignified frown. 'Possibly a little bit tipsy, but
that's not the same thing at all.'

'Oh,' he said, and his sister chimed in, 'Are you
staying for dinner?'

'Oh, I think I should probably be going,' I said, but
Rita put a surprisingly firm hand on my shoulder.

'You're not driving anywhere like this,' she said.

'Like what?'

'Tipsy,' said Cody.

'I'm not tipsy,' I said.

'You said you were,' said Cody. I couldn't remember
the last time I'd heard him put four words in a row like
that, and I was very proud of him.

'You did,' Astor added. 'You said you're not drunk, you're just a little tipsy.'

'I said that?' They both nodded. 'Oh. Well then – '

'Well then,' Rita chimed in, 'I guess you're staying for dinner.'

Well then. I guess I did. I am pretty sure I did, anyway. I do know that at some point I went to the refrigerator for a lite beer and discovered they were all gone. And at some later point I was sitting on the couch again. The television was on and I was trying to figure out what the actors were saying and why an invisible crowd thought it was the most hilarious dialogue of all time.

Rita slid onto the couch next to me. 'The kids are in bed,' she said. 'How do you feel?'

'I feel wonderful,' I said. 'If only I could figure out what's so funny.'

Rita put a hand on my shoulder. 'It really bothers you, doesn't it? Letting the bad guy go. Children . . .' She moved closer and put her arm all the way around me, laying her head on my shoulder. 'You're such a good guy, Dexter.'

'No, I'm not,' I said, wondering why she would say something so very strange.

Rita sat up and looked from my left eye to my right eye and back again. 'But you are, you KNOW you are.' She smiled and nestled her head back down on my shoulder. 'I think it's . . . nice that you came here. To see me. When you were feeling bad.'

I started to tell her that wasn't quite right, but then it occurred to me: I *had* come here when I felt bad. True, it was only to bore Doakes into going away, after the terrible frustration of losing my playdate with Reiker.

44

But it had turned out to be a pretty good idea after all, hadn't it? Good old Rita. She was very warm and she smelled nice. 'Good old Rita,' I said. I pulled her against me as tight as I could and leaned my cheek against the top of her head.

We sat that way for a few minutes, and then Rita wiggled to her feet and pulled me up by the hand. 'Come on,' she said. 'Let's get you to bed.'

Which we did, and when I had flopped down under the top sheet and she crawled in beside me, she was just so nice and smelled so good and felt so warm and comfortable that –

Well. Beer really is amazing stuff, isn't it?

CHAPTER 6

I WOKE UP WITH A HEADACHE, A FEELING OF tremendous self-loathing, and a sense of disorientation. There was a rose-colored sheet against my cheek. My sheets – the sheets I woke up to every day in my little bed – were not rose-colored, and they did not smell like this. The mattress seemed too spacious to be my modest trundle bed, and really – I was quite sure this was not my headache either.

'Good morning, handsome,' said a voice somewhere over my feet. I turned my head and saw Rita standing at the foot of the bed, looking down at me with a happy little smile.

'Ung,' I said in a voice that sounded like a toad's croak and hurt my head even more. But apparently it was an amusing kind of pain, because Rita's smile widened.

'That's what I thought,' she said. 'I'll get you some aspirin.' She leaned over and rubbed my leg. 'Mmm,' she said, and then turned and went into the bathroom.

I sat up. This may have been a strategic mistake, as it made my head pound a great deal more. I closed my eyes, breathed deeply, and waited for my aspirin.

This normal life was going to take a little getting used to.

*

But oddly enough it didn't, not really. I found that if I limited myself to one or two beers, I could relax just enough to blend in with the slipcover on the couch. And so several nights a week, with ever-faithful Sergeant Doakes in my rearview mirror, I would stop over at Rita's house after work, play with Cody and Astor, and sit with Rita after the kids were in bed. Around ten I would head for the door. Rita seemed to expect to be kissed when I left, so I generally arranged to kiss her standing in the open front door where Doakes could see me. I used all the technique I could muster from the many movies I have seen, and Rita responded happily.

I do like routine, and I settled into this new one to a point where I almost began to believe in it myself. It was so boring that I was putting my real self to sleep. From far away in the backseat of the deepest darkest corner of Dexterland I could even hear the Dark Passenger starting to snore gently, which was a little scary and made me feel a tiny bit lonesome for the first time. But I stayed the course, making a small game of my visits to Rita to see how far I could push it, knowing that Doakes was watching and, hopefully, beginning to wonder just a little bit. I brought flowers, candy, and pizza. I kissed Rita ever more outlandishly, framed in the open front door to give Doakes the best possible picture. I knew it was a ridiculous display, but it was the only weapon I had.

For days on end Doakes stayed with me. His appearances were unpredictable, which made him seem even more threatening. I never knew when or where he might turn up, and that made me feel like he was always there. If I went into the grocery store,

Doakes was waiting by the broccoli. If I rode my bicycle out Old Cutler Road, somewhere along the way I would see the maroon Taurus parked under a banyan tree. A day might go by without a Doakes sighting, but I could feel him out there, circling downwind and waiting, and I did not dare hope that he had given up; if I could not see him, he was either well hidden or waiting to spring another surprise appearance on me.

I was forced into being Daytime Dexter on a full-time basis, like an actor trapped in a movie, knowing that the real world was right there, just beyond the screen, but as unreachable as the moon. And like the moon, the thought of Reiker pulled at me. The thought of him clomping through his unworried life in those absurd red boots was almost more than I could stand.

Of course I knew that even Doakes could not keep this up forever. He was, after all, receiving a handsome salary from the people of Miami for performing a job, and every now and then he had to perform it. But Doakes understood the rising interior tide that battered at me, and he knew that if he kept the pressure on long enough, the disguise would slip, HAD to slip, as the cool whispers from the backseat became more urgent.

And so there we were, balanced on a knife edge that was unfortunately only metaphorical. Sooner or later, I had to be me. But until then I would see an awful lot of Rita. She couldn't hold a candle to my old flame, the Dark Passenger, but I did need my secret identity. And until I escaped Doakes, Rita was my cape, red tights, and utility belt – almost the entire costume.

Very well: I would sit on the couch, can of beer in

hand, watching *Survivor* and thinking of an interesting variation of the game that would never make it to the network. If you simply add Dexter to the castaways and interpret the title a bit more literally . . .

It was not all dismal, bleak, and wretched. Several times a week I got to play kick the can with Cody and Astor and the other assorted wild creatures of the neighborhood, which brings us back to where we began: Dexter Dismasted, unable to sail through his normal life, anchored instead to a gaggle of kids and a ravioli can. And on evenings when it was raining, we stayed inside around the dining table, while Rita bustled about doing laundry, washing dishes, and otherwise perfecting the domestic bliss of her little nest.

There are only so many indoor games one can play with two children of such tender ages and damaged spirits as Cody and Astor; most of the board games were uninteresting or incomprehensible to them, and too many of the card games seemed to require a lighthearted simplemindedness that even I could not fake convincingly. But we finally hit on hangman; it was educational, creative, and mildly homicidal, which made everyone happy, even Rita.

If you had asked me pre-Doakes if a life of hangman and Miller Lite sounded like my cup of tea, I would have been forced to confess that Dexter Oolong was somewhat darker. But as the days piled up and I slipped further into the reality of my disguise, I had to ask myself: Was I enjoying the life of Mr. Suburban Householder just a little too much?

Still, it was very comforting somehow to see the predatory zest Cody and Astor brought to something as harmless as hangman. Their enthusiasm for hanging the little stick figures made me feel a bit more like we might all be part of the same general species. As they happily murdered their anonymous hanged men, I felt a certain kinship.

Astor quickly learned to draw the gallows and the lines for the letters. She was, of course, much more verbal about it. 'Seven letters,' she would say, then tucking her upper lip between her teeth add, 'Wait. Six.' As Cody and I missed on our guesses she would pounce and call out, 'An *ARM*! Ha!' Cody would stare at her without expression, and then look down to the doodled figure hanging from its noose. When it was his turn and we missed a guess, he would say in his soft voice, 'Leg,' and look up at us with something that might almost have been triumph in someone who showed emotion. And when the line of dashes under the gallows was finally filled in with the spelled-out word, they would both look at the dangling man with satisfaction, and once or twice Cody even said, 'Dead,' before Astor bounced up and down and said, 'Again, Dexter! My turn!'

All very idyllic. Our perfect little family of Rita, the kids, and Monster makes four. But no matter how many stick figures we executed, it did nothing to kill my worry that time was gurgling rapidly down the drain and soon I would be a white-haired old man, too feeble to lift a carving knife, tottering through my horrifyingly ordinary days, shadowed by an ancient Sergeant Doakes and a sense of missed opportunity.

As long as I couldn't think of a way out, I was in the noose as surely as Cody and Astor's stick figures. Very depressing, and I am ashamed to admit that I almost lost hope, which I never would have done if I had remembered one important thing.

This was Miami.

CHAPTER 7

OF COURSE IT COULDN'T LAST. I SHOULD HAVE known that such an unnatural state of affairs had to give way, yield to the natural order of things. After all, I lived in a city where mayhem was like the sunshine, always right behind the next cloud. Three weeks after my first unsettling encounter with Sergeant Doakes, the clouds finally broke.

It was just a piece of luck, really – not quite the falling piano I had been hoping for, but still a happy coincidence. I was having lunch with my sister, Deborah. Excuse me; I should have said, SERGEANT Deborah. Like her father, Harry, Debs was a cop. Owing to the happy outcome of recent events, she had been promoted, pulled out of the prostitute costume she had been forced to wear by her assignment with vice, whisked off the street corner at last and into her very own set of sergeant's stripes.

It should have made her happy. After all, this was what she thought she wanted; an end to her tenure as a pretend hooker. Any young and reasonably attractive female officer assigned to vice would sooner or later find herself in a prostitution sting operation, and Deborah was very attractive. But her lush figure and healthy good looks had never done anything for my poor sister except embarrass her. She hated to wear anything that even hinted at her physical charms, and standing on the street in hot pants and a tube top had been sheer torture for her. She had been in danger of growing permanent frown lines.

Because I am an inhuman monster, I tend to be logical, and I had thought that her new assignment would end her martyrdom as Our Lady of Perpetual Grumpiness. Alas, even her transfer to homicide had failed to bring a smile to her face. Somewhere along the way she had decided that serious law enforcement personnel must reshape their faces until they look like large, mean-spirited fish, and she was still working very hard to accomplish this.

We had come to lunch together in her new motor-pool car, another of the perks of her promotion that really should have brought a small ray of sunshine into her life. It didn't seem to. I wondered if I should worry about her. I watched her as I slid into a booth at Café Relampago, our favorite Cuban restaurant. She called in her location and status and then sat across from me with a frown.

'Well, Sergeant Grouper,' I said as we picked up our menus.

'Is that funny, Dexter?'

'Yes,' I said. 'Very funny. And a little sad, too. Like life itself. Especially your life, Deborah.'

'Fuck you, Charlie,' she said. 'My life is fine.' And to prove it, she ordered a *medianoche* sandwich, the best in Miami, and a *batido de mamey*, a milk shake made from a unique tropical fruit that tastes something like a combination of peach and watermelon.

My life was every bit as fine as hers, so I ordered the same thing. Because we were regulars here, and had been coming here most of our lives, the aging, unshaven waiter snatched away our menus with a face that might have been the role model for Deborah's, and stomped off to the kitchen like Godzilla on his way to Tokyo.

'Everyone is so cheerful and happy,' I said.

'This isn't *Mister Rogers' Neighborhood*, Dex. It's Miami. Only the bad guys are happy.' She looked at me without expression, a perfect cop stare. 'How come you're not laughing and singing?'

'Unkind, Deb. Very unkind. I've been good for months.'

She took a sip of water. 'Uh-huh. And it's making you crazy.'

'Much worse than that,' I said with a shudder. 'I think it's making me normal.'

'Coulda fooled me,' she said.

'Sad but true. I've become a couch potato.' I hesitated, then blurted it out. After all, if a boy can't share his problems with his family, who can he confide in? 'It's Sergeant Doakes,' I said.

She nodded. 'He's got a real hard-on for you,' she said. 'You better keep away from him.'

'I would love to,' I said. 'But HE won't keep away from ME.'

Her cop stare got harder. 'What do you plan to do about it?'

I opened my mouth to deny all the things I had been thinking, but happily for the good of my immortal soul, before I could lie to her we were interrupted by the sound of Deb's radio. She cocked her head to one side, snatched up the radio, and said she was on her way. 'Come on,' she snapped, heading for the door. I followed meekly behind, pausing only to throw some money on the table.

Deborah was already backing out her car by the time I came out of Relampago's. I hurried over and lunged for the door. She was moving forward and out of the parking lot before I even got both feet in. 'Really, Deb,' I said. 'I almost lost a shoe. What's so important?'

Deborah frowned, accelerating through a small gap in traffic that only a Miami driver would have attempted. 'I don't know,' she said as she turned on the siren.

I blinked and raised my voice over the noise. 'Didn't the dispatcher tell you?'

'Have you ever heard the dispatcher stutter, Dexter?'

'Why no, Deb, I haven't. Did this one do that?'

Deb swerved around a school bus and roared up onto 836. 'Yeah,' she said. She turned hard to avoid a BMW full of young men, who all flipped her off. 'I think it's a homicide.'

'You think,' I said.

'Yeah,' she answered, and then she concentrated on driving and I let her. High speeds always remind me of my own mortality, especially on Miami's roads. And as for the Case of the Stuttering Dispatcher – well, Sergeant Nancy Drew and I would find out soon enough, particularly at this speed, and a little excitement is always welcome.

In a very few minutes Deb managed to get us over near the Orange Bowl without causing major loss of life, and we came down onto the surface roads and made a few quick turns before sliding into the curb at a small house on N.W. 4th Street. The street was lined with similar houses, all small and close together and each one with its own wall or chain-link fence. Many of them were brightly colored and had paved yards.

Two patrol cars had already pulled up in front of the house, their lights flashing. A pair of uniformed cops were rolling out the yellow crime-scene tape around the place, and as we got out, I saw a third cop sitting in the front seat of one of the cars, his head in his hands. On the porch of the house a fourth cop stood beside an elderly lady. There were two small steps leading up to the porch and she sat on the top one. She seemed to be alternating weeping with throwing up. Somewhere nearby a dog was howling, the same note over and over.

Deborah marched up to the nearest uniform. He was a square, middle-aged guy with dark hair and a look on his face that said he wished he was sitting in his car with his head in his hands, too. 'What have we got?' Deb asked him, holding up her badge.

The cop shook his head without looking at us and blurted out, 'I'm not going in there again, not if it costs me my pension.' And he turned away, almost walking into the side of a patrol car, rolling out the yellow tape like it could protect him from whatever was in the house.

Deborah stared after the cop, then looked at me. Quite frankly, I could think of nothing really useful or clever to say, and for a moment we just stood there looking at each other. The wind rattled the crime-scene tape, and the dog continued to howl, a kind of weird yodeling sound that did nothing to increase my affection for the canine species. Deborah shook her head. 'Somebody should shut that fucking dog up,' she said, and she ducked under the yellow tape and started up the walk to the house. I followed. After a few steps I realized that the dog sound was getting closer; it was in the house, probably the victim's pet. Quite often an animal reacts badly to its owner's death.

We stopped at the steps and Deborah looked up at the cop, reading his name tag. 'Coronel. Is this lady a witness?'

The cop didn't look at us. 'Yeah,' he said. 'Mrs. Medina. She called it in,' and the old woman leaned over and retched.

Deborah frowned. 'What's with that dog?' she asked him.

Coronel made a sort of barking noise halfway between laughing and gagging, but he didn't answer and he didn't look at us.

I suppose Deborah had had enough, and it's hard to blame her. 'What the fuck is going on here?' she demanded.

Coronel turned his head to look at us. There was no expression at all on his face. 'See for yourself,' he said, and then he turned away again. Deborah thought she was going to say something, but changed her mind. She looked at me instead and shrugged.

'We might as well take a look,' I told her, and I hoped I didn't sound too eager. In truth, I was anxious to see anything that could create this kind of reaction in Miami cops. Sergeant Doakes might very well prevent me from doing anything of my own, but he couldn't stop me from admiring someone else's creativity. After all, it was my job, and shouldn't we enjoy our work?

Deborah, on the other hand, showed uncharacteristic reluctance. She glanced back at the patrol car where the cop still sat unmoving, head in hands. Then she looked back to Coronel and the old lady, then at the front door of the little house. She took a deep breath, blew it out hard, and said, 'All right. Let's have a look.' But she still didn't move, so I slipped past her and pushed open the door.

The front room of the little house was dark, curtains and blinds all pulled closed. There was one easy chair that looked like it had come from a thrift shop. It had a slipcover that was so dirty it was impossible to tell what color it was supposed to be. The chair sat in front of a small TV on a folding card table. Other than that the room was empty. A doorway opposite the front door showed a small patch of light, and that seemed to be where the dog was yowling, so I headed that way, toward the back of the house.

Animals do not like me, which proves they are smarter than we think. They seem to sense what I am, and they disapprove, often expressing their opinion in a very pointed way. So I was a little bit reluctant to approach a dog already so obviously upset. But I moved through the doorway, slowly, calling out hopefully, 'Nice doggie!' It didn't really sound like a very nice doggie; it sounded like a brain-damaged pit bull with rabies. But I do try to put a good face on things, even with our canine friends. With a kind and animal-loving expression on my face, I stepped to the swinging door that led to what was obviously the kitchen.

As I touched the door I heard a soft and uneasy rustling from the Dark Passenger and I paused. *What?* I asked, but there was no reply. I closed my eyes for just a second, but the page was blank; no secret message flashed onto the back of my eyelids. I shrugged, pushed open the door, and stepped into the kitchen.

The upper half of the room was painted a faded, greasy yellow, and the lower half was lined with old, blue pinstriped white tiles. There was a small refrigerator in one corner and a hot plate on the counter. A palmetto bug ran across the counter and dove behind the refrigerator. A sheet of plywood had been nailed across the room's only window, and there was a single dim lightbulb hanging from the ceiling.

Under the lightbulb was a large, heavy old table, the kind with square legs and a white porcelain finish. A large mirror hung on the wall at an angle that allowed it to reflect whatever was on the table. And in that reflection, lying in the middle of the table was a . . . um . . .

Well. I assume it had started life as a human being of some kind, quite probably male and Hispanic. Very difficult to say in its present state which, I admit, left even me a bit startled. Still, in spite of being surprised, I had to admire the thoroughness of the work, and the neatness. It would have made a surgeon very jealous, although it seems likely that very few surgeons would be able to justify this kind of work to an HMO.

I would never have thought, for instance, of cutting off the lips and eyelids like that, and although I pride myself on my neat work, I could never have done so without damage to the eyes, which in this case were rolling wildly back and forth, unable to close or even blink, always returning to that mirror. Just a hunch, but I guessed that the eyelids had been done last, long after the nose and ears had been oh-so-neatly removed. I could not decide, however, if I would have done these before or after the arms, legs, genitals, etc. A difficult series of choices, but from the look of things, it had all been done properly, even expertly, by someone who'd had plenty of practice. We often speak of very neat body work as 'surgical.' But this was actual surgery. There was no bleeding at all, even from the mouth, where the lips and tongue had been removed. Even the teeth; one had to admire such amazing thoroughness. Every cut had been professionally closed; a white bandage was neatly taped to each shoulder where arms had once hung, and the rest of the cuts had already healed, in a way you might hope to find in the very best of hospitals.

Everything on the body had been cut off, absolutely everything. There was nothing left of it but a bare and featureless head attached to an unencumbered body. I could not imagine how it was possible to do this without killing the thing, and it was certainly far beyond me why anyone would want to. It revealed a cruelty that really made one wonder if the universe was such a good idea after all. Pardon me if this sounds a tad hypocritical coming from Death-head Dexter, but I know very well what I am and it is nothing like this. I do what the Dark Passenger deems necessary, to someone who truly deserves it, and it always ends in death – which I am sure the thing on the table would agree was not such a bad thing.

But this – to do all this so patiently and carefully and leave it alive in front of a mirror . . . I could feel a sense of black wonder drifting up from deep inside, as if for the very first time my Dark Passenger was feeling just a little bit insignificant.

The thing on the table did not appear to register my presence. It just kept making that deranged doggie sound, nonstop, the same horrible wavering note over and over.

I heard Deb scuffle to a halt behind me. 'Oh Jesus,' she said. 'Oh God . . . What is it?'

'I don't know,' I said. 'But at least it's not a dog.'

CHAPTER 8

THERE WAS A VERY QUIET RUSH OF AIR, AND I looked beyond Deborah to see that Sergeant Doakes had arrived. He glanced once around the room and then his eyes settled on the table. I admit that I had been curious to see what his reaction would be to something this extreme, and it was well worth the wait. When Doakes saw the kitchen's central exhibit his eyes locked onto it and he stopped moving so completely that he could have been a statue. After a long moment he moved toward it, gliding slowly as if pulled on a string. He slid past us without noticing that we were there and came to a stop at the table.

For several seconds he stared down at the thing. Then, still without even blinking, he reached inside his sport coat and drew out his pistol. Slowly, with no expression, he aimed it between the unblinkable eyes of the still-yowling thing on the table. He cocked the pistol.

'Doakes,' said Deborah in a dry croak of a voice, and she cleared her throat and tried again. 'Doakes!'

Doakes did not answer nor look away, but he didn't pull the trigger, which seemed a shame. After all, what were we going to do with this thing? It wasn't going to tell us who had done this. And I had a feeling its days as a useful member of society had come to an end. Why not let Doakes put it out of its misery? And then

Deb and I would reluctantly be compelled to report what Doakes had done, he would be fired and even imprisoned, and my problems would be over. It seemed like such a neat solution, but of course it was not the kind of thing Deborah would ever agree to. She can get so fussy and official at times.

'Put away your weapon, Doakes,' she said, and although the rest of him remained absolutely motionless, he swiveled his head to look at her.

'Only thing to do,' he said. 'Believe me.'

Deborah shook her head. 'You know you can't,' she said. They stared at each other for a moment, then his eyes clicked onto me. It was exceptionally hard for me to look back without blurting out something like, 'Oh, what the hell – go for it!' But I managed somehow, and Doakes turned the pistol up into the air. He looked back at the thing, shook his head, and put the pistol away. 'Shit,' he said. 'Shoulda let me.' And he turned, walking rapidly out of the room.

Within the next few minutes the room became crowded with people who tried desperately not to look while they went to work. Camilla Figg, a stocky, short-haired lab tech who had always seemed to be limited in expression to either blushing or staring, was crying quietly as she dusted for fingerprints. Angel Batista, or Angel-no-relation as we called him, since that is how he always introduced himself, turned pale and clamped his jaw tightly shut, but he stayed in the room. Vince Masuoka, a co-worker who normally acted like he was only pretending to be human, trembled so badly he had to go outside and sit on the porch.

I began to wonder if I should pretend to be

horrified, too, just to avoid being too noticeable. Perhaps I should go out and sit beside Vince. What did one talk about at such times? Baseball? The weather? Surely one wouldn't talk about the thing we were running from – and yet, I found to my surprise that I would not mind talking about it. In truth, the thing was beginning to raise a mild twitch of interest from a Certain Interior Party. I had always worked so hard to avoid any kind of notice at all, and here was someone doing just the opposite. Clearly this monster was showing off for some reason, and it may have been only a perfectly natural competitive spirit, but that seemed a little irritating, even while it made me want to know more. Whoever did this was unlike anyone else I had ever encountered. Should I move this anonymous predator onto my list? Or should I pretend to swoon with horror and go sit outside on the porch?

As I pondered this difficult choice, Sergeant Doakes brushed past me again, for once barely even pausing to glower at me, and I recalled that because of him I had no chance to work through a list at the moment. It was mildly disconcerting, but it did make the decision seem a little easier. I started composing a properly unsettled facial expression, but got no further than raising my eyebrows. Two paramedics came rushing in, all focused importance, and stopped dead when they saw the victim. One of them immediately ran from the room. The other, a young black woman, turned to me and said, 'What the fuck are *we* supposed to do?' Then she started crying, too.

You have to agree she had a point. Sergeant Doakes's solution was starting to look more practical, even elegant. There seemed very little point in whisking this thing onto a gurney and dashing through Miami traffic to deliver it to a hospital. As the young lady had so elegantly put it, what the fuck were they supposed to do? But clearly somebody had to do something. If we just left it there and stood around like this, eventually someone would complain about all the cops throwing up in the yard, which would be very bad for the department's image.

It was Deborah who finally got things organized. She persuaded the paramedics to sedate the victim and take it away, which allowed the surprisingly squeamish lab techs to come back inside and go to work. The quiet in the little house as the drugs took hold of the thing was close to ecstatic. The paramedics got the thing covered and onto their gurney without dropping it and wheeled it off into the sunset.

And just in time; as the ambulance pulled away from the curb the news trucks started to arrive. In a way it was a shame; I would love to have seen the reaction of one or two of the reporters, Rick Sangre in particular. He had been the area's leading devotee of 'If it bleeds, it leads,' and I had never seen him express any sense of pain or horror, except on camera or if his hair was mussed. But it was not to be. By the time Rick's cameraman was ready to roll, there was nothing left to see other than the little house fenced in by the yellow tape, and a handful of cops with clamped jaws who wouldn't have had much to say to Sangre on a good day, and today probably wouldn't have told him his own name.

There was really not a great deal for me to do. I had come in Deborah's car and so I did not have my kit, and in any case there was no visible blood spatter anywhere that I could see. Since that was my area of expertise, I felt I should find something and be useful, but our surgical friend had been too careful. Just to be sure I looked through the rest of the house, which wasn't much. There was one small bedroom, an even smaller bathroom, and a closet. They all seemed to be empty, except for a bare, battered mattress on the floor of the bedroom. It looked like it had come from the same thrift shop as the living-room chair and had been pounded flat like a Cuban steak. No other furniture or utensils, not even a plastic spoon.

The only thing that showed even the smallest hint of personality was something Angel-no-relation found under the table as I finished my quick tour of the house. 'Hola,' he said, and pulled a small piece of notepaper off the floor with his tweezers. I stepped over to see what it might be. It was hardly worth the effort; nothing but a single small page of white paper, ripped slightly at the top where a little rectangle had been torn away. I looked just above Angel's head and sure enough, there on the side of the table was the missing rectangle of paper, held to the table with a strip of Scotch tape. 'Mira,' I said, and Angel looked. 'Aha,' he said.

As he examined the tape carefully – tape holds fingerprints wonderfully well – he put the paper on the floor and I squatted down to look at it. There were some letters written on it in a spidery hand; I leaned over farther to read them: LOYALTY.

'Loyalty?' I said.

'Sure. Isn't that an important virtue?'

'Let's ask him,' I said, and Angel shuddered hard enough that he almost dropped his tweezers.

'Me cago en diez with that shit,' he said, and reached for a plastic bag to put the paper into. It hardly seemed like something worth watching, and there was really nothing else to see, so I headed for the door.

I certainly am not a professional profiler, but because of my dark hobby I often have a certain amount of insight into other crimes that seem to come from the same neighborhood. This, however, was far outside the bounds of anything I had ever seen or imagined. There was no hint of any kind that pointed toward personality or motivation, and I was intrigued nearly as much as I was irritated. What kind of predator would leave the meat lying around and still wiggling like that?

I went outside and stood on the porch. Doakes was huddled with Captain Matthews, telling him something that had the captain looking worried. Deborah was crouched beside the old lady, talking quietly with her. I could feel a breeze picking up, the squall breeze that comes right before the afternoon thunderstorm, and as I looked up the first hard spatters of rain pelted down on the sidewalk. Sangre, who had been standing at the tape waving his microphone and trying to get the attention of Captain Matthews, looked up at the clouds too and, as the thunder began to rumble, threw his microphone at his producer and lurched into the news van.

My stomach rumbled, too, and I remembered that I had missed my lunch in all the excitement. This would never do; I needed to keep up my strength. My naturally high metabolism needed constant attention: no diet for Dexter. But I had to depend on Deborah for a ride, and I had the feeling, just a hunch, that she would not be sympathetic about any mention of eating at the moment. I looked at her again. She was cradling the old lady, Mrs. Medina, who had apparently given up retching and was concentrating on sobbing.

I sighed and walked to the car through the rain. I didn't really mind getting wet. It looked like I was going to have a long wait to dry off.

It was indeed a long wait, well over two hours. I sat in the car and listened to the radio and tried to picture, bite by bite, what it was like to eat a *medianoche* sandwich: the crackle of the bread crust, so crisp and toasty it scratches the inside of your mouth as you bite down. Then the first taste of mustard, followed by the soothing cheese and the salt of the meat. Next bite – a piece of pickle. Chew it all up; let the flavors mingle. Swallow. Take a big sip of Iron Beer (pronounced Ee-roan Bay-er, and it's a soda). Sigh. Sheer bliss. I would rather eat than do anything else except play with the Passenger. It's a true miracle of genetics that I am not fat.

I was on my third imaginary sandwich when Deborah finally came back to the car. She slid into the driver's seat, closed the door, and just sat there, staring ahead through the rain-splattered windshield. And I knew it wasn't the best thing I could have said, but I couldn't help myself. 'You look beat, Deb. How about lunch?'

She shook her head but didn't say anything.

'Maybe a nice sandwich. Or a fruit salad – get your blood sugar back up? You'll feel so much better.'

Now she looked at me, but it was not a look that showed any real promise of lunch at any time in the near future. 'This is why I wanted to be a cop,' she said.

'The fruit salad?'

'That thing in there – ' she said, and then turned to look out the windshield again. 'I want to nail that – that, whatever it is that could do that to a human being. I want it so bad I can *taste* it.'

'Does it taste like a sandwich, Deborah? Because – '

She smacked the heels of her palms onto the rim of the steering wheel, hard. Then she did it again. 'GodDAMN it,' she said. 'God-fucking-DAMN it!'

I sighed. Clearly long-suffering Dexter was going to be denied his crust of bread. And all because Deborah was having some kind of epiphany from seeing a piece of wiggling meat. Of course it was a terrible thing, and the world would be a much better place without someone in it who could do that, but did that mean we had to miss lunch? Didn't we all need to keep up our strength to catch this guy? Still, it did not seem like the very best time to point this out to Deborah, so I simply sat there with her, watching the rain splat against the windshield, and ate imaginary sandwich number four.

The next morning I had hardly settled into my little cubicle at work when my phone rang. 'Captain Matthews wants to see everybody who was there yesterday,' Deborah said.

'Good morning, Sis. Fine, thanks, and you?'

'Right now,' she said, and hung up.

The police world is made up of routine, both official and unofficial. This is one of the reasons I like my job. I always know what's coming, and so there are fewer human responses for me to memorize and then fake at the appropriate times, fewer chances for me to be caught off guard and react in a way that might call into question my membership in the race.

As far as I knew, Captain Matthews had never before called in 'everybody who was there.' Even when a case was generating a great deal of publicity, it was his policy to handle the press and those above him in the command structure, and let the investigating officer handle the casework. I could think of absolutely no reason why he would violate this protocol, even with a case as unusual as this one. And especially so soon – there had barely been enough time for him to approve a press release.

But 'right now' still meant right now, as far as I could tell, so I tottered down the hall to the captain's office. His secretary, Gwen, one of the most efficient women who had ever lived, sat there at her desk. She was also one of the plainest and most serious, and I found it almost impossible to resist tweaking her. 'Gwendolyn! Vision of radiant loveliness! Fly away with me to the blood lab!' I said as I came into the office.

She nodded at the door at the far end of the room. 'They're in the conference room,' she said, completely stone-faced.

'Is that a no?'

She moved her head an inch to the right. 'That door over there,' she said. 'They're waiting.'

They were indeed. At the head of the conference table Captain Matthews sat with a cup of coffee and a scowl. Ranged around the table were Deborah and Doakes, Vince Masuoka, Camilla Figg, and the four uniformed cops who had been setting the perimeter at the little house of horror when we arrived. Matthews nodded at me and said, 'Is this everybody?'

Doakes stopped glaring at me and said, 'Paramedics.'

Matthews shook his head. 'Not our problem. Somebody will talk to them later.' He cleared his throat and looked down, as though consulting an invisible script. 'All right,' he said, and cleared his throat again. 'The, uh, the event of yesterday which occurred at, um, N.W. 4th Street has been interdicted, ah, at the very highest level.' He looked up, and for a moment I thought he was impressed. '*Very* highest,' he said. 'You are all hereby ordered to keep to yourselves what you may have seen, heard, or surmised in connection with this event and its location. No comment, public or private, of any kind.' He looked at Doakes, who nodded, and then he looked around the table at all of us. 'Therefore, ah . . .'

Captain Matthews paused and frowned as he realized that he didn't actually have a 'therefore' for us. Luckily for his reputation as a smooth talker, the door opened. We all turned to look.

The doorway was filled with a very big man in a very nice suit. He wore no tie and the top three buttons of his shirt were undone. A diamond pinkie ring glittered on the little finger of his left hand. His hair was wavy and artfully mussed. He looked to be in his forties, and time had not been kind to his nose. A scar ran across his right eyebrow and another down one side of his chin, but the overall impression was not disfigurement so much as decoration. He looked at us all with a cheerful grin and bright, empty blue eyes, pausing in the doorway for a dramatic moment before he looked to the head of the table and said, 'Captain Matthews?'

The captain was a reasonably large man and masculine in a very well-kept way, but he looked small and even effeminate compared to the man in the doorway, and I believe he felt it. Still, he clenched his manly jaw and said, 'That's right.'

The big man strode in to Matthews and held out his hand. 'Nice to meet you, Captain. I'm Kyle Chutsky. We talked on the phone.' As he shook hands, he glanced around the table, pausing at Deborah before moving back to Matthews. But after only half a second his head snapped back around and he locked stares with Doakes, just for a moment. Neither one of them said anything, moved, twitched, or offered a business card, but I was absolutely positive they knew each other. Without acknowledging this in any way, Doakes looked down at the table in front of him and Chutsky returned his attention to the captain. 'You have a great department here, Captain Matthews. I hear nothing but good things about you guys.'

'Thank you . . . Mr. Chutsky,' Matthews said stiffly. 'Have a seat?'

Chutsky gave him a big, charming smile. 'Thanks, I will,' he said, and slid into the empty seat next to Deborah. She didn't turn to look at him, but from my spot across the table I could see a slow flush climbing up her neck, all the way to her scowl.

And at this point, I could hear a little voice in the back of Dexter's brain clearing its throat and saying, 'Excuse me, just a minute – but what the hell is going on here?' Perhaps someone had slipped some LSD into my coffee, because this entire day was beginning to feel like Dexter in Wonderland. Why were we even here? Who was the battered big guy who made Captain Matthews nervous? How did he know Doakes? And why, for the love of all that is shiny, bright, and sharp, was Deborah's face turning such an unbecoming shade of red?

I often find myself in situations where it seems to me like everyone else has read the instruction book while poor Dexter is in the dark and can't even match tab A with slot B. It usually relates to some natural human emotion, something that is universally understood. Unfortunately, Dexter is from a different universe and does not feel nor understand such things. All I can do is gather a few quick clues to help me decide what kind of face to make while I wait for things to settle back onto the familiar map.

I looked at Vince Masuoka. I was probably closer to him than any of the other lab techs, and not just because we took turns bringing in doughnuts. He always seemed to be faking his way through life, too, as if he had watched a series of videos to learn how to smile and talk to people. He was not quite as talented at pretending as I was, and the results were never as convincing, but I felt a certain kinship.

Right now he looked flustered and intimidated, and he seemed to be trying hard to swallow without any real luck. No clue there.

Camilla Figg was sitting at attention, staring at a spot on the wall in front of her. Her face was pale, but there was a small and very round spot of red color on each cheek.

Deborah, as mentioned, was slumping down in her chair and seemed very busily engaged in turning bright scarlet.

Chutsky slapped the palm of his hand on the table, looked around with a big happy smile, and said, 'I want to thank you all for your cooperation with this thing. It's very important that we keep this quiet until my people can move in on it.'

Captain Matthews cleared his throat. 'Ahem. I, uh, I assume you will want us to continue our routine investigative procedures and the, uh, interrogating of witnesses and so on.'

Chutsky shook his head slowly. 'Absolutely not. I need your people all the way out of the picture immediately. I want this whole thing to cease and desist, disappear – as far as your department is concerned, Captain, I want it never to have happened at all.'

'Are YOU taking over this investigation?' Deborah demanded.

Chutsky looked at her and his smile got bigger. 'That's right,' he said. And he probably would have kept smiling at her indefinitely if not for Officer Coronel, the cop who had sat on the porch with the weeping and retching old lady. He cleared his throat and said, 'Yeah, okay, just a minute here,' and there was a certain amount of hostility in his voice that made his very slight accent a little more obvious. Chutsky turned to look at him, and the smile stayed on his face. Coronel looked flustered, but he met Chutsky's happy stare. 'Are you trying to stop us from doing our jobs here?'

'Your job is to protect and serve,' Chutsky said. 'In this case that means to protect this information and serve me.'

'That's bullshit,' Coronel said.

'It doesn't matter what kind of shit it is,' Chutsky told him. 'You're gonna do it.'

'Who the fuck are you to tell me that?'

Captain Matthews tapped the table with his fingertips. 'That's enough, Coronel. Mr. Chutsky is from Washington, and I have been instructed to render him every assistance.'

Coronel was shaking his head. 'He's no goddamn FBI,' he said.

Chutsky just smiled. Captain Matthews took a deep breath to say something – but Doakes moved his head half an inch toward Coronel and said, 'Shut your mouth.' Coronel looked at him and some of the fight went out of him. 'Don't want to mess with this shit,' Doakes went on. 'Let his people handle it.'

'It isn't right,' said Coronel.

'Leave it,' said Doakes.

Coronel opened his mouth, Doakes raised his eyebrows – and on reflection, looking at the face underneath those eyebrows, perhaps, Officer Coronel decided to leave it.

Captain Matthews cleared his throat in an attempt to take back control. 'Any more questions? All right then – Mr. Chutsky. If there's any other way we can help . . .'

'As a matter of fact, Captain, I would appreciate it if I could borrow one of your detectives for liaison. Somebody who can help me find my way around, dot all the t's, like that.'

All the heads around the table swung to Doakes in perfect unison, except for Chutsky's. He turned to his side, to Deborah, and said, 'How about it, Detective?'

CHAPTER 9

I HAVE TO ADMIT THE SURPRISE ENDING TO Captain Matthews' meeting caught me off guard, but at least I now knew why everyone was acting so much like lab rats thrown into a lion's cage. No one likes to have the Feds come in on a case; the only joy in it is making things as hard as possible for them when they do. But Chutsky was apparently such a very heavy hitter that even this small pleasure would be denied to us.

The significance of Deborah's bright red skin condition was a deeper mystery, but it wasn't my problem. My problem had suddenly become a little bit clearer. You may think that Dexter is a dull boy for not putting it together sooner, but when the nickel finally dropped it was accompanied by a desire to smack myself on the head. Perhaps all the beer at Rita's house had short-sheeted my mental powers.

But clearly this visitation from Washington had been called down upon us by none other than Dexter's personal nemesis, Sergeant Doakes. There had been some vague rumors that his service in the army had been somewhat irregular, and I was starting to believe them. His reaction when he saw the thing on the table had not been shock, outrage, disgust, or anger, but something far more interesting: recognition. Right at the scene he had told Captain Matthews what this was, and who to talk to about it. That particular who had sent Chutsky. And therefore when I had thought Chutsky and Doakes had recognized each other at the meeting, I had been right – because whatever was going on that Doakes knew about, Chutsky knew about it, too, probably even more so, and he had come to squash it. And if Doakes knew about something like this, there had to be a way to use his background against him in some small way, thus flinging the chains off poor Detained Dexter.

It was a brilliant train of pure cool logic; I welcomed the return of my giant brain and mentally patted myself on the head. Good boy, Dexter. Arf arf.

It is always nice to see the synapses clicking in a way that lets you know your opinion of yourself is sometimes justified. But in this particular case, there was just a chance that more was at stake than Dexter's self-esteem. If Doakes had something to hide, I was a step closer to being back in business.

There are several things that Dashing Dexter is good at, and some of them can actually be legally performed in public. One of these things is using a computer to find information. This was a skill I had developed to help me be absolutely sure about new friends like MacGregor and Reiker. Aside from avoiding the unpleasantness of cutting up the wrong person, I like to confront my fellow hobbyists with the evidence of their past indiscretions before I send them off to dreamland. Computers and the Internet were wonderful means of finding this stuff.

So if Doakes had something to hide, I thought I could probably find it, or at least some small thread of it that I could yank on until his whole dark past began to unravel. Knowing him as I did, I was quite sure it would be dismal and Dexter-like. And when I found that certain something . . . Perhaps I was being naïve to think I could use this hypothetical information to get him off my case, but I thought there was a very good chance. Not by confronting him directly and demanding that he cease and desist or else, which might not be entirely wise with someone like Doakes. Besides, that was blackmail, which I am told is very wrong. But information is power, and I would certainly find some small way to use whatever I found – a way to give Doakes something to think about that did not involve shadowing Dexter and curtailing his Crusade for Decency. And a man who discovers his pants are on fire tends to have very little time to worry about somebody else's box of matches.

I went happily down the hall from the captain's office, back to my little cubicle off the forensics lab, and got right to work.

A few hours later I had just about all I could find. There were surprisingly few details in Sergeant Doakes's file. The few that I found left me gasping for breath: Doakes had a first name! It was Albert – had anyone ever really called him that? Unthinkable. I had assumed his name was Sergeant. And he had been born, too – in Waycross, Georgia. Where would the wonders end? There was more, even better; before he had come to the department, Sergeant Doakes had been – Sergeant Doakes! In the army – the Special Forces, of all things! Picturing Doakes in one of those jaunty green beanies marching alongside John Wayne was almost more than I could think about without bursting into military song.

Several commendations and medals were listed, but I could find no mention of any heroic actions that had earned them. Still, I felt much more patriotic just knowing the man. The rest of his record was almost completely empty of details. The only thing that stood out at all was an eighteen-month stretch of something called 'detached service.' Doakes had served it as a military adviser in El Salvador, returned home to a six-month stretch at the Pentagon, and then retired to our fortunate city. Miami's police department had been happy to scoop up a decorated veteran and offer him gainful employment.

But El Salvador – I was not a history buff, but I seemed to recall that it had been something of a horror show. There had been protest marches down on Brickell Avenue at the time. I didn't remember why, but I knew how to find out. I fired up my computer again and went online, and oh dear – find out I did. El Salvador at the time Doakes was there had been a true three-ring circus of torture, rape, murder, and name-calling. And no one had thought to invite me.

I found an awful lot of information posted by various human rights groups. They were quite serious, almost shrill, in the things they had to say about what had been done down there. Still, as far as I could tell, nothing had ever come of their protests. After all, it was only human rights. It must be terribly frustrating; PETA seems to get much better results. These poor souls had done their research, published their results detailing rapes, electrodes, and cattle prods, complete with photos, diagrams, and the names of the hideous inhuman monsters who reveled in inflicting this suffering on the masses. And the hideous inhuman monsters in question retired to the south of France, while the rest of the world boycotted restaurants for mistreating chickens.

It gave me a great deal of hope. If I was ever caught, perhaps I could simply protest dairy products and they'd let me go.

The El Salvadoran names and historical details I found meant very little to me. Neither did the organizations involved. Apparently it had developed into one of those wonderful free-for-alls where there were no actual good guys, merely several teams of bad guys with the campesinos caught in the middle. The United States had covertly backed one side, however, in spite of the fact that this team seemed just as eager to hammer suspicious poor persons into paste. And it was this side that got my attention. Something had turned the tide in their favor, some terrible threat that was not specified, something that was apparently so awful it left people nostalgic for cattle prods in the rectum.

Whatever it was, it seemed to coincide with the period of Sergeant Doakes's detached service.

I sat back in my rickety swivel chair. Well, well, well, I thought. What an interesting coincidence. At approximately the same time, we had Doakes, hideous unnamed torture, and covert U.S. involvement all buzzing about together. Naturally enough there was no proof that these three things were in any way linked, no reason at all to suspect any kind of connection. Just as naturally, I was as sure as I could be that they were very much three peas in one pod. Because twenty-some years later they had all come back together for a reunion party in Miami: Doakes, Chutsky, and whatever had made the thing on the table. It was starting to look like tab A would fit into slot B after all.

I had found my little string. And if only I could think of a way to pull on it –

Peekaboo, Albert.

Of course, having information to use is one thing. Knowing what it means and how to use it is a different story. And all I really knew was that Doakes had been there when some bad things happened. He probably hadn't done them himself, and in any case they were sanctioned by the government. Covertly, of course – which made one wonder how everyone knew about it.

On the other hand, there was certainly somebody out there who still wanted to keep this quiet. And at the moment, that somebody was represented by Chutsky – who was being chaperoned by my dear sister, Deborah. If I could get her help, I might be able to squeeze a few details out of Chutsky. What I could do then remained to be seen, but at least I could begin.

It sounded too simple, and of course it was. I called Deborah right away, and got her answering machine. I tried her cell phone and it was the same thing. For the rest of the day, Debs was out of the office please leave a message. When I tried her at home that evening it was the same thing. And when I hung up the phone and looked out the window of my apartment, Sergeant Doakes was parked in his favorite spot across the street.

A half-moon came out from behind a tattered cloud and muttered at me, but it was wasting its breath. No matter how much I wanted to slip away and have an adventure named Reiker, I could not; not with that awful maroon Taurus parked there like a discount conscience. I turned away, looking for something to kick. Here it was Friday night, and I was prevented from stepping out and strolling through the shadows with the Dark Passenger – and now I couldn't even get my sister on the phone. What a terrible thing life can be.

I paced around my apartment for a while but accomplished nothing except stubbing my toe. I called Deborah two more times and she was not home two more times. I looked out the window again. The moon had moved slightly; Doakes had not.

All righty then. Back to plan B.

Half an hour later I was sitting on Rita's couch with a can of beer in my hand. Doakes had followed me, and I had to assume he was waiting across the street in his car. I hoped he was enjoying this as much as I was, which was to say not very much at all. Was this what it was like to be human? Were people actually so miserable and brainless that they looked forward to this – to spending Friday night, precious time off from wage slave drudgery, sitting in front of a television with a can of beer? It was mind-numbingly dull, and to my horror, I found that I was getting used to it.

Curses on you, Doakes. You're driving me normal.

'Hey, mister,' Rita said, plunking herself down next to me, where she curled her feet under her, 'why so quiet?'

'I think I'm working too hard,' I told her. 'And enjoying it less.'

She was quiet for a moment, then she said, 'It's that thing with the guy you had to let go, isn't it? The guy who was . . . he killed the kids?'

'That's part of it,' I said. 'I don't like unfinished business.'

Rita nodded, almost as if she actually understood what I was saying. 'That's very . . . I mean, I can tell it's bothering you. Maybe you should – I don't know. What do you usually do to relax?'

It certainly conjured up some funny pictures to think of telling her what I did to relax, but it was probably not a very good idea. So instead I said, 'Well, I like to take my boat out. Go fishing.'

And a small, very soft voice behind me said, 'Me, too.' Only my highly trained nerves of steel prevented me from bumping my head on the ceiling fan; I am nearly impossible to sneak up on, and yet I'd had no idea there was anyone else in the room. But I turned around and there was Cody, looking at me with his large, unblinking eyes. 'You too?' I said. 'You like to go fishing?'

He nodded; two words at a time was close to his daily limit.

'Well, then,' I said. 'I guess it's settled. How about tomorrow morning?'

'Oh,' Rita said, 'I don't think – I mean, he isn't – You don't have to, Dexter.'

Cody looked at me. Naturally enough he didn't say anything, but he didn't need to. It was all there in his eyes. 'Rita,' I said, 'sometimes the boys need to get away from the girls. Cody and I are going fishing in the morning. Bright and early,' I said to Cody.

'Why?'

'I don't know why,' I said. 'But you're supposed to go early, so we will.' Cody nodded, looked at his mother, and then turned around and walked down the hall.

'Really, Dexter,' Rita said. 'You really don't have to.'

And, of course, I knew I didn't have to. But why shouldn't I? It probably wouldn't cause me actual physical pain. Besides that, it would be nice to get away for a few hours. Especially from Doakes. And in any case – again, I don't know why it should be, but kids really do matter to me. I certainly don't get all gooey-eyed at the sight of training wheels on a bicycle, but on the whole I find children far more interesting than their parents.

The next morning, as the sun was coming up, Cody and I were motoring slowly out of the canal by my apartment in my seventeen-foot Whaler. Cody wore a blue-and-yellow life vest and sat very still on the cooler. He slumped down just a little so that his head almost vanished inside the vest, making him look like a brightly colored turtle.

Inside the cooler was soda and a lunch Rita had made for us, a light snack for ten or twelve people. I had brought frozen shrimp for bait, since this was Cody's first trip and I didn't know how he might react to sticking a sharp metal hook into something that was still alive. I rather enjoyed it, of course – the more alive, the better! – but one can't expect sophisticated tastes from a child.

Out the canal, into Biscayne Bay, and I headed across to Cape Florida, steering for the channel that cut past the lighthouse. Cody didn't say anything until we came within sight of Stiltsville, that odd collection of houses built on pilings in the middle of the bay. Then he tugged at my sleeve. I bent down to hear him over the roar of the engine and the wind.

'Houses,' he said.

'Yes,' I yelled. 'Sometimes there are even people in them.'

He watched the houses go by and then, when they began to disappear behind us, he sat back down on the cooler. He turned around once more to look at them when they were almost out of sight. After that he just sat until we got to Fowey Rock and I idled down. I put the motor in neutral and slid the anchor over the bow, waiting to make sure it caught before turning the engine off.

'All right, Cody,' I said. 'It's time to kill some fish.'

He smiled, a very rare event. 'Okay,' he said.

He watched me with unblinking attention as I showed him how to thread the shrimp onto the hook. Then he tried it himself, very slowly and carefully pushing the hook in until the point came out again. He looked at the hook and then up at me. I nodded, and he looked back at the shrimp, reaching out to touch the place where the hook broke through the shell.

'All right,' I said. 'Now drop it in the water.' He looked up at me. 'That's where the fish are,' I said. Cody nodded, pointed his rod tip over the side of the boat, and pushed the release button on his little Zebco reel to drop the bait into the water. I flicked my bait over the side, too, and we sat there rocking slowly on the waves.

I watched Cody fish with his fierce blank concentration. Perhaps it was the combination of open water and a small boy, but I couldn't help but think of Reiker. Even though I could not safely investigate him, I was assuming that he was guilty. When would he know that MacGregor was gone, and what would he do about it? It seemed most likely that he would panic and try to disappear – and yet, the more I thought about it, the more I wondered. There is a natural human reluctance to abandon an entire life and start over somewhere else. Perhaps he would just be cautious for a while. And if so, I could fill my time with the new entry on my rather exclusive social register, whoever had created the Howling Vegetable of N.W. 4th Street, and the fact that this sounded rather like a Sherlock Holmes title made it no less urgent. Somehow I had to neutralize Doakes. Somehow someway sometime soon I had to –

'Are you going to be my dad?' Cody asked suddenly.

Luckily I had nothing in my mouth which might choke me, but for a moment it felt like there was something in my throat, something the approximate size of a Thanksgiving turkey. When I could breathe again, I managed to stammer out, 'Why do you ask?'

He was still watching his rod tip. 'Mom says maybe,' he said.

'Did she?' I said, and he nodded without looking up.

My head whirled. What was Rita thinking? I had been so wrapped up in the hard work of ramming my disguise down Doakes's throat that I had never really thought about what was going on in Rita's head. Apparently, I should have. Could she truly be thinking that, that – it was unthinkable. But I suppose in a strange way it might make sense if one was a human being. Fortunately I am not, and the thought seemed completely bizarre to me. *Mom says maybe?* Maybe I would be Cody's dad? Meaning, um –

'Well,' I said, which was a very good start considering I had absolutely no idea what I might say next. Happily for me, just as I realized nothing resembling a coherent answer was going to come out of my mouth, Cody's rod tip jerked savagely. 'You have a fish!' I said, and for the next few minutes it was all he could do to hang on as the line whirred off his reel. The fish made repeated ferocious, slashing zigzags to the right, the left, under the boat, and then straight for the horizon. But slowly, in spite of several long runs away from the boat, Cody worked the fish closer. I coached him to keep the rod tip up, wind in the line, work the fish in to where I could get a hand on the leader and bring it into the boat. Cody watched it flop on the deck, its forked tail still flipping wildly.

'A blue runner,' I said. 'That is one wild fish.' I bent to release it, but it was bucking too much for me to get a hand on it. A thin stream of blood came from its mouth and onto my clean white deck, which was a bit upsetting. 'Ick,' I said. 'I think he swallowed the hook. We'll have to cut it out.' I pulled my fillet knife from its black plastic sheath and laid it on the deck. 'There's going to be a lot of blood,' I warned Cody. I do not like blood, and I did not want it in my boat, not even fish blood. I took the two steps forward to open the dry locker and get an old towel I kept for cleaning up.

'Ha,' I heard behind me, softly. I turned around.

Cody had taken the knife and stuck it into the fish, watching it struggle away from the blade, and then carefully sticking the point in again. This second time he pushed the blade deep into the fish's gills, and a gout of blood ran out onto the deck.

'Cody,' I said.

He looked up at me and, wonder of wonders, he smiled. 'I like fishing, Dexter,' he said.

CHAPTER 10

BY MONDAY MORNING I STILL HAD NOT GOTTEN in touch with Deborah. I called repeatedly, and although I became so familiar with the sound of the tone that I could hum it, Deborah did not respond. It was increasingly frustrating; here I was with a possible way out of the stranglehold Doakes had put me in, and I could get no further with it than the telephone. It's terrible to have to depend on someone else.

But I am persistent and patient, among my many other Boy Scout virtues. I left dozens of messages, all of them cheerful and clever, and that positive attitude must have done the trick, because I finally got an answer.

I had just settled into my desk chair to finish a report on a double homicide, nothing exciting. A single weapon, probably a machete, and a few moments of wild abandon. The initial wounds on both victims had been delivered in bed, where they had apparently been caught in flagrante delicto. The man had managed to raise one arm, but a little too late to save his neck. The woman made it all the way to the door before a blow to the upper spine sent a spurt of blood onto the wall beside the door frame. Routine stuff, the kind of thing that makes up most of my work, and extremely unpleasant. There is just so very much blood in two human beings, and when somebody decides to let it all out at once it makes a terrible and unattractive mess, which I find deeply offensive. Organizing and analyzing it makes me feel a great deal better, and my job can be deeply satisfying on occasion.

But this one was a real mess. I had found spatter on the ceiling fan, most likely from the machete blade as the killer raised his arm between strokes. And because the fan was on, it flung more spatter to the far corners of the room.

It had been a busy day for Dexter. I was just trying to word a paragraph in the report properly to indicate that it had been what we like to call a 'crime of passion' when my phone rang.

'Hey, Dex,' the voice said, and it sounded so relaxed, even sleepy, that it took me a moment to realize it was Deborah.

'Well,' I said. 'The rumors of your death were exaggerated.'

She laughed, and again the sound of it was downright mellow, unlike her usual hard-edged chuckle. 'Yeah,' she said. 'I'm alive. But Kyle has kept me pretty busy.'

'Remind him of the labor laws, Sis. Even sergeants need their rest.'

'Mm, I don't know about that,' she said. 'I feel pretty good without it.' And she gave a throaty, two-syllable chuckle that sounded as unlike Debs as if she had asked me to show her the best way to cut through living human bone.

I tried to remember when I had heard Deborah say she felt pretty good and actually sound like she meant it at the same time. I came up blank. 'You sound very unlike yourself, Deborah,' I said. 'What on earth has gotten into you?'

This time her laugh was a bit longer, but just as happy. 'The usual,' she said. And then she laughed again. 'Anyway, what's up?'

'Oh, not a thing,' I said, with innocence blooming from my tongue. 'My only sister disappears for days and nights on end without a word and then turns up sounding like she stepped out of *Stepford Sergeants*. So I am naturally curious to know what the hell is going on, that's all.'

'Well, hell,' she said. 'I'm touched. It's almost like having a real human brother.'

'Let's hope it goes no further than almost.'

'How about we get together for lunch?' she said.

'I'm already hungry,' I said. 'Relampago's?'

'Mm, no,' she said. 'How about Azul?'

I suppose her choice of restaurant made as much sense as everything else about her this morning, because it made no sense at all. Deborah was a blue-collar diner, and Azul was the kind of place where Saudi royalty ate when they were in town. Apparently her transformation into an alien was now complete.

'Certainly, Deb, Azul. I'll just sell my car to pay for it and meet you there.'

'One o'clock,' she said. 'And don't worry about the money. Kyle will pick up the tab.' She hung up. And I didn't actually say AHA! But a small light flickered on.

Kyle would pay, would he? Well, well. And at Azul, too.

If the glittery ticky-tack of South Beach is the part of Miami designed for insecure wannabe celebrities, Azul is for people who find the glamour amusing. The little cafés that crowd South Beach compete for attention with a shrill clamor of bright and cheap gaudiness.

Azul is so understated by comparison that you wonder if they had ever seen even a single episode of *Miami Vice*.

I left my car with the mandatory valet parking attendant in a small cobblestone circle out front. I am fond of my car, but I will admit that it did not compare favorably to the line of Ferraris and Rolls-Royces. Even so, the attendant did not actually decline to park it for me, although he must have guessed that it would not result in the kind of tip he was used to. I suppose my bowling shirt and khaki pants were an unmistakable clue that I didn't have even a single bearer bond or Krugerrand for him.

The restaurant itself was dark and cool and so quiet you could hear an American Express Black Card drop. The far wall was tinted glass with a door that led out to a terrace. And there was Deborah, sitting at a small corner table outside, looking out over the water. Across from her, facing back toward the door in to the restaurant, sat Kyle Chutsky, who would pick up the tab. He was wearing very expensive sunglasses, so perhaps he really would. I approached the table and a waiter materialized to pull out a chair that was certainly far too heavy for anyone who could afford to eat here. The waiter didn't actually bow, but I could tell that the restraint was an effort.

'Hey, buddy,' Kyle said as I sat down. He stretched his hand across the table. Since he seemed to believe I was his new best friend, I leaned in and shook hands with him. 'How's the spatter trade?'

'Always plenty of work,' I said. 'And how's the mysterious visitor from Washington trade?'

'Never better,' he said. He held my hand in his just

a moment too long. I looked down at it; his knuckles were enlarged, as if he had spent too much time sparring with a concrete wall. He slapped his left hand on the table, and I got a glimpse of his pinkie ring. It was startlingly effeminate, almost an engagement ring. When he finally let go of my hand, he smiled and swiveled his head toward Deborah, although with his sunglasses it was impossible to tell if he was looking at her or just moving his neck around.

Deborah smiled back at him. 'Dexter was worried about me.'

'Hey,' Chutsky said, 'what are brothers for?'

She glanced at me. 'Sometimes I wonder,' she said.

'Why Deborah, you know I'm only watching your back,' I said.

Kyle chuckled. 'Good deal. I got the front,' he said, and they both laughed. She reached across and took his hand.

'All the hormones and happiness are setting my teeth on edge,' I said. 'Tell me, is anybody actually trying to catch that inhuman monster, or are we just going to sit around and make tragic puns?'

Kyle swiveled his head back to me and raised an eyebrow. 'What's your interest in this, buddy?'

'Dexter has a fondness for inhuman monsters,' Deborah said. 'Like a hobby.'

'A hobby,' Kyle said, keeping the sunglasses turned to my face. I think it was supposed to intimidate me, but for all I knew his eyes could be closed. Somehow, I managed not to tremble.

'He's kind of an amateur profiler,' Deborah said.

Kyle didn't move for a moment and I wondered if he had gone to sleep behind his dark lenses. 'Huh,' he finally said, and he leaned back in his chair. 'Well, what do you think about this guy, Dexter?'

'Oh, just the basics so far,' I said. 'Somebody with a lot of training in the medical area and in covert activities who came unhinged and needs to make a statement, something to do with Central America. He'll probably do it again timed for maximum impact, rather than because he feels he *has* to. So he's not really a standard serial type of – What?' I said. Kyle had lost his laid-back smile and was sitting straight up with his fists clenched.

'What do you mean, Central America?'

I was fairly sure we both knew exactly what I meant by Central America, but I thought saying El Salvador might have been a bit too much; it wouldn't do to lose my casual, it's-just-a-hobby credentials. But my whole purpose for coming had been to find out about Doakes, and when you see an opening – well, I admit it had been a little obvious, but it had apparently worked. 'Oh,' I said. 'Isn't that right?' All those years of practice in imitating human expressions paid off for me here as I put on my best innocently curious face.

Kyle apparently couldn't decide if that was right. He worked his jaw muscles and unclenched his fists.

'I should have warned you,' Deborah said. 'He's good at this.'

Chutsky let out a big breath and shook his head. 'Yeah,' he said. With a visible effort he leaned back and flicked on his smile again. 'Pretty good, buddy. How'd you come up with all that?'

'Oh, I don't know,' I said modestly. 'It just seemed obvious. The hard part is figuring out how Sergeant Doakes is involved.'

'Jesus H. Christ,' he said, and clenched his fists again. Deborah looked at me and laughed, not exactly the same kind of laugh she had given Kyle, but still, it felt good to know she could remember now and then that we were on the same team. 'I told you he's good,' she said.

'Jesus Christ,' Kyle said again. He pumped one index finger unconsciously, as if squeezing an invisible trigger, then turned his sunglasses in Deb's direction. 'You're right about that,' he said, and turned back to me. He watched me hard for a moment, possibly to see if I would bolt for the door or start speaking Arabic, and then he nodded. 'What's this about Sergeant Doakes?'

'You're not just trying to drop Doakes in the shit, are you?' Deborah asked me.

'In Captain Matthews's conference room,' I said, 'when Kyle saw Doakes for the first time, there was a moment when I thought they recognized each other.'

'I didn't notice that,' Deborah said with a frown.

'You were busy blushing,' I said. She blushed again, which I thought was a little redundant. 'Besides, Doakes was the one who knew who to call when he saw the crime scene.'

'Doakes knows some stuff,' Chutsky admitted. 'From his military service.'

'What kind of stuff?' I asked. Chutsky looked at me for a long time, or anyway his sunglasses did. He tapped on the table with that silly pinkie ring and the sunlight flashed off the large diamond in the center. When he finally spoke it felt like the temperature at our table had dropped ten degrees.

'Buddy,' he said, 'I don't want to cause you any

trouble, but you have to let go of this. Back off. Find a different hobby. Or else you are in a world of shit – and you will get flushed.' The waiter materialized at Kyle's elbow before I could think of something wonderful to say to that. Chutsky kept the sunglasses turned toward me for a long moment. Then he handed the menu to the waiter. 'The bouillabaisse is really good here,' he said.

Deborah disappeared for the rest of the week, which did very little for my self-esteem, because no matter how terrible it was for me to admit it, without her help I was stuck. I could not come up with any sort of alternative plan for ditching Doakes. He was still there, parked under the tree across from my apartment, following me to Rita's house, and I had no answers. My once-proud brain chased its tail and caught nothing but air.

I could feel the Dark Passenger roiling and whimpering and struggling to climb out and take the steering wheel, but there was Doakes looming up through the windshield, forcing me to clamp down and reach for another can of beer. I had worked too hard and too long to achieve my perfect little life and I was not going to ruin it now. The Passenger and I could wait a bit longer. Harry had taught me discipline, and that would have to see me through to happier days.

'Patience,' Harry said. He paused to cough into a Kleenex. 'Patient is more important than smart, Dex. You're already smart.'

'Thank you,' I said. And I meant it politely, really,

because I was not at all comfortable sitting there in Harry's hospital room. The smell of medicine and disinfectant and urine mixed with the air of restrained suffering and clinical death made me wish I was almost anywhere else. Of course, as a callow young monster, I never wondered if Harry might not feel the same.

'In your case, you have to be *more* patient, because you'll be thinking you're clever enough to get away with it,' he said. 'You're not. Nobody is.' He paused to cough again, and this time it took longer and seemed to go deeper. To see Harry like this – indestructible, supercop, foster-father Harry, shaking, turning red and weepy-eyed from the strain – was almost too much. I had to look away. When I looked back a moment later, Harry was watching me again.

'I know you, Dexter. Better than you know yourself.' And this was easy to believe until he followed up with, 'You're basically a good guy.'

'No I'm not,' I said, thinking of the wonderful things I had not yet been allowed to do; even wanting to do them pretty much ruled out any kind of association with goodness. There was also the fact that most of the other pimple-headed hormone-churning twinkies my age who were considered good guys were no more like me than an orangutan was. But Harry wouldn't hear it.

'Yes, you are,' he said. 'And you have to believe that you are. Your heart is pretty much in the right place, Dex,' he said, and with that he collapsed into a truly epic fit of coughing. It lasted for what seemed like several minutes, and then he leaned weakly back onto his pillow. He closed his eyes for a moment, but when he opened them again they were steely Harry blue, brighter than ever in the pale green of his dying face. 'Patience,' he said. And he made it sound strong, in spite of the terrible pain and weakness he must have felt. 'You still have a long way to go, and I don't have a whole lot of time, Dexter.'

'Yes, I know,' I said. He closed his eyes.

'That's just what I mean,' he said. 'You're supposed to say no, don't worry, you have plenty of time.'

'But you don't,' I said, not sure where this was going.

'No, I don't,' he said. 'But people pretend. To make me feel better about it.'

'Would you feel better?'

'No,' he said, and opened his eyes again. 'But you can't use logic on human behavior. You have to be patient, watch and learn. Otherwise, you screw up. Get caught and . . . Half my legacy.' He closed his eyes again and I could hear the strain in his voice. 'Your sister will be a good cop. You,' he smiled slowly, a little sadly, 'you will be something else. Real justice. But only if you're patient. If your chance isn't there, Dexter, wait until it is.'

It all seemed so overwhelming to an eighteen-year-old apprentice monster. All I wanted was to do The Thing, very simple really, just go dancing in the moonlight with the bright blade flowing free – such an easy thing, so natural and sweet – to cut through all the nonsense and right down to the heart of things. But I could not. Harry made it complicated.

'I don't know what I'll do when you're dead,' I said.

'You'll do fine,' he said.

'There's so much to remember.'

97

Harry reached a hand out and pushed the button that hung on a cord beside his bed. 'You'll remember it,' he said. He dropped the cord and it was almost as though it pulled the last of the strength from him as it flopped back down by the bedside. 'You'll remember.' He closed his eyes and for a moment I was all alone in the room. Then the nurse bustled in with a syringe and Harry opened one eye. 'We can't always do what we think we have to do. So when there's nothing else you can do, you wait,' he said, and held out his arm for his shot. 'No matter what . . . pressure . . . you might feel.'

I watched him as he lay there, taking the needle without flinching and knowing that even the relief it brought was temporary, that his end was coming and he could not stop it – and knowing, too, that he was not afraid, and that he would do this the right way, as he had done everything else in his life the right way. And I knew this, too: Harry understood me. No one else ever had, and no one else ever would, through all time in all the world. Only Harry.

The only reason I ever thought about being human was to be more like him.

CHAPTER 11

AND SO I WAS PATIENT. IT WAS NOT AN EASY thing, but it was the Harry thing. Let the bright steely spring inside stay coiled and quiet and wait, watch, hold the hot sweet release locked tight in its cold box until it was Harry-right to let it skitter out and cartwheel through the night. Sooner or later some small opening would show and we could vault through it. Sooner or later I would find a way to make Doakes blink.

I waited.

Some of us, of course, find that harder to do than others, and it was several days later, a Saturday morning, that my telephone rang.

'Goddamn it,' said Deborah without any preamble. It was almost a relief to hear that she was her recognizable cranky self again.

'Fine, thanks, and you?' I said.

'Kyle is making me nuts,' she said. 'He says there's nothing we can do but wait, but he won't tell me what we're waiting for. He disappears for ten or twelve hours and won't tell me where he was. And then we just wait some more. I am so fucking tired of waiting my teeth hurt.'

'Patience is a virtue,' I said.

'I'm tired of being virtuous, too,' she said. 'And I am sick to death of Kyle's patronizing smile when I ask him what we can do to find this guy.'

'Well, Debs, I don't know what I can do except offer my sympathy,' I said. 'I'm sorry.'

'I think you can do a whole hell of a lot more than that, Bro,' she said.

I sighed heavily, mostly for her benefit. Sighs register so nicely on the telephone. 'This is the trouble with having a reputation as a gunslinger, Debs,' I said. 'Everybody thinks I can shoot the eye out of a jack at thirty paces, every single time.'

'I still think it,' she said.

'Your confidence warms my heart, but I don't understand a thing about this kind of adventure, Deborah. It leaves me completely cold.'

'I have to find this guy, Dexter. And I want to rub Kyle's nose in it,' she said.

'I thought you liked him.'

She snorted. 'Jesus, Dexter. You don't know anything about women, do you? Of course I like him. That's *why* I want to rub his nose in it.'

'Oh, good, *now* it makes sense,' I said.

She paused, and then very casually said, 'Kyle said some interesting things about Doakes.'

I felt my long-fanged friend inside stretch just a little and absolutely purr. 'You're getting very subtle all of a sudden, Deborah,' I said. 'All you had to do was ask me.'

'I just asked, and you gave me all that crap about how you can't help,' she said, suddenly good old plain-speaking Debs again. 'So how about it. What have you got?'

'Nothing at the moment,' I said.

'Shit,' said Deborah.

'But I might be able to find something.'

'How soon?'

I admit that I was feeling irked by Kyle's attitude toward me. What had he said? I would be 'in the shit and you will get flushed'? Seriously – who wrote his dialogue? And Deborah's sudden onset of subtlety, which had been my traditional bailiwick, had done nothing to calm me down. So I shouldn't have said it, but I did. 'How about by lunchtime?' I said. 'Let's say I'll have something by one o'clock. Baleen, since Kyle can pick up the check.'

'This I gotta see,' she said, and then added, 'The stuff about Doakes? It's pretty good.' She hung up.

Well, well, I said to myself. Suddenly, I did not mind the thought of working a little bit on a Saturday. After all, the only alternative was to hang out at Rita's and watch moss grow on Sergeant Doakes. But if I found something for Debs, I might at long last have the small opening I had hoped for. I merely had to be the clever boy we all believed I was.

But where to start? There was precious little to go on, since Kyle had pulled the department away from the crime scene before we had done much more than dust for prints. Many times in the past I had earned a few modest brownie points with my police colleagues by helping them track down the sick and twisted demons who lived only to kill. But that was because I understood them, since I am a sick and twisted demon myself. This time, I could not rely on getting any hints from the Dark Passenger, who had been lulled into an uneasy sleep, poor fellow. I had to depend on my own bare-naked native wit, which was also being alarmingly silent at the moment.

Perhaps if I gave my brain some fuel, it would kick into high gear. I went to the kitchen and found a banana. It was very nice, but for some reason it did not launch any mental rockets.

I threw the peel in the garbage and looked at the clock. Well, dear boy, that was five whole minutes gone by. Excellent. And you have already managed to figure out that you can't figure anything out. Bravo, Dexter.

There really were very few places to start. In fact, all I had was the victim and the house. And since I was fairly certain that the victim would not have a lot to say, even if we gave him back his tongue, that left the house. Of course it was possible that the house belonged to the victim. But the decor had such a temporary look to it, I was sure it did not.

Strange to simply walk away from an entire house like that. But he had done so, and with no one breathing down his neck and forcing a hasty and panicked retreat – which meant that he had done it deliberately, as part of his plan.

And that should imply that he had somewhere else to go. Presumably still in the Miami area, since Kyle was here looking for him. It was a starting point, and I thought of it all by myself. Welcome home, Mr. Brain.

Real estate leaves fairly large footprints, even when you try to cover them up. Within fifteen minutes of sitting down at my computer I had found something – not actually a whole footprint, but certainly enough to make out the shape of a couple of toes.

The house on N.W. 4th Street was registered to Ramon Puntia. How he expected to get away with that in Miami, I don't know, but Ramon Puntia was a

Cuban joke name, like 'Joe Blow' in English. But the house was paid for and no taxes were due, a sound arrangement for someone who valued privacy as much as I assumed our new friend did. The house had been bought with a single cash payment, a wire transfer from a bank in Guatemala. This seemed a bit odd; with our trail starting in El Salvador and leading through the murky depths of a mysterious government agency in Washington, why take a left turn into Guatemala? But a quick online study of contemporary money laundering showed that it fit very well. Apparently Switzerland and the Cayman Islands were no longer à la mode, and if one wished for discreet banking in the Spanish-speaking world, Guatemala was all the rage.

This raised the interesting question of how much money Dr. Dismember had, and where it came from. But it was a question that led nowhere at the moment. I had to assume that he had enough for another house when he was done with the first one, and probably in the same approximate price range.

All right then. I went back to my Dade County real estate database and looked for other properties recently purchased the same way, from the same bank. There were seven; four of them had sold for more than a million dollars, which struck me as a bit high for disposable property. They had probably been bought by nothing more sinister than run-of-the-mill drug lords and Fortune 500 CEOs on the run.

That left three properties that seemed possible. One of them was in Liberty City, a predominantly black inner-city area of Miami. But on closer inspection, it turned out to be a block of apartments.

Of the two remaining properties, one was in Homestead, within sight of the gigantic dump heap of city garbage known locally as Mount Trashmore. The other was also in the south end of town, just off Quail Roost Drive.

Two houses: I was willing to bet that someone new had just moved in to one of them, and was doing things that might startle the ladies from the welcome wagon. No guarantees, of course, but it certainly seemed likely, and it was, after all, just in time for lunch.

Baleen was a very pricey place that I would not have attempted on my own modest means. It has the kind of oak-paneled elegance that makes you feel the need for a cravat and spats. It also has one of the best views of Biscayne Bay in the city, and if one is lucky there are a handful of tables that take advantage of this.

Either Kyle was lucky or his mojo had bowled over the headwaiter, because he and Deborah were waiting outside at one of these tables working on a bottle of mineral water and a plate of what appeared to be crab cakes. I grabbed one and took a bite as I slid into a chair facing Kyle.

'Yummy,' I said. 'This must be where good crabs go when they die.'

'Debbie says you have something for us,' Kyle said. I looked at my sister, who had always been Deborah or Debs but certainly never Debbie. She said nothing, however, and appeared willing to let this egregious liberty go by, so I turned my attention back to Kyle. He was wearing the designer sunglasses again, and his ridiculous pinkie ring sparkled as he brushed the hair carelessly back from his forehead.

'I hope I have something,' I said. 'But I do want to be careful not to get flushed.'

Kyle looked at me for a long moment, then he shook his head and a reluctant smile moved his mouth perhaps a quarter of an inch upward. 'All right,' he said. 'Busted. But you'd be surprised how often that kind of line really works.'

'I'm sure I'd be flabbergasted,' I said. I passed him the printout from my computer. 'While I catch my breath, you might want to look at this.'

Kyle frowned and unfolded the paper. 'What's this?'

Deborah leaned forward, looking like the eager young police hound she was. 'You found something! I knew you would,' she said.

'It's just two addresses,' said Kyle.

'One of them may very well be the hiding place of a certain unorthodox medical practitioner with a Central American past,' I said, and I told him how I found the addresses. To his credit, he looked impressed, even with the sunglasses on.

'I should have thought of this,' he said. 'That's very good.' He nodded and flicked the paper with a finger. 'Follow the money. Works every time.'

'Of course I can't be positive,' I said.

'Well, I'd bet on it,' he said. 'I think you found Dr. Danco.'

I looked at Deborah. She shook her head, so I looked back at Kyle's sunglasses. 'Interesting name. Is it Polish?'

Chutsky cleared his throat and looked out over the water. 'Before your time, I guess. There was a commercial back then. Danco presents the autoveggie. It slices, it dices – ' He swiveled his dark lenses back to me. 'That's what we called him. Dr. Danco. He made chopped-up vegetables. It's the kind of joke you like when you're far from home and seeing terrible things,' he said.

'But now we're seeing them close to home,' I said. 'Why is he here?'

'Long story,' Kyle said.

'That means he doesn't want to tell you,' Deborah said.

'In that case, I'll have another crab cake,' I said. I leaned over and took the last one off the plate. They really were quite good.

'Come on, Chutsky,' Deborah said. 'There's a good chance we know where this guy is. Now what are you going to do about it?'

He put a hand on top of hers and smiled. 'I'm going to have lunch,' he said. And he picked up a menu with his other hand.

Deborah looked at his profile for a minute. Then she pulled her hand away. 'Shit,' she said.

The food actually was excellent, and Chutsky tried very hard to be chummy and pleasant, as if he had decided that when you can't tell the truth you might as well be charming. In fairness, I couldn't complain, since I generally get away with the same trick, but Deborah didn't seem very happy. She sulked and poked at her food while Kyle told jokes and asked me if I liked the Dolphins' chances to go all the way this year. I didn't really care if the Dolphins won the Nobel Prize for Literature, but as a well-designed artificial human I had several authentic-sounding prepared remarks on the subject, which seemed to satisfy Chutsky, and he chattered on in the chummiest way possible.

We even had dessert, which seemed to me to be pushing the distract-them-with-food ploy a little far, particularly since neither Deborah nor I was at all distracted. But it was quite good food, so it would have been barbaric of me to complain.

Of course, Deborah had worked very hard her whole life to become barbaric, so when the waiter placed an enormous chocolate thing in front of Chutsky, who turned to Debs with two forks and said, 'Well . . .' she took the opportunity to fling a spoon into the center of the table.

'No,' she said to him. 'I don't want another fucking cup of coffee, and I don't want a fucking chocolate foo-foo. I want a fucking answer. When are we going to go get this guy?'

He looked at her with mild surprise and even a certain fondness, as though people in his line of work found spoon-throwing women quite useful and charming, but he thought her timing might be slightly off. 'Can I finish my dessert first?' he said.

CHAPTER 12

DEBORAH DROVE US SOUTH ON DIXIE HIGHWAY. Yes, I did say 'us.' To my surprise, I had become a valuable member of the Justice League and was informed that I was being honored with the opportunity to put my irreplaceable self in harm's way. Although I was far from delighted, one small incident almost made it worthwhile.

As we stood outside the restaurant waiting for the valet to bring Deborah's car, Chutsky had quietly muttered, 'What the fuck . . . ?' and sauntered away down the driveway. I watched him as he walked out to the gate and gestured at a maroon Taurus that had casually parked there beside a palm tree. Debs glared at me as if it was all my fault, and we both watched Chutsky wave at the driver's window, which rolled down to reveal, of course, the ever-watchful Sergeant Doakes. Chutsky leaned on the gate and said something to Doakes, who glanced up the drive to me, shook his head, and then rolled up the window and drove away.

Chutsky didn't say anything when he rejoined us. But he did look at me a little differently before he climbed into the front seat of the car.

It was a twenty-minute drive south to where Quail Roost Drive runs east and west and crosses Dixie Highway, right beside a mall. Just two blocks in, a series of side streets leads into a quiet, working-class neighborhood made up of small, mostly neat houses, usually with two cars in the short driveway and several bicycles scattered across the lawn.

One of these streets bent to the left and led to a cul-de-sac, and it was here, at the end of the street, that we found the house, a pale yellow stucco dwelling with an overgrown yard. There was a battered gray van in the driveway with dark red lettering that said HERMANOS CRUZ LIMPIADORES – Cruz Brothers Cleaners.

Debs drove around the cul-de-sac and up the street about half a block to a house with half a dozen cars parked out front and on the lawn, and loud rap music coming from inside. Debs turned our car around to face our target and parked under a tree. 'What do you think?' she said.

Chutsky just shrugged. 'Uh-huh. Could be,' he said. 'Let's watch a while.' And that was the entire extent of our sparkling conversation for a good half hour. Hardly enough to keep the mind alive, and I found myself mentally drifting off to the small shelf in my apartment, where a little rosewood box holds a number of glass slides, the kind you place under a microscope. Each slide contained a single drop of blood – very well-dried blood, of course. I wouldn't have the nasty stuff in my home otherwise. Forty tiny windows into my shadow other self. One drop from each of my small adventures. There had been First Nurse, so long ago, who had killed her patients by careful overdose, under the guise of easing pain. And the very next slot in the box, the high-school shop teacher who strangled nurses. Wonderful contrast, and I do love irony.

So many memories, and as I stroked each one it

made me even more eager to make a new one, number forty-one, even though number forty, MacGregor, was hardly dry. But because it was connected to my next project, and therefore felt incomplete, I was anxious to get on with it. As soon as I could be sure about Reiker and then find some way –

I sat up. Perhaps the rich dessert had clogged my cranial arteries, but I had temporarily forgotten Deborah's bribe. 'Deborah?' I said.

She glanced back at me, with a small frown of concentration on her face. 'What.'

'Here we are,' I said.

'No shit.'

'None whatsoever. A complete lack of shit, in fact – and all thanks to my mighty mental labors. Wasn't there some mention of a few things you were going to tell me?'

She glanced at Chutsky. He was staring straight ahead, still wearing the sunglasses, which did not blink. 'Yeah, all right,' she said. 'In the army Doakes was in Special Forces.'

'I know that. It's in his personnel file.'

'What you don't know, buddy,' said Kyle without moving, 'is that there's a dark side to Special Forces. Doakes was with them.' A very tiny smile creased his face for just a second, so small and sudden I might have imagined it. 'Once you go over to the dark side, it's forever. You can't go back.'

I watched Chutsky sit completely motionless for a moment longer and then I looked at Debs. She shrugged. 'Doakes was a shooter,' she said. 'The army let the guys in El Salvador borrow him, and he killed people for them.'

'Have gun will travel,' Chutsky said.

'That explains his personality,' I said, thinking it also explained a great deal more, like the echo I heard coming from his direction when my Dark Passenger called out.

'You have to understand how it was,' Chutsky said. It was a little eerie to hear his voice coming from a completely unmoving and unemotional face, as if the voice was really coming from a tape recorder somebody had put in his body. 'We believed we were saving the world. Giving up our lives and any hope for something normal and decent, for the cause. Turns out we were just selling our souls. Me, Doakes . . .'

'And Dr. Danco,' I said.

'And Dr. Danco.' Chutsky sighed and finally moved, turning his head briefly to Deborah, then looking forward again. He shook his head, and the movement seemed so large and theatrical after his stillness that I felt like applauding. 'Dr. Danco started out as an idealist, just like the rest of us. He found out in med school there was something missing inside him and he could do things to people and not feel any empathy at all. Nothing at all. It's a lot rarer than you think.'

'Oh, I'm sure it is,' I said, and Debs glared at me.

'Danco loved his country,' Chutsky went on. 'So he switched to the dark side, too. On purpose, to use this talent. And in El Salvador it . . . blossomed. He would take somebody that we brought him and just – ' He paused and took a breath, blew it out slowly. 'Shit. You saw what he does.'

'Very original,' I said. 'Creative.'

Chutsky gave a small snort of laughter that had no

humor in it. 'Creative. Yeah. You could say that.' Chutsky swung his head slowly left, right, left. 'I said it didn't bother him to do that stuff – in El Salvador he got to like it. He'd sit in on the interrogation and ask personal questions. Then when he started to – He'd call the person by name, like he was a dentist or something, and say, "Let's try number five," or number seven, whatever. Like there were all these different patterns.'

'What kind of patterns?' I asked. It seemed like a perfectly natural question, showing polite interest and keeping the conversation moving. But Chutsky swiveled around in his seat and looked at me as if I was something that might require a whole bottle of floor cleaner.

'This is funny to you,' he said.

'Not yet,' I said.

He stared at me for what seemed like an awfully long time; then he just shook his head and faced front again. 'I don't know what kind of pattern, buddy. Never asked. Sorry. Probably something to do with what he cut off first. Just something to keep himself amused. And he'd talk to them, call them by name, show them what he was doing.' Chutsky shuddered. 'Somehow that made it worse. You should have seen what it did to the other side.'

'How about what it did to you?' Deborah demanded.

He let his chin fall forward to his chest, then straightened again. 'That too,' he said. 'Anyway, something finally changed at home, the politics, back in the Pentagon. New regime and all that, and they didn't want anything to do with what we had been doing down there. So very quietly the word came that Dr. Danco might buy us a small piece of political accommodation with the other side if we delivered him.'

'You gave up your own guy to be killed?' I asked. It hardly seemed fair – I mean, I may be untroubled by a sense of morals, but at least I play by the rules.

Kyle was silent for a long moment. 'I told you we sold our souls, buddy,' he said at last. He smiled again, a little longer this time. 'Yeah, we set him up and they took him down.'

'But he's not dead,' Deborah said, always practical.

'We got scammed,' Chutsky said. 'The Cubans took him.'

'What Cubans?' Deborah asked. 'You said El Salvador.'

'Back in the day, anytime there was trouble in the Americas, there were Cubans. They were propping up one side, just like we did with the other. And they wanted our doctor. I told you, he was special. So they took him, tried to turn him. Put him in the Isle of Pines.'

'Is that a resort?' I asked.

Chutsky gave a single small snort of a laugh. 'The last resort, maybe. Isle of Pines is one of the hardest prisons in the world. Dr. Danco spent some real quality time there. They let him know his own side had given him up, and they really put him through it. And a few years later, one of our guys gets caught and turns up like that. No arms or legs, the whole deal. Danco is working for them. And now – ' He shrugged. 'Either they turned him loose or he skipped. Doesn't matter which. He knows who set him up, and he's got a list.'

'Is your name on that list?' Deborah demanded.

'Maybe,' Chutsky said.

'Is Doakes's?' I asked. After all, I can be practical, too.

'Maybe,' he said again, which didn't seem very helpful. All the stuff about Danco was interesting, of course, but I was here for a reason. 'Anyway,' Chutsky said, 'that's what we're up against.'

Nobody seemed to have much to say to that, including me. I turned the things I'd heard from side to side, looking for some way to make it help me with my Doakes infestation. I will admit that I saw nothing at the moment, which was humbling. But I did seem to have a slightly better understanding of dear Dr. Danco. So he was empty inside, too, was he? A raptor in sheep's clothing. And he, too, had found a way to use his talent for the greater good – again, just like dear old Dexter. But now he had come off the rails, and he began to seem a little bit more like just another predator, no matter the unsettling direction his technique took him.

And oddly enough, with that insight, another thought nosed its way back into the bubbling cauldron of Dexter's dark underbrain. It had been a passing fancy before – now it began to seem like a very good idea. Why not find Dr. Danco myself, and do a little Dark Dance with him? He was a predator gone bad, just like all the others on my list. No one, not even Doakes, could possibly object to his demise. If I had wondered casually about finding the Doctor before, now it began to take on an urgency that drove away my frustration with missing out on Reiker. So he was like me, was he? We would see about that. A jolt of something cold bristled up my spine and I found that I truly looked forward to meeting the Doctor and discussing his work in depth.

In the distance I heard the first rumble of thunder as the afternoon storm moved in. 'Shit,' said Chutsky. 'Is it going to rain?'

'Every day at this time,' I said.

'That's no good,' he said. 'We gotta do something before it rains. You're up, Dexter.'

'Me?' I said, startled out of my meditations on maverick medical malpractice. I had adjusted to going along for the ride, but to actually have to *do* something was a little more than I had bargained for. I mean, here we had two hardened warriors sitting idly by, while we sent Delicate Dimpled Dexter into danger? Where's the sense in that?

'You,' Chutsky said. 'I need to hang back and see what happens. If it's him, I can take him out better. And Debbie – ' He smiled at her, even though she seemed to be scowling at him. 'Debbie is too much of a cop. She walks like a cop, she stares like a cop, and she might try to write him a ticket. He'd make her from a mile away. So it's you, Dex.'

'It's me doing what?' I asked, and I admit that I was still feeling some righteous indignation.

'Just walk by the house one time, around the cul-de-sac and back. Keep your eyes and ears open, but don't be too obvious.'

'I don't know how to be obvious,' I said.

'Great. Then this should be a piece of cake.'

It was clear that neither logic nor completely justified irritation was going to do any good, so I opened the door and got out, but I couldn't resist a parting shot. I leaned in Deborah's window and said, 'I hope I live to regret this.' And very obligingly, the thunder rumbled again nearby.

I strolled down the sidewalk toward the house. There were leaves underfoot, a couple of crushed juice cartons from some kid's lunch box. A cat rushed out onto a lawn as I passed and sat down very suddenly to lick its paws and stare at me from a safe distance.

At the house with all the cars in front the music changed and someone yelled, 'Whoo!' It was nice to know that somebody was having a good time while I strolled into mortal danger.

I turned left and began to walk the curve around the cul-de-sac. I glanced at the house with the van in front, feeling very proud of the completely nonobvious way I pulled it off. The lawn was shaggy and there were several soggy newspapers in the driveway. There didn't seem to be any visible pile of discarded body parts, and no one rushed out and tried to kill me. But as I passed by I could hear a TV blaring a game show in Spanish. A male voice rose above the hysterical announcer's and a dish clattered. And as a puff of wind brought the first large and hard raindrops, it also carried the smell of ammonia from the house.

I continued on past the house and back to the car. A few more drops of rain pelted down and a rumble of thunder rolled by, but the downpour held off. I climbed back into the car. 'Nothing terribly sinister,' I reported. 'The lawn needs mowing and there's a smell of ammonia. Voices in the house. Either he talks to himself or there's more than one of him.'

'Ammonia,' Kyle said.

'Yes, I think so,' I said. 'Probably just cleaning supplies.'

Kyle shook his head. 'Cleaning services don't use ammonia, the smell's too strong. But I know who does.'

'Who?' Deborah demanded.

He grinned at her. 'I'll be right back,' he said, and got out of the car.

'Kyle!' Deborah said, but he just waved a hand and walked right up to the front door of the house. 'Shit,' Deborah muttered as he knocked and stood glancing up at the dark clouds of the approaching storm.

The front door opened. A short and stocky man with a dark complexion and black hair falling over his forehead stared out. Chutsky said something to him and for a moment neither of them moved. The small man looked up the street, then at Kyle. Kyle slowly pulled a hand from his pocket and showed the dark man something – money? The man looked at whatever it was, looked at Chutsky again, and then held the door open. Chutsky went in. The door slammed shut.

'Shit,' Deborah said again. She chewed on a fingernail, a habit I hadn't seen from her since she was a teenager. Apparently it tasted good, because when it was gone she started on another. She was on her third fingernail when the door to the little house opened and Chutsky came back out, smiling and waving. The door closed and he disappeared behind a wall of water as the clouds finally opened wide. He came pounding up the street to the car and slid into the front seat, dripping wet.

'GodDAMN!' he said. 'I'm totally soaked!'

'What the fuck was that all about?' Deborah demanded.

Chutsky cocked an eyebrow at me and pushed the hair off his forehead. 'Don't she talk elegant?' he said.

'Kyle, goddamn it,' she said.

'The smell of ammonia,' he said. 'No surgical use, and no commercial cleaning crew would use it.'

'We did this already,' Deborah snapped.

He smiled. 'But ammonia IS used for cooking methamphetamine,' he said. 'Which turns out to be what these guys are doing.'

'You just walked right into a meth kitchen?' Deb said. 'What the hell did you do in there?'

He smiled and pulled a Baggie out of his pocket. 'Bought an ounce of meth,' he said.

CHAPTER 13

DEBORAH DIDN'T SPEAK FOR ALMOST TEN MINUTES, just drove the car and stared ahead with her jaw clamped shut. I could see the muscles flexing along the side of her face and all the way down into her shoulders. Knowing her as I did I was quite sure that an explosion was brewing, but since I knew nothing at all about how Debs in Love might behave, I couldn't tell how soon. The target of her impending meltdown, Chutsky, sat beside her in the front seat, equally silent, but apparently quite happy to sit quietly and look at the scenery.

We were almost to the second address and well into the shadow of Mount Trashmore when Debs finally erupted.

'Goddamn it, that's *illegal!*' she said, smacking the steering wheel with the palm of her hand for emphasis.

Chutsky looked at her with mild affection. 'Yes, I know,' he said.

'I am a sworn fucking officer of the law!' Deborah told him. 'I took an oath to stop this kind of shit – and you – !' She sputtered to a halt.

'I had to be sure,' he said calmly. 'This seemed like the best way.'

'I ought to put the cuffs on *YOU!*' she said.

'That might be fun,' he said.

'You SON of a bitch!'

'At least.'

'I will not cross over to your motherfucking dark side!'

'No, you won't,' he said. 'I won't let you, Deborah.'

The breath whooshed out of her and she turned to look at him. He looked back. I had never seen a silent conversation, and this one was a doozy. Her eyes clicked anxiously from the left side of his face to the right and then left again. He simply looked back, calm and unblinking. It was elegant and fascinating and almost as interesting as the fact that Debs had apparently forgotten she was driving.

'I hate to interrupt,' I said. 'But I believe that's a beer truck right ahead?'

Her head snapped back around and she braked, just in time to avoid turning us into a bumper sticker on a load of Miller Lite. 'I'm calling that address in to vice. Tomorrow,' she said.

'All right,' Chutsky said.

'And you're throwing away that Baggie.'

He looked mildly surprised. 'It cost me two grand,' he said.

'You're throwing it away,' she repeated.

'All right,' he said. They looked at each other again, leaving me to watch for lethal beer trucks. Still, it was nice to see everything settled and harmony restored to the universe so we could get on with finding our hideous inhuman monster of the week, secure in the knowledge that love will always prevail. And so it was a great satisfaction to cruise down South Dixie Highway through the last of the rainstorm, and as the sun broke out of the clouds we turned onto a road that led us into a twisty series of streets, all with a terrific view of the gigantic pile of garbage known as Mount Trashmore.

The house we were looking for was in the middle of what looked like the last row of houses before civilization ended and garbage reigned supreme. It was at the bend of a circular street and we went past it twice before we were sure that we had found it. It was a modest dwelling of the three-bedroom two-mortgage kind, painted a pale yellow with white trim, and the lawn was very neatly cropped. There was no car visible in the driveway or the carport, and a FOR SALE sign on the front lawn had been covered with another that said SOLD! in bright red letters.

'Maybe he hasn't moved in yet,' Deborah said.

'He has to be somewhere,' Chutsky said, and it was hard to argue with his logic. 'Pull over. Have you got a clipboard?'

Deborah parked the car, frowning. 'Under the seat. I need it for my paperwork.'

'I won't smudge it,' he said, and fumbled under the seat for a second before pulling out a plain metal clipboard with a stack of official forms clamped onto it. 'Perfect,' he said. 'Gimme a pen.'

'What are you going to do?' she asked, handing him a cheap white ballpoint with a blue top.

'Nobody ever stops a guy with a clipboard,' Chutsky said with a grin. And before either of us could say anything, he was out of the car and walking up the short driveway in a steady, nine-to-five-bureaucrat kind of pace. He stopped halfway and looked at the clipboard, turning over a couple of pages and reading something before looking at the house and shaking his head.

'He seems very good at this kind of thing,' I said to Deborah.

'He'd goddamned well better be,' she said. She bit another nail and I worried that soon she would run out.

Chutsky continued up the drive, consulting his clipboard, apparently unaware that he was causing a fingernail shortage in the car behind him. He looked natural and unrushed, and had obviously had a lot of experience at either chicanery or skulduggery, depending on which word was better suited for describing officially sanctioned mischief. And he had Debs biting her nails and almost ramming beer trucks. Perhaps he was not a good influence on her after all, although it was nice to have another target for her scowling and her vicious arm punches. I am always willing to let someone else wear the bruises for a while.

Chutsky paused outside the front door and wrote something down. And then, although I did not see how he did it, he unlocked the front door and went in. The door closed behind him.

'Shit,' said Deborah. 'Breaking and entering on top of possession. He'll have me hijacking an airliner next.'

'I've always wanted to see Havana,' I said helpfully.

'Two minutes,' she said tersely. 'Then I call for backup and go in after him.'

To judge from the way her hand was twitching toward the radio, it was one minute and fifty-nine seconds when the front door opened again and Chutsky came back out. He paused in the driveway, wrote something on the clipboard, and returned to the car.

'All right,' he said as he slid into the front seat. 'Let's go home.'

'The house is empty?' Deborah demanded.

'Clean as a whistle,' he said. 'Not a towel or a soup can anywhere.'

'So now what?' she asked as she put the car in gear.

He shook his head. 'Back to plan A,' he said.

'And what the hell is plan A?' Deborah asked him.

'Patience,' he said.

And so in spite of a delightful lunch and a truly original little shopping trip afterward, we were back to waiting. A week passed in the now typically boring way. It didn't seem like Sergeant Doakes would give up before my conversion to a beer-bellied sofa ornament was complete, and I could see nothing else to do except play kick the can and hangman with Cody and Astor, performing outrageously theatrical goodbye kisses with Rita afterward for the benefit of my stalker.

Then came the telephone ringing in the middle of the night. It was Sunday night, and I had to leave for work early the next day; Vince Masuoka and I had an arrangement, and it was my turn to pick up doughnuts. And now here was the telephone, brazenly ringing as if I had no cares in the world and the doughnuts would deliver themselves. I glanced at the clock on my bedside table: 2:38. I admit I was somewhat cranky as I lifted the receiver and said, 'Leave me alone.'

'Dexter. Kyle is gone,' Deborah said. She sounded far beyond tired, totally tense, and unsure whether she wanted to shoot someone or cry.

It took me just a moment to get my powerful intellect up to speed. 'Uh, well Deb,' I said, 'a guy like that, maybe you're better off – '

'He's *gone*, Dexter. Taken. The, the guy has him. The guy who did that thing to the guy,' she said, and although I felt like I was suddenly thrust into an episode of *The Sopranos*, I knew what she meant. Whoever had turned the thing on the table into a yodeling potato had taken Kyle, presumably to do something similar to him.

'Dr. Danco,' I said.

'Yes.'

'How do you know?' I asked her.

'He said it could happen. Kyle is the only one who knows what the guy looks like. He said when Danco found out Kyle was here, he'd make a try. We had a – a signal set up, and – Shit Dexter, just get over here. We have to find him,' she said, and hung up.

It's always me, isn't it? I'm not really a very nice person, but for some reason it's always me that they come to with their problems. *Oh, Dexter, a savage inhuman monster has taken my boyfriend!* Well damn it, I'm a savage inhuman monster, too – didn't that entitle me to some rest?

I sighed. Apparently not.

I hoped Vince would understand about the doughnuts.

CHAPTER 14

IT WAS A FIFTEEN-MINUTE DRIVE TO DEBORAH'S house from where I lived in the Grove. For once, I did not see Sergeant Doakes following me, but perhaps he was using a Klingon cloaking device. In any case, the traffic was very sparse and I even made the light at U.S. 1. Deborah lived in a small house on Medina in Coral Gables, overgrown with some neglected fruit trees and a crumbling coral-rock wall. I nosed my car in next to hers in the short driveway and was only two steps away when Deborah opened her front door. 'Where have you been?' she said.

'I went to yoga class, and then out to the mall to buy shoes,' I said. In truth, I had actually hurried over, getting there less than twenty minutes after her call, and I was a little miffed at the tone she was taking.

'Get in here,' she said, peering around into the darkness and holding on to the door as if she thought it might fly away.

'Yes, O Mighty One,' I said, and I got in.

Deborah's little house was lavishly decorated in I-have-no-life modern. Her living area generally looked like a cheap hotel room that had been occupied by a rock band and looted of everything except a TV and VCR. There was a chair and a small table by French doors that led out to a patio that was almost lost in a tangle of bushes. She had found another chair somewhere, though, a rickety folding chair, and she pulled it over to the table for me. I was so touched by her hospitable gesture that I risked life and limb by sitting in the flimsy thing. 'Well,' I said. 'How long has he been gone?'

'Shit,' she said. 'About three and a half hours. I think.' She shook her head and slumped into the other chair. 'We were supposed to meet here, and – he didn't show up. I went to his hotel, and he wasn't there.'

'Isn't it possible he just went away somewhere?' I asked – and I'm not proud of it, but I admit I sounded a little hopeful.

Deborah shook her head. 'His wallet and keys were still on the dresser. The guy has him, Dex. We gotta find him before – ' She bit her lip and looked away.

I was not at all sure what I could do to find Kyle. As I said, this was not the kind of thing I generally had any insight into, and I had already given it my best shot tracking down the real estate. But since Deborah was already saying 'we' it seemed that I didn't have a lot of choice in the matter. Family ties and all that. Still, I tried to make a little bit of wiggle room. 'I'm sorry if this sounds stupid, Debs, but did you report this?'

She looked up with a half snarl. 'Yeah, I did. I called Captain Matthews. He sounded relieved. He told me not to get hysterical, like I'm some kind of old lady with the vapors.' She shook her head. 'I asked him to put out an APB, and he said, "For what?" ' She hissed out her breath. 'For what . . . Goddamn it, Dexter, I wanted to strangle him, but . . .' She shrugged.

'But he was right,' I said.

'Yeah. Kyle is the only one who knows what the guy looks like,' she said. 'We don't know what he's driving or what his real name is or – Shit, Dexter. All I know is he's got Kyle.' She took a ragged breath. 'Anyway, Matthews called Kyle's people in Washington. Said that was all he could do.' She shook her head and looked very bleak. 'They're sending somebody Tuesday morning.'

'Well then,' I said hopefully. 'I mean, we know that this guy works very slowly.'

'Tuesday morning,' she said. 'Almost two days. Where do you think he starts, Dex? Does he take a leg off first? Or an arm? Will he do them both at the same time?'

'No,' I said. 'One at a time.' She looked at me hard. 'Well, it just makes sense, doesn't it?'

'Not to me,' she said. 'Nothing about this makes sense.'

'Deborah, cutting off the arms and legs is not *what* this guy wants to do. It's just *how* he does it.'

'Goddamn it, Dexter, talk English.'

'What he *wants* to do is totally destroy his victims. Break them inside and out, way beyond repair. Turn them into musical beanbags that will never again have a moment of anything except total endless insane horror. Cutting off limbs and lips is just the way he – What?'

'Oh, Jesus, Dexter,' Deborah said. Her face had screwed up into something I hadn't seen since our mom died. She turned away, and her shoulders began to shake. It made me just a little uneasy. I mean, I do not feel emotions, and I know Deborah quite often does. But she was not the kind of person who showed them, unless irritation is an emotion. And now she was making wet snuffly sounds, and I knew that I should probably pat her shoulder and say, 'There there,' or something equally profound and human, but I couldn't quite make myself do it. This was Deb, my sister. She would know I was faking it and –

And what? Cut off my arms and legs? The worst she would do would be to tell me to stop it, and go back to being Sergeant Sourpuss again. Even that would be a great improvement over her wilting-lily act. In any case, this was clearly one of those times where some human response was called for, and since I knew from long study what a human would do, I did it. I stood up and stepped over to her. I put my arm on her shoulder, patted her, and said, 'All right, Deb. There there.' It sounded even stupider than I had feared, but she leaned against me and snuffled, so I suppose it was the right thing to do after all.

'Can you really fall in *love* with somebody in a week?' she asked me.

'I don't think I can do it at all,' I said.

'I can't take this, Dexter,' she said. 'If Kyle gets killed, or turned into – Oh, God, I don't know what I'll do.' And she collapsed against me again and cried.

'There there,' I said.

She gave a long hard snuffle, and then blew her nose on a paper towel from the table beside her. 'I wish you'd stop saying that,' she said.

'I'm sorry,' I said. 'I don't know what else to tell you.'

'Tell me what this guy is up to. Tell me how to find him.'

I sat back down in the wobbly little chair. 'I don't think I can, Debs. I don't really have much of a feel for what he's doing.'

'Bullshit,' she said.

'Seriously. I mean, technically speaking, he hasn't actually killed anybody, you know.'

'Dexter,' she said, 'you already understand more about this guy than Kyle did, and he knows who it is. We've got to find him. We've GOT to.' She bit her lower lip, and I was afraid she would start blubbering again, which would have left me totally helpless since she had already told me I couldn't say 'There there' again. But she pulled it together like the tough sergeant sister she was and merely blew her nose again.

'I'll try, Deb. Can I assume that you and Kyle have done all the basic work? Talked to witnesses and so on?'

She shook her head. 'We didn't need to. Kyle knew – ' She paused at that past tense, and then went on, very determined. 'Kyle KNOWS who did it, and he KNOWS who should be next.'

'Excuse me. He knows who's next?'

Deborah frowned. 'Don't sound like that. Kyle said there are four guys in Miami who are on the list. One of them is missing, Kyle figured he was already taken, but that gave us a little time to set up surveillance on the other three.'

'Who are these four guys, Deborah? And how does Kyle know them?'

She sighed. 'Kyle didn't tell me their names. But they were all part of a team of some kind. In El Salvador. Along with this . . . Dr. Danco guy. So – ' She spread her hands and looked helpless, a new look for her. And although it gave her a certain little-girl charm, the only thing it did for me was to make me feel even more put-upon. The whole world goes spinning merrily along, getting itself into the most God-awful trouble, and then it's all up to Dashing Dexter to tidy things up again. It didn't seem fair, but what can you do?

More to the point – what could I do now? I didn't see any way to find Kyle before it was too late. And although I am fairly sure I didn't say that out loud, Deborah reacted as if I had. She slapped one hand on the table and said, 'We have to find him before he starts on Kyle. Before he even STARTS, Dexter. Because – I mean, am I supposed to hope Kyle will only lose an arm before we get there? Or a leg? Either way, Kyle is . . .' She turned away without finishing, looking out into the darkness through the French doors by the little table.

She was right, of course. It looked like there was very little we could do to get Kyle back intact. Because with all the luck in the world, even my dazzling intellect couldn't possibly lead us to him before the work started. And then – how long could Kyle hold out? Presumably he'd had some sort of training in dealing with this sort of thing, and he knew what was coming, so –

But wait a moment. I closed my eyes and tried to think about it. Dr. Danco would know that Kyle was a pro. And as I had already told Deborah, the whole purpose was to shatter the victim into screaming unfixable pieces. Therefore . . .

I opened my eyes. 'Deb,' I said. She looked at me. 'I am in the rare position of having some hope to offer.'

'Spill it,' she said.

'This is only a guess,' I said. 'But I think Dr.

Demented will probably keep Kyle around for a while, without working on him.'

She frowned. 'Why would he do that?'

'To make it last longer, and to soften him up. Kyle knows what's coming. He's braced for it. But now, imagine he's just left lying in the dark, tied up, so his imagination goes to work. And so I think maybe,' I added as it occurred to me, 'there's another victim ahead of him. The guy who's missing. So Kyle hears it – the saws and scalpels, the moans and whispers. He even smells it, knows it's coming but doesn't know when. He'll be half crazy before he even loses a toenail.'

'Jesus,' she said. 'That's your version of hope?'

'Absolutely. It gives us a little extra time to find him.'

'Jesus,' she said again.

'I could be wrong,' I said.

She looked back out the window. 'Don't be wrong, Dex. Not this time,' she said.

I shook my head. This was going to be pure drudgery, no fun at all. I could only think of two things to try, and neither of them were possible until the morning. I glanced around for a clock. According to the VCR, it was 12:00. 12:00. 12:00. 'Do you have a clock?' I asked.

Deborah frowned. 'What do you want a clock for?'

'To find out what time it is,' I said. 'I think that's the usual purpose.'

'What the hell difference does that make?' she demanded.

'Deborah. There is very little to go on here. We will have to go back and do all the routine stuff that

131

Chutsky pulled the department away from. Luckily, we can use your badge to barge around and ask questions. But we will have to wait until morning.'

'Shit,' she said. 'I hate waiting.'

'There there,' I said. Deborah gave me a very sour look, but didn't say anything.

I didn't like waiting either, but I had done so much of it lately that perhaps it came easier to me. In any case, wait we did, dozing in our chairs until the sun came up. And then, since I was the domestic one lately, I made coffee for the two of us – one cup at a time, since Deborah's coffeemaker was one of those single-cup things for people who don't expect to be entertaining a great deal and don't actually have a life. There was nothing in the refrigerator remotely worth eating, unless you were a feral dog. Very disappointing: Dexter is a healthy boy with a high metabolism, and facing what was sure to be a difficult day on an empty stomach was not a happy thought. I know family comes first, but shouldn't that mean after breakfast?

Ah, well. Dauntless Dexter would make the sacrifice once again. Pure nobility of spirit, and I could expect no thanks, but one does what one must.

CHAPTER 15

DR. MARK SPIELMAN WAS A LARGE MAN WHO looked more like a retired linebacker than an ER physician. But he had been the physician on duty when the ambulance delivered The Thing to Jackson Memorial Hospital, and he was not at all happy about it. 'If I ever have to see something like that again,' he told us, 'I will retire and raise dachshunds.' He shook his head. 'You know what the ER at Jackson is like. One of the busiest. All the crazy stuff comes here, from one of the craziest cities in the world. But this – ' Spielman knocked twice on the table in the mild green staff lounge where we sat with him. 'Something else,' he said.

'What's the prognosis?' Deborah asked him, and he looked at her sharply.

'Is that a joke?' he said. 'There's no prognosis, and there's not going to be one. Physically, there's not enough left to do anything but sustain life, if you want to call it that. Mentally?' He put both hands palm up and then dropped them on the table. 'I'm not a shrink, but there's nothing left in there and no way that he'll ever have a single lucid moment, ever again. The only hope he has is that we keep him so doped up he doesn't know who he is, until he dies. Which for his sake we should all hope is soon.' He looked at his watch, a very nice Rolex. 'Is this going to take long? I am on duty, you know.'

'Were there traces of any drugs in the blood?' Deborah asked.

Spielman snorted. 'Traces, hell. The guy's blood is a cocktail sauce. I've never seen such a mix before. All designed to keep him awake, but deaden the physical pain so the shock of the multiple amputations didn't kill him.'

'Was there anything unusual about the cuts?' I asked him.

'The guy's had training,' Spielman said. 'They were all done with very good surgical technique. But any medical school in the world could have taught him that.' He blew out a breath and an apologetic smile flickered quickly across his face. 'Some of them were already healed.'

'What kind of time frame does that give us?' Deborah asked him.

Spielman shrugged. 'Four to six weeks, start to finish,' he said. 'He took at least a month to surgically dismember this guy, one small piece at a time. I can't imagine anything more horrible.'

'He did it in front of a mirror,' I said, ever-helpful. 'So the victim had to watch.'

Spielman looked appalled. 'My God,' he said. He just sat there for a minute, and then said, 'Oh, my God.' Then he shook his head and looked at his Rolex again. 'Listen, I'd like to help out here, but this is . . .' He spread his hands and then dropped them on the table again. 'I don't think there's really anything I can tell you that's going to do any good. So let me save you some time here. That Mister, uh – Chesney?'

'Chutsky,' Deborah said.

'Yes, that was it. He called in and suggested I might

get an ID with a retinal scan at, um, a certain database in Virginia.' He raised an eyebrow and pursed his lips. 'Anyway. I got a fax yesterday, with a positive identification of the victim. I'll get it for you.' He stood up and disappeared into the hall. A moment later he returned with a sheet of paper. 'Here it is. Name is Manuel Borges. A native of El Salvador, in the import business.' He put the paper down in front of Deborah. 'I know it's not much, but believe me, that's it. The shape he's in . . .' He shrugged. 'I didn't think we'd get this much.'

A small intercom speaker in the ceiling muttered something that might have come from a TV show. Spielman cocked his head, frowned, and said, 'Gotta go. Hope you catch him.' And he was out the door and down the hall so quickly that the fax paper he had dropped on the table fluttered.

I looked at Deborah. She did not seem particularly encouraged that we had found the victim's name. 'Well,' I said. 'I know it isn't much.'

She shook her head. 'Not much would be a big improvement. This is nothing.' She looked at the fax, read it through one time. 'El Salvador. Connected to something called FLANGE.'

'That was our side,' I said. She looked up at me. 'The side the United States supported. I looked it up on the Internet.'

'Swell. So we just found out something we already knew.' She got up and headed for the door, not quite as quickly as Dr. Spielman but fast enough that I had to hurry and I didn't catch up until she was at the door to the parking lot.

Deborah drove rapidly and silently, with her jaw

clenched, all the way to the little house on N.W. 4th Street where it had all started. The yellow tape was gone, of course, but Deborah parked haphazardly anyway, cop fashion, and got out of the car. I followed her up the short walkway to the house next door to the one where we had found the human doorstop. Deborah rang the bell, still without speaking, and a moment later it swung open. A middle-aged man wearing gold-rimmed glasses and a tan guayabera shirt looked out at us inquiringly.

'We need to speak to Ariel Medina,' Deborah said, holding up her badge.

'My mother is resting now,' he said.

'It's urgent,' Deborah said.

The man looked at her, then at me. 'Just a moment,' he said. He closed the door. Deborah stared straight ahead at the door, and I watched her jaw muscles working for a couple of minutes before the man opened the door again and held it wide. 'Come in,' he said.

We followed him into a small dark room crowded with dozens of end tables, each one festooned with religious articles and framed photographs. Ariel, the old lady who had discovered the thing next door and cried on Deb's shoulder, sat on a large overstuffed sofa with doilies on the arms and across the back. When she saw Deborah she said, 'Aaahhh,' and stood up to give her a hug. Deborah, who really should have been expecting an *abrazo* from an elderly Cuban lady, stood stiffly for a moment before awkwardly returning the embrace with a few pats on the woman's back. Deborah backed off as soon as she decently could. Ariel sat back down on the couch and patted the cushion beside her. Deborah sat.

The old lady immediately launched into a very rapid stream of Spanish. I speak some Spanish, and often I can even understand Cuban, but I was getting only one word in ten of Ariel's harangue. Deborah looked at me helplessly; for whatever quixotic reasons, she had chosen to study French in school, and as far as she was concerned the woman might as well have been speaking ancient Etruscan.

'Por favor, Señora,' I said. 'Mi hermana no habla español.'

'Ah?' Ariel looked at Deborah with a little less enthusiasm and shook her head. 'Lázaro!' Her son stepped forward, and as she resumed her monologue with barely a pause, he began to translate for her. 'I came here from Santiago de Cuba in 1962,' Lázaro said for his mother. 'Under Batista I saw some terrible things. People disappeared. Then Castro came and for a while I had hope.' She shook her head and spread her hands. 'Believe it or not, but this is what we thought at the time. Things would be different. But soon it was the same thing again. Worse. So I came here. To the United States. Because here, people don't disappear. People are not shot in the street or tortured. That's what I thought. And now this.' She waved an arm toward the house next door.

'I need to ask you a few questions,' Deborah said, and Lázaro translated.

Ariel simply nodded and went right on with her riveting tale. 'Even with Castro, they would never do a thing like that,' she said. 'Yes, they kill people. Or they put you in the Isle of Pines. But never a thing like this. Not in Cuba. Only in America,' she said.

'Did you ever see the man next door?' Deborah

interrupted. 'The man who did this?' Ariel studied Deborah for a moment. 'I need to know,' Deb said. 'There's going to be another one if we can't find him.'

'Why is it you who asks me?' Ariel said through her son. 'This is no job for you. A pretty woman like you, you should have a husband. A family.'

'El victimo proximo es el novio de mi hermana,' I said. *The next victim is my sister's sweetheart.* Deborah glared at me, but Ariel said, 'Aaahhh,' clucked her tongue, and nodded her head. 'Well, I don't know what I can tell you. I did see the man, maybe two times.' She shrugged and Deborah leaned forward impatiently. 'Always at night, never very close. I can say, the man was small, very short. And skinny as well. With big glasses. More than this, I don't know. He never came out, he was very quiet. Sometimes we would hear music.' She smiled just a little and added, 'Tito Puente.' And Lázaro echoed unnecessarily, 'Tito Puente.'

'Ah,' I said, and they all looked at me. 'It would hide the noise,' I said, a little embarrassed at all the attention.

'Did he have a car?' Deborah asked, and Ariel frowned.

'A van,' she said. 'He drove an old white van with no windows. It was very clean, but had many rust spots and dents. I saw it a few times, but he usually kept it in his garage.'

'I don't suppose you saw the license plate?' I asked her, and she looked at me.

'But I did,' she said through her son, and held up one hand, palm outward. 'Not to get the number, that only happens in the old movies. But I know it was a Florida license plate. The yellow one with the cartoon of a child,' she said, and she stopped talking and

138

glared at me, because I was giggling. It's not at all dignified, and certainly not something I practice on a regular basis, but I was actually giggling and I could not help myself.

Deborah glared at me, too. 'What is so goddamned funny?' she demanded.

'The license plate,' I said. 'I'm sorry, Debs, but my God, don't you know what the yellow Florida plate is? And for this guy to have one and do what he does . . .' I swallowed hard to keep from laughing again, but it took all my self-control.

'All right, damn it, what's so funny about the yellow license plate?'

'It's a specialty plate, Deb,' I said. 'The one that says, CHOOSE LIFE.'

And then, picturing Dr. Danco carting around his wriggling victims, filling them with chemicals and cutting so very perfectly to keep them alive through it all, I'm afraid I giggled again. 'Choose life,' I said.

I really wanted to meet this guy.

We walked back to the car in silence. Deborah got in and called in the description of the van to Captain Matthews, and he agreed that he could probably put out an APB. While she talked to the captain, I looked around. Neatly manicured yards, mostly consisting of colored rocks. A few children's bicycles chained to the front porch, and the Orange Bowl looming in the background. A nice little neighborhood to live in, work in, raise a family in – or chop off somebody's arms and legs.

'Get in,' said Deborah, interrupting my rustic reverie. I got in and we drove off. At one point, stopped at a red light, Deb glanced at me and said,

'You pick a funny time to start laughing.'

'Really, Deb,' I said. 'This is the first hint of personality we've got from the guy. We know he has a sense of humor. I think that's a big step forward.'

'Sure. Maybe we'll catch him at a comedy club.'

'We will catch him, Deb,' I said, although neither one of us believed me. She just grunted; the light changed and she stomped on the gas as if she was killing a poisonous snake.

We moved through the traffic back to Deb's house. The morning rush hour was coming to an end. At the corner of Flagler and 34th a car had run up onto the sidewalk and smacked into a light pole in front of a church. A cop stood beside the car between two men who were screaming at each other. A little girl sat on the curb crying. Ah, the enchanting rhythms of another magical day in paradise.

A few moments later we turned down Medina and Deborah parked her car beside mine in the driveway. She switched off the engine and for a moment we both just sat there listening to the ticking of the cooling motor. 'Shit,' she said.

'I agree.'

'What do we do now?' she said.

'Sleep,' I said. 'I'm too tired to think.'

She pounded both hands on the steering wheel. 'How can I sleep, Dexter? Knowing that Kyle is . . .' She hit the wheel again. 'Shit,' she said.

'The van will turn up, Deb. You know that. The database will spit out every white van with a CHOOSE LIFE tag, and with an APB out it's just a matter of time.'

'Kyle doesn't have time,' she said.

'Human beings need sleep, Debs,' I said. 'And so do I.'

A courier's van squealed around the corner and clunked to a halt in front of Deborah's house. The driver jumped out with a small package and approached Deb's front door. She said, 'Shit,' one last time and got out of the car to collect the package.

I closed my eyes and sat for just a moment longer, pondering, which is what I do instead of thinking when I am very tired. It really seemed like wasted effort; nothing came to me except to wonder where I'd left my running shoes. With my new sense of humor apparently still idling, that seemed funny to me and, to my great surprise I heard a very faint echo from the Dark Passenger. *Why is that funny?* I asked. *Is it because I left the shoes at Rita's?* Of course it didn't answer. The poor thing was probably still sulking. And yet it had chuckled. *Is it something else altogether that seems funny?* I asked. But again there was no answer; just a faint sense of anticipation and hunger.

The courier rattled and roared away. Just as I was about to yawn, stretch, and admit that my finely tuned cerebral powers were on hiatus, I heard a kind of retching moan. I opened my eyes and looked up to see Deborah stagger forward a step and then sit down hard on her front walk. I got out of the car and hurried over to her.

'Deb?' I said. 'What is it?'

She dropped the package and hid her face in her hands, making more unlikely noises. I squatted beside her and picked up the package. It was a small box, about the right size to hold a wristwatch. I pried the end up. Inside was a ziplock bag. And inside the bag was a human finger.

A finger with a big, flashy pinkie ring.

CHAPTER 16

IT TOOK A VERY GREAT DEAL MORE THAN PATTING Deborah on the shoulder and saying 'There there' to get her calmed down this time. In fact I had to force-feed her a large glass of peppermint schnapps. I knew that she needed some kind of chemical help to relax and even sleep if possible, but Debs had nothing in her medicine chest stronger than Tylenol, and she was not a drinker. I finally found the schnapps bottle under her kitchen sink, and after making sure it wasn't actually drain cleaner I made her chug down a glass of it. From the apparent taste, it might as well have been drain cleaner. She shuddered and gagged but she drank it, too bone weary and brain numb to fight.

While she slumped in her chair I threw a few changes of her clothing into a grocery bag and dropped it by the front door. She stared at the bags and then at me. 'What are you doing,' she said. Her voice was slurred and she sounded uninterested in the answer.

'You're staying at my place for a few days,' I said.

'Don't want to,' she said.

'It doesn't matter,' I said. 'You have to.'

She shifted her gaze to the bag of clothing by the door. 'Why.'

I walked over to her and squatted beside her chair. 'Deborah. He knows who you are and where you are.

142

Let's try to make it just a little bit of a challenge for him, all right?'

She shuddered again, but she didn't say anything more as I helped her to her feet and out the door. Half an hour and one more slug of peppermint schnapps later she was in my bed, snoring lightly. I left her a note to call me when she woke up, and then I took her little surprise package with me and headed in to work.

I didn't expect to find any important clues from running the finger through a lab check, but since I do forensics for a living it seemed like I really ought to give it a professional once-over. And because I take all my obligations very seriously, I stopped on the way and bought doughnuts. As I approached my second-floor cubbyhole, Vince Masuoka came down the hall from the opposite direction. I bowed humbly and held up the bag. 'Greetings, Sensei,' I said. 'I bring gifts.'

'Greetings, Grasshopper,' he said. 'There is a thing called time. You must explore its mysteries.' He held up his wrist and pointed to his watch. 'I'm on my way to lunch, and now you bring me my breakfast?'

'Better late than never,' I said, but he shook his head.

'Nah,' he said. 'My mouth has already changed gears. I'm gonna go get some *ropa vieja* and *plátanos*.'

'If you spurn my gift of food,' I said, 'I will give you the finger.' He raised an eyebrow, and I handed him Deb's package. 'Can I have half an hour of your time before lunch?'

He looked at the small box. 'I don't think I want to open this on an empty stomach, do I?' he said.

'Well then, how about a doughnut?'

It took more than half an hour, but by the time Vince left for lunch we had learned that there was nothing to learn from Kyle's finger. The cut was extremely clean and professional, done with a very sharp instrument that left no trace behind in the wound. There was nothing under the fingernail except a little dirt that could have come from anywhere. I removed the ring, but we found no threads or hairs or telltale fabric swatches, and Kyle had somehow failed to etch an address or phone number onto the inside of the ring. Kyle's blood type was AB positive.

I put the finger into cold storage, and slipped the ring into my pocket. That wasn't exactly standard procedure, but I was fairly sure that Deborah would want it if we didn't get Kyle back. As it was, it looked like if we did get him back it would be by messenger, one piece at a time. Of course, I'm not a sentimental person, but that didn't seem like something that would warm her heart.

By now I was very tired indeed, and since Debs hadn't called yet I decided that I was well within my rights to head for home and take a nap. The afternoon rain started as I climbed into my car. I shot straight down LeJeune in the relatively light traffic and got home after being screamed at only one time, which was a new record. I dashed in through the rain and found Deborah gone. She had scribbled a note on a Post-it saying she would call later. I was relieved, since I had not been looking forward to sleeping on my half-size couch. I crawled right into my own bed and slept without interruption until a little after six o'clock in the evening.

Naturally, even the mighty machine that is my body needs a certain amount of maintenance, and when I sat up in bed I felt very much in need of an oil change. The long night with so little sleep, the missed breakfast, the tension and suspense of trying to think of something besides 'There there' to say to Deborah – all these things had taken their toll. I felt as though someone had snuck in and packed my head with beach sand, even including the bottle caps and cigarette butts.

There is only one solution to this occasional condition, and that is exercise. But as I decided that what I really needed was a pleasant two- or three-mile jog, I remembered again that I had misplaced my running shoes. They were not in their usual spot by the door, and they were not in my car. This was Miami, so it was possible that someone had broken into my apartment and stolen them; they were, after all, very nice New Balance shoes. But I thought it more likely that I had left them over at Rita's. For me, to decide is to act. I toddled down to my car and drove over to Rita's house.

The rain was long gone – it seldom lasts even an hour – and the streets were already dry and filled with the usual cheerfully homicidal crowd. My people. The maroon Taurus showed up behind me at Sunset, and stayed with me all the way. It was nice to see Doakes back on the job. I had felt just a little bit neglected. Once again he parked across the street as I knocked on the door. He had just turned off the engine when Rita opened the door. 'Well,' she said. 'What a surprise!' She lifted her face for a kiss.

I gave her one, putting a little extra English on it to entertain Sergeant Doakes. 'There's no easy way to say this,' I said, 'but I've come for my running shoes.'

Rita smiled. 'Actually, I just put mine on. Care to get sweaty together?' And she held the door wide for me.

'That's the best invitation I've had all day,' I said.

I found my shoes in her garage beside the washing machine, along with a pair of shorts and a sleeveless sweatshirt, laundered and ready to go. I went into the bathroom and changed clothes, leaving my work clothes folded neatly on the toilet seat. In just a few minutes Rita and I were trotting up the block together. I waved to Sergeant Doakes as we went by. We ran down the street, turned right for a few blocks, and then around the perimeter of the nearby park. We had run this route together before, had even measured it out at just under three miles, and we were used to each other's pace. And so about half an hour later, sweaty and once again willing to face the challenges of another evening of life on Planet Earth, we stood at the front door of Rita's house.

'If you don't mind, I'll take the first shower,' she said. 'That way I can start dinner while you clean up.'

'Absolutely,' I said. 'I'll just sit out here and drip.'

Rita smiled. 'I'll get you a beer,' she said. A moment later she handed me one and then went in and closed the door. I sat on the step and sipped my beer. The last few days had gone by in a savage blur, and I had been so entirely upended from my normal life that I actually enjoyed the moment of peaceful contemplation, calmly sitting there and drinking a beer while somewhere in the city Chutsky was shedding spare parts. Life whirled on around me with its sundry slashings, strangulations, and dismemberings, but in Dexter's Domain it was Miller Time. I raised the can in a toast to Sergeant Doakes.

Somewhere in the house I heard a commotion. There was shouting and a little bit of squealing, as if

Rita had just discovered the Beatles in her bathroom. Then the front door slammed open and Rita grabbed me around the neck in a stranglehold. I dropped my beer and gasped for air. 'What? What did I do?' I said. I saw Astor and Cody watching from just inside the door. 'I'm terribly sorry, and I'll never do it again,' I added, but Rita kept squeezing.

'Oh, Dexter,' she said, and now she was crying. Astor smiled at me and clasped her hands together under her chin. Cody just watched, nodding a little bit. 'Oh, Dexter,' Rita said again.

'Please,' I said, struggling desperately to get some air, 'I promise it was an accident and I didn't mean it. What did I do?' Rita finally relented and loosened her death grip.

'Oh, Dexter,' she said one more time, and she put her hands on my face and looked at me with a blinding smile and a faceful of tears. 'Oh, YOU!' she said, although to be honest it didn't seem very much like me at the moment. 'I'm sorry, it was an accident,' she said, snuffling now. 'I hope you didn't have anything really special planned.'

'Rita. Please. What is going on?'

Her smile got bigger and bigger. 'Oh, Dexter. I really – it was just – Astor needed to use the toilet, and when she picked up your clothes, it just fell out onto the floor and – Oh, Dexter, it's so beautiful!' She had now said Oh Dexter so many times that I began to feel Irish, but I still had no idea what was going on.

Until Rita lifted up her hand in front of her. Her left hand. Now with a large diamond ring sparkling on her ring finger.

Chutsky's ring.

'Oh, Dexter,' she said again, and then buried her face in my shoulder. 'Yes yes YES! Oh, you've made me so happy!'

'All right,' Cody said softly.

And after that, what can you say except congratulations?

The rest of the evening passed in a blur of disbelief and Miller Lite. I knew very well that hovering somewhere out in space was a perfect, calm, logical series of words that I could put together and say to Rita to make her understand that I had not actually proposed to her, and we would all have a good laugh and say good night. But the harder I searched for that magical elusive sentence, the faster it ran away from me. And I found myself reasoning that perhaps one more beer would unlock the doors of perception, and after several cans Rita went up to the corner store and returned with a bottle of champagne. We drank the champagne and everyone seemed so very happy, and one thing led to another and somehow I ended up in Rita's bed once again, witness to some exceedingly unlikely and undignified events.

And once again I found myself wondering, as I drifted off to stunned and unbelieving sleep: *How do these terrible things always happen to me?*

Waking up after a night like that is never very pleasant. Waking up in the middle of the night and thinking, *Oh God – Deborah!* is even worse. You may think I was guilty or uneasy about neglecting someone who depended on me, in which case you would be very wrong. As I have said, I don't really feel emotions. I can, however, experience fear, and the idea of

Deborah's potential rage pulled the trigger. I hurried into my clothes and managed to slip out to my car without waking anyone. Sergeant Doakes was no longer in his position across the street. It was nice to know that even Doakes needed to sleep sometime. Or perhaps he had thought that someone who just got engaged deserved a little privacy. Knowing him as I did, however, this didn't seem likely. It was far more likely that he had been elected pope and had to fly off to the Vatican.

I drove home quickly, and checked my answering machine. There was one automated message urging me to buy a new set of tires before it was too late, which seemed ominous enough, but no message from Debs. I made coffee and waited for the thump of the morning paper against my door. There was a sense of unreality to the morning that was not entirely caused by the aftereffects of the champagne. Engaged, was I? Well well. I wished that I could scold myself and demand to know what I thought I had been doing. But the truth was that, unfortunately, I hadn't been doing anything wrong; I was entirely clothed in virtue and diligence. And I had done nothing that could be called spectacularly stupid – far from it. I had been proceeding with life in a noble and even exemplary manner, minding my own business and trying to help my sister recover her boyfriend, exercising, eating plenty of green vegetables, and not even slicing up other monsters. And somehow all this pure and decent behavior had snuck around behind me and bitten me on the ass. Never a good deed goes unpunished, as Harry used to say.

And what could I do about it now? Surely Rita

would come to her senses. I mean, really: *ME?* Who could possibly want to marry *ME?!* There had to be better alternatives, like becoming a nun, or joining the Peace Corps. This was Dexter we were talking about. In a city the size of Miami, couldn't she find somebody who was at least human? And what was her rush to get married again anyway? It hadn't worked out terribly well for her the first time, but she was apparently willing to plunge right back into it again. Were women really this desperate to get married?

Of course there were the children to think about. Conventional wisdom would say they needed a father, and there was something to that, because where would I have been without Harry? And Astor and Cody had looked so happy. Even if I made Rita see that a comical mistake had happened, would the kids ever understand?

I was on my second cup of coffee when the paper came. I glanced through the main sections, relieved to find that terrible things were still happening almost everywhere. At least the rest of the world hadn't gone crazy.

By seven o'clock I thought it would be safe to call Deborah on her cell phone. There was no answer; I left a message, and fifteen minutes later she called back. 'Good morning, Sis,' I said, and I marveled at the way I managed to sound cheerful. 'Did you get some sleep?'

'A little,' she grumbled. 'I woke up around four yesterday. I traced the package to a place in Hialeah. I drove around the area most of the night looking for the white van.'

'If he dropped the package way up in Hialeah, he

150

probably drove in from Key West to do it,' I said.

'I know that, goddamn it,' she snapped. 'But what the hell else am I supposed to do?'

'I don't know,' I admitted. 'But doesn't the guy from Washington get here today?'

'We don't know anything about him,' she said. 'Just because Kyle is good, doesn't mean this guy will be.'

She apparently didn't remember that Kyle had not shown himself to be particularly good, at least in public. He'd done nothing at all, in fact, except get himself captured and have his finger nipped off. But it didn't seem politic for me to comment on how good he was, so I simply said, 'Well, we have to assume the new guy knows something about this that we don't know.'

Deborah snorted. 'That wouldn't be too hard,' she said. 'I'll call you when he gets in.' She hung up, and I got ready for work.

CHAPTER 17

AT 12:30 DEB STALKED INTO MY MODEST RETREAT off the forensics lab and threw a cassette tape on my desk. I looked up at her; she didn't seem happy, but that really wasn't much of a novelty. 'From my answering machine at home,' she said. 'Listen to it.'

I lifted the hatch on my boom box and put in the tape Deb had flung at me. I pushed play: the tape beeped loudly, and then an unfamiliar voice said, 'Sergeant, um, Morgan. Right? This is Dan Burdett, from uh – Kyle Chutsky said I should call you. I'm on the ground at the airport, and I'll call you about getting together when I get to my hotel, which is – ' There was a rustling sound and he obviously moved the cell phone away from his mouth, since his voice got fainter. 'What? Oh, hey, that's nice. All right, thanks.' His voice got louder again. 'I just met your driver. Thanks for sending somebody. All right, I'll call from the hotel.'

Deborah reached across my desk and switched off the machine. 'I didn't send anybody to the fucking airport,' she said. 'And Captain Matthews damn sure didn't either. Did you send somebody to the fucking airport, Dexter?'

'My limo was out of gas,' I said.

'Well then GOD*DAMN* it!' she said, and I had to agree with her analysis.

'Anyway,' I said, 'at least we found out how good Kyle's replacement is.'

Deborah slumped into the folding chair by my desk. 'Square fucking one,' she said. 'And Kyle is . . .' She bit her lip and didn't finish the sentence.

'Did you tell Captain Matthews about this yet?' I asked her. She shook her head. 'Well, he has to call them. They'll send somebody else.'

'Sure, great. They send somebody else, who might make it all the way to baggage claim this time. Shit, Dexter.'

'We have to tell them, Debs,' I said. 'By the way, who are *them*? Did Kyle ever tell you exactly who he works for?'

She sighed. 'No. He joked about working for the OGA, but he never said why that was funny.'

'Well, whoever they are, they need to know,' I said. I pried the cassette out of my boom box and put it on the desk in front of her. 'There has to be something they can do.'

Deborah didn't move for a moment. 'Why do I get the feeling they've already done it, and Burdett was it?' she said. Then she scooped up the tape and trudged out of my office.

I was sipping coffee and digesting my lunch with the help of a jumbo chocolate-chip cookie when the call came to report to the scene of a homicide in the Miami Shores area. Angel-no-relation and I drove over to where a body had been found in the shell of a small house on a canal that was being ripped apart and rebuilt. Construction had been temporarily halted while the owner and the contractor sued each other. Two teenaged boys skipping school had snuck into the house and found the body. It was laid out on heavy plastic on top of a sheet of plywood which had been placed over two sawhorses. Someone had taken a power saw and neatly lopped off the head, legs, and arms. The whole thing had been left like that, with the trunk in the middle and the pieces simply trimmed off and moved a few inches away.

And although the Dark Passenger had chuckled and whispered little dark nothings in my ear, I put it down to pure envy and went on with my work. There was certainly plenty of blood spatter for me to work with, still very fresh, and I probably would have spent a cheerfully efficient day finding and analyzing it if I hadn't happened to overhear the uniformed officer who had been first on the scene talking with a detective.

'The wallet was right there by the body,' Officer Snyder was saying. 'Got a Virginia driver's license in the name of Daniel Chester Burdett.'

Oh, well then, I said to the happy chattering voice in the backseat of my brain. *That would certainly explain a lot, wouldn't it?* I looked again at the body. Although the removal of the head and limbs had been fast and savage, there was a neatness to the arrangement that I could now recognize as slightly familiar, and the Dark Passenger chuckled happily in agreement. Between the trunk and each part, the gap was as precise as if it had been measured, and the whole presentation was arranged almost like an anatomy lesson. The hip bone disconnected from the leg bone.

'Got the two boys who found it in the squad car,' Snyder said to the detective. I glanced back at the two of them, wondering how to tell them my news. Of course, it was possible that I was wrong, but –

'Sonamabeech,' I heard someone mutter. I looked back to where Angel-no-relation was squatting on the far side of the body. Once again he was using his tweezers to hold up a small piece of paper. I stepped behind him and looked over his shoulder.

In a clear and spidery hand, someone had written 'POGUE,' and crossed it out with a single line. 'Whassa pogue?' Angel asked. 'His name?'

'It's somebody who sits behind a desk and orders around the real troops,' I told him.

He looked at me. 'How you know all this shit?' he asked.

'I see a lot of movies,' I said.

Angel glanced back down at the paper. 'I think the handwriting is the same,' he said.

'Like the other one,' I said.

'The one that never happened,' he said. 'I know, I was there.'

I straightened up and took a breath, thinking how nice it was to be right. 'This one never happened, either,' I said, and walked over to where Officer Snyder was chatting with the detective.

The detective in question was a pear-shaped man named Coulter. He was sipping from a large plastic bottle of Mountain Dew and looking out at the canal that ran by the backyard. 'What do you think a place like this goes for?' he asked Snyder. 'On a canal like that. Less than a mile from the bay, huh? Figure maybe what. Half a million? More?'

'Excuse me, Detective,' I said. 'I think we have a situation here.' I'd always wanted to say that, but it didn't seem to impress Coulter.

'A situation. You been watching *CSI* or something?'

'Burdett is a federal agent,' I said. 'You have to call Captain Matthews right away and tell him.'

'I *have* to,' Coulter said.

'This is connected to something we're not supposed to touch,' I said. 'They came down from Washington and told the captain to back off.'

Coulter took a swig from his bottle. 'And did the captain back off?'

'Like a rabbit in reverse,' I said.

Coulter turned and looked at Burdett's body. 'A fed,' he said. He took one more swig as he stared at the severed head and limbs. Then he shook his head. 'Those guys always come apart under pressure.' He looked back out the window and pulled out his cell phone.

Deborah got to the scene just as Angel-no-relation was putting his kit back in the van, which was three minutes before Captain Matthews. I don't mean to seem critical of the captain. To be perfectly fair, Debs didn't have to put on a fresh spray of Aramis, and he did, and redoing the knot in his tie must have taken some time, too. Just moments behind Matthews came a car I had come to know as well as my own; a maroon Ford Taurus, piloted by Sergeant Doakes. 'Hail, hail, the gang's all here,' I said cheerfully. Officer Snyder looked at me like I had suggested we dance naked, but Coulter just pushed his index finger into the mouth of his soda bottle and let it dangle as he walked away to meet the captain.

Deborah had been looking the scene over from the outside and directing Snyder's partner to move the perimeter tape back a little. By the time she finally walked over to talk to me, I had reached a startling conclusion. It had started as an exercise in ironic whimsy, but it grew into something that I couldn't argue with, as much as I tried. I stepped over to Coulter's expensive window and stared out, leaning on the wall and looking hard at the idea. For some reason, the Dark Passenger found the notion hugely amusing and began whispering frightful counterpoint. And finally, feeling like I was selling nuclear secrets to the Taliban, I realized it was all we could do.

'Deborah,' I said as she stalked over to where I stood by the window, 'the cavalry isn't coming this time.'

'No shit, Sherlock,' she said.

'We are all there is, and we are not enough.'

She pushed a lock of hair away from her face and blew out a deep breath. 'What have I been saying?'

'But you didn't take the next step, Sis. Since we are not enough, we need help, somebody who knows something about this – '

'For Christ's sake, Dexter! We've been *feeding* people like that to this guy!'

'Which means the only remaining candidate at the moment is Sergeant Doakes,' I said.

It might not be fair to say that her jaw dropped. But she did stare at me with her mouth open before turning to look at Doakes, where he stood beside Burdett's body, talking to Captain Matthews.

'Sergeant Doakes,' I repeated. 'Formerly *Sergeant* Doakes. Of the Special Forces. On detached service in El Salvador.'

She looked back at me, and then at Doakes again.

'Deborah,' I said, 'if we want to find Kyle, we need to know more about this. We need to know the names on Kyle's list and we need to know what kind of team it was and why all this is happening. And Doakes is the only one I can think of who knows any of it.'

'Doakes wants you dead,' she said.

'No working situation is ever ideal,' I said with my best smile of cheerful perseverance. 'And I think he wants this to go away as badly as Kyle does.'

'Probably not as much as Kyle,' Deborah said. 'Not as much as I do, either.'

'Well then,' I said. 'This looks like your best shot.'

Deborah still didn't look convinced for some reason. 'Captain Matthews won't want to lose Doakes for this. We'd have to clear it with him.'

I pointed to where that very same captain was conferring with Doakes. 'Behold,' I said.

Deborah chewed her lip for a moment before she finally said, 'Shit. It might work.'

'I can't think of anything else that might,' I said.

She took another breath, and then as if someone had clicked a switch, she stepped toward Matthews and Doakes with her jaw clenched. I trailed along behind, trying hard to blend in with the bare walls so Doakes wouldn't pounce and rip out my heart.

'Captain,' Deborah said, 'we need to get proactive with this.'

Even though 'proactive' was one of his favorite words, Matthews stared at her like she was a cockroach in the salad. 'What we need,' he said, 'is for these . . . *people* . . . in Washington to send somebody competent to clean up this situation.'

Deborah pointed at Burdett. 'They sent him,' she said.

Matthews glanced down at Burdett and pushed his

lips out thoughtfully. 'What do you suggest?'

'We have a couple of leads,' she said, nodding toward me. I really wished she hadn't, since Matthews swung his head in my direction and, much worse, so did Doakes. If his hungry-dog expression was any indication, he apparently hadn't mellowed in his feelings toward me.

'What is your involvement with this?' Matthews asked me.

'He's providing forensic assistance,' Deborah said, and I nodded modestly.

'Shit,' Doakes said.

'There's a time factor here,' Deborah said. 'We need to find this guy before he – before more of these turn up. We can't keep a lid on it forever.'

'I think the term 'media feeding frenzy' might be appropriate,' I offered, always helpful. Matthews glared at me.

'I know the overall shape of what Kyle – of what Chutsky was trying to do,' Deborah went on. 'But I can't go on with it because I don't know any background details.' She stuck her chin out in the direction of Doakes. 'Sergeant Doakes does.'

Doakes looked surprised, which was obviously an expression he hadn't practiced enough. But before he could speak Deborah plowed ahead. 'I think the three of us together can catch this guy before another fed gets on the ground and catches up to what's happened so far.'

'Shit,' Doakes said again. 'You want me to work with *him*?' He didn't need to point to let everyone know he meant me, but he did anyway, pushing a muscular, knobby index finger at my face.

'Yeah, I do,' Deborah said. Captain Matthews was chewing on his lip and looking undecided, and Doakes said, 'Shit,' again. I did hope that his conversational skills would improve if we were going to work together.

'You said you know something about this,' Matthews said to Doakes, and the sergeant reluctantly turned his glare away from me and onto the captain.

'Uh-huh,' said Doakes.

'From your, uh – From the army,' Matthews said. He didn't seem terribly frightened by Doakes's expression of petulant rage, but perhaps that was just the habit of command.

'Uh-huh,' Doakes said again.

Captain Matthews frowned, looking as much as he possibly could like a man of action making an important decision. The rest of us managed to control our goose bumps.

'Morgan,' Captain Matthews finally said. He looked at Debs, and then he paused. A van that said Action News on the side pulled up in front of the little house and people began to get out. 'Goddamn it,' Matthews said. He glanced at the body and then at Doakes. 'Can you do it, Sergeant?'

'They're not going to like it in Washington,' Doakes said. 'And I don't much like it here.'

'I'm beginning to lose interest in what they like in Washington,' Matthews said. 'We have our own problems. Can you handle this?'

Doakes looked at me. I tried to look serious and dedicated, but he just shook his head. 'Yeah,' he said. 'I can do this.'

Matthews clapped him on the shoulder. 'Good

160

man,' he said, and he hurried away to talk to the news crew.

Doakes was still looking at me. I looked back. 'Think how much easier it's going to be to keep track of me,' I said.

'When this is over,' he said. 'Just you and me.'

'But not until it's over,' I said, and he finally nodded, just once.

'Until then,' he said.

CHAPTER 18

DOAKES TOOK US TO A COFFEE SHOP ON CALLED Ocho, just across the street from a car dealership. He led us to a small table in the back corner and sat down facing the door. 'We can talk here,' he said, and he made it sound so much like a spy movie that I wished I had brought sunglasses. Still, perhaps Chutsky's would come in the mail. Hopefully without his nose attached.

Before we could actually talk, a man came from the back room and shook Doakes's hand. 'Alberto,' he said. 'Como estas?' And Doakes answered him in very good Spanish – better than mine, to be honest, although I do like to think that my accent is better. 'Luis,' he said. 'Mas o menos.' They chattered away for a minute, and then Luis brought us all tiny cups of horribly sweet Cuban coffee and a plate of *pastelitos*. He nodded once at Doakes and then disappeared into the back room.

Deborah watched the whole performance with growing impatience, and when Luis finally left us she opened up. 'We need the names of everybody from El Salvador,' she blurted out.

Doakes just looked at her and sipped his coffee. 'Be a big list,' he said.

Deborah frowned. 'You know what I mean,' she said. 'Goddamn it, Doakes, he's got Kyle.'

Doakes showed his teeth. 'Yeah, Kyle getting old. Never would have got him in his prime.'

'What exactly were *you* doing down there?' I asked him. I know it was a bit off message, but my curiosity about how he would answer got the best of me.

Still smiling, if that's what it was, Doakes looked at me and said, 'What do you think?' And just underneath the threshold of hearing there came a quiet rumble of savage glee, answered right away from deep inside my dark backseat, one predator calling across a moonlit night to another. And really and truly, what else could he have been doing? Just as Doakes knew me, I knew Doakes for what he was: a cold killer. Even without what Chutsky had said, it was very clear what Doakes would have been doing in a homicidal carnival like El Salvador. He would have been one of the ringmasters.

'Cut the staring contest,' Deborah said. 'I need some names.'

Doakes picked up one of the *pastelitos* and leaned back. 'Why don't you-all bring me up to date,' he said. He took a bite, and Deborah tapped a finger on the table before deciding that made sense.

'All right,' she said. 'We got a rough description of the guy who's doing this, and his van. A white van.'

Doakes shook his head. 'Don't matter. We *know* who's doing this.'

'We also got an ID on the first victim,' I said. 'A man named Manuel Borges.'

'Well, well,' Doakes said. 'Old Manny, huh? Really should've let me shoot him.'

'A friend of yours?' I asked, but Doakes ignored me.

'What else you got?' he said.

'Kyle had a list of names,' Deborah said. 'Other men from the same unit. He said one of them would be the next victim. But he didn't tell me the names.'

'No, he wouldn't,' Doakes said.

'So we need you to tell us,' she said.

Doakes appeared to think this over. 'If I was a hotshot like Kyle, I'd pick one of these guys and stake him out.' Deborah pursed her lips and nodded. 'Problem is, I am *not* a hotshot like Kyle. Just a simple cop from the country.'

'Would you like a banjo?' I asked, but for some reason he didn't laugh.

'I only know about one guy from the old team here in Miami,' he said, after a quick and savage glance at me. 'Oscar Acosta. Saw him at Publix two years ago. We could run him down.' He pointed his chin at Deborah. 'Two other names I can think of. You look 'em up, see if they're here.' He spread his hands. 'About all I got. I could maybe call some old buddies in Virginia, but no telling what that might stir up.' He snorted. 'Anyway, take them two days to decide what I was really asking and what they ought to do about it.'

'So what do we do?' Deborah said. 'We stake this guy out? The one you saw? Or do we talk to him?'

Doakes shook his head. 'He remembered me. I can talk to him. You try to watch him, he'll know it and probably disappear.' He looked at his watch. 'Quarter of three. Oscar be home in a couple of hours. You-all wait for my call.' And then he gave me his 150-watt I'm-watching-you smile, and said, 'Why don't you go wait with your pretty fiancée?' And he got up and walked out, leaving us with the check.

Deborah stared at me. 'Fiancée?' she said.

'It's not really definite,' I said.

'You're *engaged*!?'

'I was going to tell you,' I said.

'When? On your third anniversary?'

'When I know how it happened,' I said. 'I still don't really believe it.'

She snorted. 'I don't either.' She stood up. 'Come on. I'll take you back to work. Then you can go wait with your *fiancée*,' she said. I left some money on the table and followed meekly.

Vince Masuoka was passing by in the hall when Deborah and I got off the elevator. 'Shalom, boy-chick,' he said. 'How's by you?'

'He's engaged,' Deborah said before I could speak. Vince looked at her like she had said I was pregnant.

'He's *what*?' he said.

'Engaged. About to be married,' she said.

'*Married*? Dexter?' His face seemed to struggle with finding the right expression, which was not an easy task since he always seemed to be faking it, one of the reasons I got along with him; two artificial humans, like plastic peas in a real pod. He finally settled on what looked like delighted surprise – not very convincing, but still a sound choice. 'Mazel tov!' he said, and gave me an awkward hug.

'Thank you,' I said, still feeling completely baffled by the whole thing and wondering if I would actually have to go through with it.

'Well then,' he said, rubbing his hands together, 'we can't let this go unpunished. Tomorrow night at my house?'

'For what?' I asked.

He gave me his very best phony smile. 'Ancient

Japanese ritual, dating back to the Tokugawa shogunate. We get smashed and watch dirty movies,' he said, and then he turned to leer at Deborah. 'We can get your sister to jump out of a cake.'

'How about if you jump up your ass instead?' Debs said.

'That's very nice, Vince, but I don't think – ' I said, trying to avoid anything that made my engagement more official, and also trying to stop the two of them from trading their clever put-downs before I got a headache. But Vince wouldn't let me finish.

'No, no,' he said, 'this is highly necessary. A matter of honor, no escape. Tomorrow night, eight o'clock,' he said, and, looking at Deborah as he walked away, he added, 'and you only have twenty-four hours to practice twirling your tassels.'

'Go twirl your own tassel,' she said.

'Ha! Ha!' he said with his terrible fake laugh, and he disappeared down the hall.

'Little freak,' Deborah muttered, and she turned to go in the other direction. 'Stick with your *fiancée* after work. I'll call you when I hear from Doakes.'

There wasn't a great deal left of the workday. I filed a few things, ordered a case of Luminol from our supplier, and acknowledged receiving half a dozen memos that had piled up in my e-mail in-box. And with a feeling of real accomplishment, I headed down to my car and drove through the soothing carnage of rush hour. I stopped at my apartment for a change of clothes; Debs was nowhere to be seen, but the bed was unmade so I knew she had been here. I stuffed my things into a carry-on bag and headed for Rita's.

It was fully dark by the time I got to Rita's house. I

166

didn't really want to go there, but was not quite sure what else to do. Deborah expected me to be there if she needed to find me, and she was using my apartment. So I parked in Rita's driveway and got out of my car. Purely from reflex, I glanced across the street to Sergeant Doakes's parking spot. It was empty, of course. He was occupied talking with Oscar, his old army buddy. And the sudden realization grew on me that I was free, away from the unfriendly bloodhound eyes that had for so long now kept me from being me. A slow, swelling hymn of pure dark joy rose up inside me and the counterpoint thumped down from a sudden moon oozing out from a low cloud bank, a lurid, guttering three-quarter moon still low and huge in the dark sky. And the music blared from the loudspeakers and climbed into the upper decks of Dexter's Dark Arena, where the sly whispers grew into a roaring cheer to match the moon music, a rousing chant of *Do it, do it, do it*, and my body quivered from the inside out as I came up on point and thought, *Why not?*

Why not indeed? I could slip away for a few happy hours – taking my cell phone with me, of course, I wouldn't want to be irresponsible about it. But why not take advantage of the Doakes-less moony night and slide away into the dark breeze? The thought of those red boots pulled at me like a spring tide. Reiker lived just a few miles from here. I could be there in ten minutes. I could slip in and find the proof I needed, and then – I suppose I would have to improvise, but the voice just under the edge of sound was full of ideas tonight and we could certainly come up with something to lead to the sweet release we both needed so much. *Oh, do it, Dexter*, the voices howled and as I paused on tiptoe to listen and think again *Why not?* and came up with no reasonable answer . . .

. . . the front door of Rita's house swung wide and Astor peered out. 'It's him!' she called back into the house. 'He's here!'

And so I was. Here, instead of there. Reeling in to the couch instead of dancing away into darkness. Wearing the weary mask of Dexter the Sofa Spud instead of the bright silver gleam of the Dark Avenger.

'Come on in, you,' Rita said, filling the doorway with such warm good cheer that I felt my teeth grind together, and the crowd inside howled with disappointment but slowly filed out of the stadium, game over, because after all, what could we do? Nothing, of course, which was what we did, trailing meekly into the house behind the happy parade of Rita, Astor, and ever-quiet Cody. I managed not to whimper, but really: Wasn't this pushing the envelope a tiny bit? Weren't we all taking advantage of Dexter's cheerful good nature just a trifle too much?

Dinner was annoyingly pleasant, as if to prove to me that I was buying into a lifetime of happiness and pork chops, and I played along even though my heart was not in it. I cut the meat into small chunks, wishing I was cutting something else and thinking of the South Pacific cannibals who referred to humans as 'long pork.' It was appropriate, really, because it was that other pork I truly longed to slice into and not this tepid mushroom soup-covered thing on my plate. But I smiled and stabbed the green beans and made it all the way through to coffee somehow. Ordeal by pork chop, but I survived.

After dinner, Rita and I sipped our coffee as the kids

ate small portions of frozen yogurt. Although coffee is supposed to be a stimulant, it gave me no help in thinking of a way out of this – not even a way to slip out for a few hours, let alone avoid this lifelong bliss that had snuck up behind me and grabbed me around the neck. I felt like I was slowly fading away at the edges and melting into my disguise, until eventually the happy rubber mask would meld with my actual features and I would truly become the thing I had been pretending to be, taking the kids to soccer, buying flowers when I drank too many beers, comparing detergents and cutting costs instead of flensing the wicked of their unneeded flesh. It was a very depressing line of thought, and I might have grown unhappy if the doorbell had not rung just in time.

'That must be Deborah,' I said. I'm fairly sure I kept most of the hope for rescue out of my voice. I got up and went to the front door, swinging it open to reveal a pleasant-looking, overweight woman with long blond hair.

'Oh,' she said. 'You must be, ahm – Is Rita here?'

Well, I suppose I was ahm, although until now I hadn't been aware of it. I called Rita to the door and she came, smiling. 'Kathy!' she said. 'So nice to see you. How are the boys? Kathy lives next door,' she explained to me.

'Aha,' I said. I knew most of the kids in the area, but not their parents. But this one was apparently the mother of the faintly sleazy eleven-year-old boy next door, and his nearly always-absent older brother. Since that meant she was probably not carrying a car bomb or a vial of anthrax, I smiled and went back to the table with Cody and Astor.

'Jason's at band camp,' she said. 'Nick is lounging around the house trying to reach puberty so he can grow a mustache.'

'Oh Lord,' Rita said.

'Nicky is a creep,' Astor whispered. 'He wanted me to pull down my pants so he could see.' Cody stirred his frozen yogurt into a frozen pudding.

'Listen, Rita, I'm sorry to bother you at dinnertime,' Kathy said.

'We just finished. Would you like some coffee?'

'Oh, no, I'm down to one cup a day,' she said. 'Doctor's orders. But it's about our dog – I just wanted to ask if you had seen Rascal? He's been missing for a couple of days now, and Nick is so worried.'

'I haven't seen him. Let me ask the kids,' Rita said. But as she turned to ask, Cody looked at me, got up without a sound, and walked out of the room. Astor stood up, too.

'We haven't seen him,' she said. 'Not since he knocked over the trash last week.' And she followed Cody out of the room. They left their desserts on the table, still only half eaten.

Rita watched them go with her mouth open, and then turned back to her neighbor. 'I'm sorry, Kathy. I guess nobody's seen him. But we'll keep an eye open, all right? I'm sure he'll turn up, tell Nick not to worry.' She prattled on for another minute with Kathy, while I looked at the frozen yogurt and wondered what I had just seen.

The front door closed and Rita came back to her cooling coffee. 'Kathy's a nice person,' she said. 'But her boys can be a handful. She's divorced, her ex bought a place in Islamorada, he's a lawyer? But he

170

stays down there, so Kathy's had to raise the boys alone and I don't think she's very firm sometimes. She's a nurse with a podiatrist over by the university.'

'And her shoe size?' I asked.

'Am I blathering?' Rita asked. She bit her lip. 'I'm sorry. I guess I was just worrying a little bit . . . I'm sure it's just . . .' She shook her head and looked at me. 'Dexter. Did you – '

I never got to find out if I did, because my cell phone chirped. 'Excuse me,' I said, and I went over to the table by the front door where I had left it.

'Doakes just called,' Deborah said to me without even saying hello. 'The guy he went to talk to is running. Doakes is following to see where he goes, but he needs us for backup.'

'Quickly, Watson, the game's afoot,' I said, but Deborah was not in a literary mood.

'I'll pick you up in five minutes,' she said.

CHAPTER 19

I LEFT RITA WITH A HURRIED EXPLANATION AND
went outside to wait. Deborah was as good as her
word, and in five and a half minutes we were heading
north on Dixie Highway.

'They're out on Miami Beach,' she told me. 'Doakes
said he approached the guy, Oscar, and told him
what's up. Oscar says, let me think about it, Doakes
says okay, I'll call you. But he watches the house from
up the street, and ten minutes later the guy is out the
door and into his car with an overnight bag.'

'Why would he run now?'

'Wouldn't you run if you knew Danco was after
you?'

'No,' I said, thinking happily of what I might
actually do if I came face-to-face with the Doctor. 'I
would set some kind of trap for him, and let him
come.' *And then*, I thought, but did not say aloud to
Deborah.

'Well, Oscar isn't you,' she said.

'So few of us are,' I said. 'Where is he headed?'

She frowned and shook her head. 'Right now he's
just cruising around, and Doakes is tailing him.'

'Where do we think he's going to lead us?' I asked.

Deborah shook her head and cut around an old
ragtop Cadillac loaded with yelling teenagers. 'It
doesn't matter,' she said, and headed up the on-ramp

onto the Palmetto Expressway with the pedal to the floor. 'Oscar is still our best chance. If he tries to leave the area we'll pick him up, but until then we need to stick with him to see what happens.'

'Very good, a really terrific idea – but what exactly do we think might happen?'

'I don't know, Dexter!' she snapped at me. 'But we know this guy is a target sooner or later, all right? And now he knows it, too. So maybe he's just trying to see if he's being followed before he runs. Shit,' she said, and swerved around an old flatbed truck loaded with crates of chickens. The truck was going possibly thirty-five miles per hour, had no taillights, and three men sat on top of the load, hanging on to battered hats with one hand and the load with the other. Deborah gave them a quick blast of the siren as she pulled around them. It didn't seem to have any effect. The men on top of the load didn't even blink.

'Anyway,' she said as she straightened out the wheel and accelerated again, 'Doakes wants us on the Miami side for backup. So Oscar can't get too fancy. We'll run parallel along Biscayne.'

It made sense; as long as Oscar was on Miami Beach, he couldn't escape in any other direction. If he tried to dash across a causeway or head north to the far side of Haulover Park and cross, we were there to pick him up. Unless he had a helicopter stashed, we had him cornered. I let Deborah drive, and she headed north rapidly without actually killing anyone.

At the airport we swung east on the 836. The traffic picked up a little here, and Deborah wove in and out, concentrating fiercely. I kept my thoughts to myself and she displayed her years of training with Miami traffic by winning what amounted to a nonstop free-for-all high-speed game of chicken. We made it safely through the interchange with I-95 and slid down onto Biscayne Boulevard. I took a deep breath and let it out carefully as Deborah eased back into street traffic and down to normal speed.

The radio crackled once and Doakes's voice came over the speaker. 'Morgan, what's your twenty?'

Deborah lifted the microphone and told him. 'Biscayne at the MacArthur Causeway.'

There was a short pause, and then Doakes said, 'He's pulled over by the drawbridge at the Venetian Causeway. Cover it on your side.'

'Ten-four,' Deborah said.

And I couldn't help saying, 'I feel so *official* when you say that.'

'What does that mean?' she said.

'Nothing, really,' I said.

She glanced at me, a serious cop look, but her face was still young and for just a moment it felt like we were kids again, sitting in Harry's patrol car and playing cops and robbers – except that this time, I got to be a good guy, a very unsettling feeling.

'This isn't a game, Dexter,' she said, because of course she shared that same memory. 'Kyle's life is at stake here.' And her features dropped back into her Serious Large-Fish Face as she went on. 'I know it probably doesn't make sense to you, but I care about that man. He makes me feel so – Shit. You're getting *married* and you still won't ever get it.' We had come to the traffic light at N.E. 15th Street and she turned right. What was left of the Omni Mall loomed up on the left and ahead of us was the Venetian Causeway.

'I'm not very good at feeling things, Debs,' I said. 'And I really don't know at all about this marriage thing. But I don't much like it when you're unhappy.'

Deborah pulled off opposite the little marina by the old Herald building and parked the car facing back toward the Venetian Causeway. She was quiet for a moment, and then she hissed out her breath and said, 'I'm sorry.'

That caught me a bit off guard, since I admit that I had been preparing to say something very similar, just to keep the social wheels greased. Almost certainly I would have phrased it in a slightly more clever way, but the same essence. 'For what?'

'I don't mean to – I know you're different, Dex. I'm really trying to get used to that and – But you're still my brother.'

'Adopted,' I said.

'That's horseshit and you know it. You're my brother. And I know you're only here because of me.'

'Actually, I was hoping I'd get to say "ten-four" on the radio later.'

She snorted. 'All right, be an asshole. But thanks anyway.'

'You're welcome.'

She picked up the radio. 'Doakes. What's he doing?'

After a brief pause, Doakes replied, 'Looks like he's talking on a cell phone.'

Deborah frowned and looked at me. 'If he's running, who's he going to talk to on the phone?'

I shrugged. 'He might be arranging a way out of the country. Or – '

I stopped. The idea was far too stupid to think about, and that should have kept it out of my head automatically, but somehow there it was, bouncing off the gray matter and waving a small red flag.

'What?' Deborah demanded.

I shook my head. 'Not possible. Stupid. Just a wild thought that won't go away.'

'All right. How wild?'

'What if – Now I did say this was stupid.'

'It's a lot stupider to dick around like this,' she snapped. 'What's the idea?'

'What if Oscar is calling the good Doctor and trying to bargain his way out?' I said. And I was right; it did sound stupid.

Debs snorted. 'Bargain with what?'

'Well,' I said, 'Doakes said he's carrying a bag. So he could have money, bearer bonds, a stamp collection. I don't know. But he probably has something that might be even more valuable to our surgical friend.'

'Like what?'

'He probably knows where everybody else from the old team is hiding.'

'Shit,' she said. 'Give up everybody else in exchange for his life?' She chewed on her lip as she thought that over. After a minute she shook her head. 'That's pretty far-fetched,' she said.

'Far-fetched is a big step up from stupid,' I said.

'Oscar would have to know how to get in touch with the Doctor.'

'One spook can always find a way to get to another. There are lists and databases and mutual contacts, you know that. Didn't you see *Bourne Identity*?'

'Yeah, but how do we know Oscar saw it?' she said.

'I'm just saying it's possible.'

'Uh-huh,' she said. She looked out the window,

thinking, then made a face and shook her head. 'Kyle said something – that after a while you'd forget what team you were on, like baseball with free agency. So you'd get friendly with guys on the other side, and – Shit, that's stupid.'

'So whatever side Danco is on, Oscar *could* find a way to reach him.'

'So fucking what. We can't,' she said.

We were both quiet for a few minutes after that. I suppose Debs was thinking about Kyle and wondering if we would find him in time. I tried to imagine caring about Rita the same way and came up blank. As Deborah had so astutely pointed out, I was engaged and still didn't get it. And I never would, either, which I usually regard as a blessing. I have always felt that it was preferable to think with my brain, rather than with certain other wrinkled parts located slightly south. I mean, seriously, don't people ever *see* themselves, staggering around drooling and mooning, all weepy-eyed and weak-kneed and rendered completely idiotic over something even animals have enough sense to finish quickly so they can get on with more sensible pursuits, like finding fresh meat?

Well, as we all agreed, I didn't get it. So I just looked out across the water to the subdued lights of the homes on the far side of the causeway. There were a few apartment buildings close to the toll booth, and then a scattering of houses almost as big. Maybe if I won the lottery I could get a real estate agent to show me something with a small cellar, just big enough for one homicidal photographer to fit in snugly under the floor. And as I thought it a soft whisper came from my personal backseat voice, but of course there was nothing I could do about that, except perhaps applaud the moon that hung over the water. And across that same moon-painted water floated the sound of a clanging bell, signaling that the drawbridge was about to go up.

The radio crackled. 'He's moving,' Doakes said. 'Gonna run the drawbridge. Watch for him – white Toyota 4Runner.'

'I see him,' Deborah said into the radio. 'We're on him.'

The white SUV came across the causeway and onto 15th Street just moments before the bridge went up. After a slight pause to let him get ahead, Deborah pulled out and followed. At Biscayne Boulevard he turned right and a moment later we did, too. 'He's headed north on Biscayne,' she said into the radio.

'Copy that,' Doakes said. 'I'll follow out here.'

The 4Runner moved at normal speed through moderate traffic, keeping to a mere five miles per hour above the speed limit, which in Miami is considered tourist speed, slow enough to justify a blast of the horn from the drivers who passed him. But Oscar didn't seem to mind. He obeyed all the traffic signals and stayed in the right lane, cruising along as if he had no particular place to go and was merely out for a relaxing after-dinner drive.

As we came up on the 79th Street Causeway, Deborah picked up the radio. 'We're passing 79th Street,' she said. 'He's in no hurry, proceeding north.'

'Ten-four,' Doakes said, and Deborah glanced at me.

'I didn't say anything,' I said.

'You thought the hell out of it,' she said.

We moved on north, stopping twice at traffic

signals. Deborah was careful to stay several cars behind, no mean feat in Miami traffic, with most of the cars trying to go around, over, or through all the others. A fire engine went wailing past in the other direction, blasting its horn at the intersections. For all the effect it had on the other drivers, it might have been a lamb bleating. They ignored the siren and clung to their hard-won places in the scrambled line of traffic. The man behind the wheel of the fire engine, being a Miami driver himself, simply wove in and out with the horn and siren playing: Duet for Traffic.

We reached 123d Street, the last place to cross back to Miami Beach before 826 ran across at North Miami Beach, and Oscar kept heading north. Deborah told Doakes by radio as we passed it.

'Where the hell is he going?' Deborah muttered as she put down the radio.

'Maybe he's just driving around,' I said. 'It's a beautiful night.'

'Uh-huh. You want to write a sonnet?'

Under normal circumstances, I would have had a splendid comeback for that, but perhaps due to the thrilling nature of our chase, nothing occurred to me. And anyway, Debs looked like she could use a victory, however small.

A few blocks later, Oscar suddenly accelerated into the left lane and turned left across oncoming traffic, raising an entire concerto of angry horns from drivers moving in both directions.

'He's making a move,' Deborah told Doakes, 'west on 135th Street.'

'I'm crossing behind you,' Doakes said. 'On the Broad Causeway.'

'What's on 135th Street?' Debs wondered aloud.

'Opa-Locka Airport,' I said. 'A couple of miles straight ahead.'

'Shit,' she said, and picked up the radio. 'Doakes – Opa-Locka Airport is out this way.'

'On my way,' he said, and I could hear his siren cutting on before his radio clicked off.

Opa-Locka Airport had long been popular with people in the drug trade, as well as with those in covert operations. This was a handy arrangement, considering that the line between the two was often quite blurry. Oscar could very easily have a small plane waiting there, ready to whisk him out of the country and off to almost anyplace in the Caribbean or Central or South America – with connections to the rest of the world, of course, although I doubted he would be headed for the Sudan, or even Beirut. Someplace in the Caribbean was more likely, but in any case fleeing the country seemed like a reasonable move under the circumstances, and Opa-Locka Airport was a logical place to start.

Oscar was going a little faster now, although 135th Street was not as wide and well traveled as Biscayne Boulevard. We came up over a small bridge across a canal and as Oscar came down the far side he suddenly accelerated, squealing through traffic around an S curve in the road.

'Goddamn it, something spooked him,' Deborah said. 'He must have spotted us.' She sped up to stay with him, still keeping two or three cars back, even though there seemed little point now to pretending we weren't following him.

Something had indeed spooked him, because Oscar

was driving wildly, dangerously close to slamming into the traffic or running up onto the sidewalk, and naturally enough, Debs was not going to let herself lose this kind of pissing contest. She stayed with him, swerving around cars that were still trying to recover from their encounters with Oscar. Just ahead he swung into the far left lane, forcing an old Buick to spin away, hit the curb, and crash through a chain-link fence into the front yard of a light blue house.

Would the sight of our little unmarked car be enough to cause Oscar to behave this way? It was nice to think so and made me feel very important, but I didn't believe it – so far, he had acted in a cool and controlled way. If he wanted to ditch us it seemed more likely that he would have made some kind of sudden and tricky move, like going over the drawbridge as it went up. So why had he suddenly panicked? Just for something to do, I leaned forward and looked into the side mirror. The block letters on the surface of the mirror told me that objects were closer than they appeared. Things being what they were, this was a very unhappy thought, because only one object appeared in the mirror at the moment.

It was a battered white van.

And it was following us, and following Oscar. Matching our speed, moving in and out of traffic. 'Well,' I said, 'not stupid after all.' And I raised my voice to go over the squeal of tires and the horns of the other motorists.

'Oh, Deborah?' I said. 'I don't want to distract you from your driving chores, but if you have a moment, could you look in your rearview mirror?'

'What the fuck is that supposed to mean,' she

181

snarled, but she flicked her eyes to the mirror. It was a piece of good luck that we were on a straight stretch of road, because for just a second she almost forgot to steer. 'Oh, shit,' she whispered.

'Yes, that's what I thought,' I said.

The I-95 overpass stretched across the road directly ahead, and just before he passed under it Oscar swerved violently to the right across three lanes and turned down a side street that ran parallel to the freeway. Deborah swore and wrenched her car around to follow. 'Tell Doakes!' she said, and I obediently picked up the radio.

'Sergeant Doakes,' I said. 'We are not alone.'

The radio hissed once. 'The fuck does that mean?' Doakes said, almost as if he had heard Deborah's response and admired it so much he had to repeat it.

'We have just turned right on 6th Avenue, and we are being followed by a white van.' There was no answer, so I said again, 'Did I mention that the van is white?' and this time I had the great satisfaction of hearing Doakes grunt, 'Motherfucker.'

'That's exactly what we thought,' I said.

'Let the van in front and stay with him,' he said.

'No shit,' Deborah muttered through clenched teeth, and then she said something much worse. I was tempted to say something similar, because as Doakes clicked off his radio, Oscar headed up the on-ramp onto I-95 with us following, and at the very last second he yanked his car back down the paved slope and onto 6th Avenue. His 4Runner bounced as it hit the road and teetered drunkenly to the right for a moment, then accelerated and straightened up. Deborah hit the brakes and we spun through half a turn; the white van slid ahead of us, bounced down the slope, and closed the gap with the 4Runner. After half a second, Debs straightened us out of our slide and followed them down onto the street.

The side road here was narrow, with a row of houses on the right and a high yellow-cement embankment on the left with I-95 on top. We ran along for several blocks, picking up speed. A tiny old couple holding hands paused on the sidewalk to watch our strange parade rocket past. It may have been my imagination, but they seemed to flutter in the wind from Oscar's car and the van going by.

We closed the gap just a little, and the white van closed on the 4Runner, too. But Oscar picked up the pace; he ran a stop sign, leaving us to veer around a pickup truck that was spinning in a circle in its attempt to avoid the 4Runner and the van. The truck wobbled through a clumsy doughnut turn and slammed into a fire hydrant. But Debs just clamped her jaw tight and squealed around the truck and through the intersection, ignoring the horns and the fountain of water from the ruptured hydrant, and closing the gap again in the next block.

Several blocks ahead of Oscar I could see the red light of a major cross street. Even from this far I could see a steady stream of traffic moving through the intersection. Of course nobody lives forever, but this was really not the way I would choose to die if given a vote. Watching TV with Rita suddenly seemed a lot more attractive. I tried to think of a polite but very convincing way to persuade Deborah to stop and smell the roses for a moment, but just when I needed it the most my powerful brain seemed to shut down, and before I could get it going again Oscar was approaching the traffic light.

Quite possibly Oscar had been to church this week, because the light turned green as he rocketed through the intersection. The white van followed close behind, braking hard to avoid a small blue car trying to beat the light, and then it was our turn, with the light fully green now. We swerved around the van and almost made it through – but this was Miami, after all, and a cement truck ran the red light behind the blue car, right in front of us. I swallowed hard as Deborah stood on the brake pedal and spun around the truck. We thumped hard against the curb, running the two left wheels up onto the sidewalk for just a moment before bouncing down onto the road again. 'Very nice,' I said as Deborah accelerated once again. And quite possibly, she might have taken the time to thank me for my compliment, if only the white van had not chosen that moment to take advantage of our slow-down to drop back beside our car and swerve into us. The rear end of our car slewed around to the left, but Deborah fought it back around again.

The van popped us again, harder, right behind my door, and as I lurched away from the blow the door sprung open. Our car swerved and Deborah braked – perhaps not the best strategy, since the van accelerated at the same moment and this time clipped my door so hard that it came loose and bounced away, hitting the van a solid smack near the rear wheel before spinning off like a deformed wheel, spitting sparks.

I saw the van wobble slightly, and heard the slack rattling sound of a blown tire. Then the wall of white slammed into us one more time. Our car bucked violently, lurched to the left, hopped the curb and burst through a chain-link fence separating the side road from the ramp leading down off I-95. We twirled around as if the tires were made of butter. Deborah fought the wheel with her teeth showing, and we very nearly made it across the off-ramp. But of course, I had *not* been to church this week, and as our two front wheels hit the curb on the far side of the off-ramp, a large red SUV banged into our rear fender. We spun up onto the grassy area of the freeway intersection that surrounded a large pond. I had only a moment to notice that the cropped grass seemed to be switching places with the night sky. Then the car bounced hard and the passenger air bag exploded into my face. It felt like I had been in a pillow fight with Mike Tyson; I was still stunned as the car flipped onto its roof, hit the pond, and began to fill with water.

CHAPTER 20

I AM NOT SHY ABOUT ADMITTING MY MODEST talents. For example, I am happy to admit that I am better than average at clever remarks, and I also have a flair for getting people to like me. But to be perfectly fair to myself, I am ever-ready to confess my shortcomings, too, and a quick round of soul-searching forced me to admit that I had never been any good at all at breathing water. As I hung there from the seat belt, dazed and watching the water pour in and swirl around my head, this began to seem like a very large character flaw.

The last look I had at Deborah before the water closed over her head was not encouraging, either. She was hanging from her seat belt unmoving, with her eyes closed and her mouth open, just the opposite of her usual state, which was probably not a good sign. And then the water flooded up around my eyes, and I could see nothing at all.

I also like to think that I react well to the occasional unexpected emergency, so I'm quite sure my sudden stunned apathy was the result of being rattled around and then smacked with an air bag. In any case, I hung there upside down in the water for what seemed like quite a long time, and I am ashamed to admit that for the most part, I simply mourned my own passing. Dear Departed Dexter, so much potential, so many dark fellow travelers still to dissect, and now so tragically cut short in his prime. Alas, Dark Passenger, I knew him well. And the poor boy was finally just about to get married, too. How more than sad – I pictured Rita in white, weeping at the altar, two small children wailing at her feet. Sweet little Astor, her hair done up in a bouffant bubble, a pale green bridesmaid dress now soaked with tears. And quiet Cody in his tiny tuxedo, staring at the back of the church and waiting, thinking of our last fishing trip and wondering when he would ever get to push the knife in again and twist it so slowly, watching the bright red blood burble out onto the blade and smiling, and then –

Slow down, Dexter. Where did that thought come from? Rhetorical question, of course, and I did not need the low rumble of amusement from my old interior friend to give me the answer. But with his prompting I put together a few scattered pieces into half a puzzle and realized that Cody –

Isn't it odd what we think about when we're dying? The car had settled onto its flattened roof, moving with no more than a gentle rocking now and completely filled with water so thick and mucky that I could not have seen a flare gun firing from the end of my nose. And yet I could see Cody perfectly clearly, more clearly now than the last time we had been in the same room together; and standing behind this sharp image of his small form towered a gigantic dark shadow, a black shape with no features that somehow seemed to be laughing.

Could it be? I thought again about the way he had put the knife so happily into his fish. I thought about his strange reaction to the neighbor's missing dog – much like mine when I had been asked as a boy about a neighborhood dog I had taken and experimented with. And I remembered that he, too, had gone through a traumatic event like I had, when his biological father had attacked him and his sister in a terrifying drug-induced rage and beat them with a chair.

It was a totally unthinkable thing to think. A ridiculous thought, but – All the pieces were there. It made perfect, poetic sense.

I had a son.

Someone Just Like Me.

But there was no wise foster father to guide his first baby steps into the world of slice and dice; no all-seeing Harry to teach him how to be all he could be, to help change him from an aimless child with a random urge to kill into a caped avenger; no one to carefully and patiently steer him past the pitfalls and into the gleaming knife blade of the future – no one at all for Cody, not if Dexter died here and now.

It would sound far too melodramatic for me to say, 'The thought spurred me to furious action,' and I am only melodramatic on purpose, when there is an audience. However, as the realization of Cody's true nature hit me, I also heard, almost like an echo, a deep unbodied voice saying, 'Undo the seat belt, Dexter.' And somehow I managed to make my suddenly huge and clumsy fingers move to the belt's lock and fumble with the release. It felt like trying to thread a needle with a ham, but I poked and pushed and finally felt something give. Of course this meant that I bumped down onto the ceiling on my head, a little hard considering that I was under water. But the shock of getting thumped on the head cleared away a few more cobwebs, and I righted myself and reached for the opening where the car's door had been knocked away. I managed to pull myself through and face-first into several inches of muck on the bottom of the pond.

I righted myself and kicked hard for the surface. It was a fairly feeble kick, but quite good enough since the water was only about three feet deep. The kick sent me shooting up to my knees and then staggering to my feet, and I stood there in the water for just a moment retching and sucking in the wonderful air. A marvelous and underrated thing, air. How true it was that we never appreciate things until we must do without them. What a terrible thought to picture all the poor people of this world who must do without air, people like . . .

. . . Deborah?

A real human being might have thought of his drowning sister much sooner, but really, let's be fair, one can only expect so much from an imitation after what I had been through. And I did actually think of her now, possibly still in time to do something meaningful. But although I was not really reluctant to rush to the rescue, I couldn't help thinking that we were asking a bit much of Dutifully Dashing Dexter this evening, weren't we? No sooner out of it than I had to go right back in again.

Still, family was family, and complaining had never done me a bit of good. I took a deep breath and slid back under the muddy water, feeling my way through the doorway and into the front seat of Deborah's topsy-turvy car. Something smacked me across the face and then grabbed me brutally by the hair – Debs herself, I hoped, since anything else moving around in the water would surely have much sharper teeth. I reached up and tried to pry apart her fingers. It was hard enough to hold my breath and fumble around blindly without receiving an impromptu haircut at the same time. But Deborah held tight – which was a good sign, in a way, since it meant she was still alive, but it left me wondering whether my lungs or my scalp would give out first. This would never do; I put both my hands on the job and managed to pry her fingers away from my poor tender hairdo. Then I followed her arm up to the shoulder and felt across her body until I found the strap of the seat belt. I slid my hand down the strap to the buckle and pushed the release.

Well of course it was jammed. I mean, we already knew it was one of those days, didn't we? It was one thing after another, and really, it would have been far too much to hope that even one small thing might go right. Just to underline the point, something went *blurp* in my ear, and I realized that Deborah had run out of time and was now trying her luck at breathing water. It was possible that she would be better at it than I was, but I didn't think so.

I slid lower in the water and braced my knees against the roof of the car, wedging my shoulder against Deb's midsection and pushing up to take her weight off the seat belt. Then I pulled as much slack as I could get down to the buckle and slid it through, making the belt very floppy and loose. I braced my feet and pulled Deborah through the belt and toward the door. She seemed a bit loose and floppy herself; perhaps after all my valiant effort I was too late. I squeezed through the door and pulled her after me. My shirt caught on something in the doorway and ripped, but I pulled myself through anyway, staggering upright once again into the night air.

Deborah was dead weight in my arms and a thin stream of mucky water dribbled from the corner of her mouth. I hoisted her onto my shoulder and sloshed through the muck to the grass. The muck fought back every step of the way, and I lost my left shoe before I got more than three steps from the car. But shoes are, after all, much easier to replace than sisters, so I soldiered on until I could climb up onto the grass and dump Deborah on her back on the solid earth.

In the near distance a siren wailed, and was almost immediately joined by another. Joy and bliss: help was on the way. Perhaps they would even have a towel. In the meantime, I was not certain it would arrive in time to do Deborah any good. So I dropped down beside her, slung her facedown over my knee, and forced out as much water as I could. Then I rolled her onto her back, cleared a finger-load of mud from her mouth, and began to give her mouth-to-mouth resuscitation.

At first my only reward was another gout of mucky water, which did nothing to make the job more pleasant. But I kept at it, and soon Debs gave a convulsive shudder and vomited a great deal more water – most of it on me, unfortunately. She coughed horribly, took a breath that sounded like rusty door hinges swinging open, and said, 'Fuck . . .'

For once, I truly appreciated her hard-boiled eloquence. 'Welcome back,' I said. Deborah rolled weakly onto her face and tried to push herself up onto her hands and knees. But she collapsed onto her face again, gasping with pain.

'Oh, God. Oh, shit, something's broken,' she moaned. She turned her head to the side and threw up a little more, arching her back and sucking in great ratcheting breaths in between spasms of nausea. I watched her, and I admit I felt a little pleased with myself. Dexter the Diving Duck had come through and saved the day. 'Isn't throwing up great?' I asked her. 'I mean, considering the alternative?' Of course a really biting reply was beyond the poor girl in her weakened condition, but I was pleased to see that she was strong enough to whisper, 'Fuck you.'

'Where does it hurt?' I asked her.

'Goddamn it,' she said, sounding very weak, 'I can't move my left arm. The whole arm – ' She broke off and tried to move the arm in question and succeeded only in causing herself what looked like a great deal of pain. She hissed in a breath, which set her coughing weakly again, and then just flopped over onto her back and gasped.

I knelt beside her and probed gently at the upper arm. 'Here?' I asked her. She shook her head. I moved my hand up, over the shoulder joint and to the collarbone, and I didn't have to ask her if that was the place. She gasped, her eyes fluttered, and even through the mud on her face I could see her turn several shades paler. 'Your collarbone is broken,' I said.

'It can't be,' she said with a weak and raspy voice. 'I have to find Kyle.'

'No,' I said. 'You have to go to the emergency room. If you go stumbling around like this you'll end up right next to him, all tied and taped, and that won't do anyone any good.'

'I *have* to,' she said.

'Deborah, I just pulled you out of an underwater car, ruining a very nice bowling shirt. Do you want to waste my perfectly good heroic rescue?'

She coughed again, and grunted from the pain of her collarbone as it moved with her spasmodic breathing. I could tell that she wasn't finished arguing yet, but it was starting to register with her that she was in a great deal of pain. And since our conversation was going nowhere, it was just as well that Doakes arrived, followed almost immediately by a pair of paramedics.

The good sergeant looked hard at me, as if I had personally shoved the car into the pond and flipped it on its back. 'Lost 'em, huh,' he said, which seemed terribly unfair.

'Yes, it turned out to be much harder than I thought to follow him when we were upside down and under water,' I said. 'Next time you try that part and we'll stand here and complain.'

Doakes just glared at me and grunted. Then he knelt beside Deborah and said, 'You hurt?'

'Collarbone,' she said. 'It's broken.' The shock was wearing off rapidly and she was fighting the pain by biting her lip and taking ragged breaths. I hoped the paramedics had something a little more effective for her.

Doakes said nothing; he just lifted his glare up to me. Deborah reached out with her good arm and grabbed his arm. 'Doakes,' she said, and he looked back at her. 'Find him,' she said. He just watched her as she gritted her teeth and gasped through another wave of pain.

'Coming through here,' one of the paramedics said. He was a wiry young guy with a spiky haircut, and he and his older, thicker partner had maneuvered their gurney through the chain-link fence where Deb's car had torn a gap. Doakes tried to stand to let them get to Deborah, but she pulled on his arm with surprising strength.

'Find him,' she said again. Doakes just nodded, but it was enough for her. Deborah let go of his arm and he stood up to give the paramedics room. They swooped in and gave Debs a once-over, and they moved her onto their gurney, raised it up, and began to wheel her toward the waiting ambulance. I watched her go, wondering what had happened to our dear friend in the white van. He had a flat tire – how far could he get? It seemed likely that he would try to switch to a different vehicle, rather than stop and call AAA to help him change the tire. So somewhere nearby, we would be very likely to find the abandoned van and a missing car.

Out of an impulse that seemed extremely generous, considering his attitude toward me, I moved over to tell Doakes my thoughts. But I only made it a step and a half in his direction when I heard a commotion coming our way. I turned to look.

Running at us up the middle of the street was a chunky middle-aged guy in a pair of boxer shorts and nothing else. His belly hung over the band of his shorts and wobbled wildly as he came and it was clear that he had not had much practice at running, and he made it harder on himself by waving his arms around over his head and shouting, 'Hey! Hey! Hey!' as he ran. By the time he crossed the ramp from I-95 and got to us he was breathless, gasping too hard to say anything coherent, but I had a pretty good idea what he wanted to say.

'De bang,' he gasped out, and I realized that his breathlessness and his Cuban accent had combined, and he was trying to say, 'The van.'

'A white van? With a flat tire? And your car is gone,' I said, and Doakes looked at me.

But the gasping man was shaking his head. 'White van, sure. I hear I thought it's a dog inside, maybe hurt,' he said, and paused to breathe deeply so he could properly convey the full horror of what he had seen. 'And then – '

But he was wasting his precious breath. Doakes and I were already sprinting up the street in the direction he had come from.

CHAPTER 21

SERGEANT DOAKES APPARENTLY FORGOT HE WAS supposed to be following me, because he beat me to the van by a good twenty yards. Of course he had the very large advantage of having both shoes, but still, he moved quite well. The van was run up on the sidewalk in front of a pale orange house surrounded by a coral-rock wall. The front bumper had thumped a rock corner post and toppled it, and the rear of the vehicle was skewed around to face the street so we could see the bright yellow of the Choose Life license plate.

By the time I caught up with Doakes he already had the rear door open and I heard the mewling noise coming from inside. It really didn't sound quite so much like a dog this time, or maybe I was just getting used to it. It was a slightly higher pitch than before, and a little bit choppier, more of a shrill gurgle than a yodel, but still recognizable as the call of one of the living dead.

It was strapped to a backless car seat that had been turned sideways, so it ran the length of the interior. The eyes in their lidless sockets were rolling wildly back and forth, up and down, and the lipless, toothless mouth was frozen into a round O and it was squirming the way a baby squirms, but without arms and legs it couldn't manage any significant movement.

Doakes was crouched over it, looking down at the remainder of its face with an intense lack of expression. 'Frank,' he said, and the thing rolled its eyes to him. The yowling paused for just a moment, and then resumed on a higher note, keening with a new agony that seemed to be begging for something.

'You recognize this one?' I asked.

Doakes nodded. 'Frank Aubrey,' he said.

'How can you tell?' I asked. Because really, you would think that all former humans in this condition would be awfully hard to tell apart. The only distinguishing mark I could see was forehead wrinkles.

Doakes kept looking at it, but he grunted once and nodded at the side of the neck. 'Tattoo. It's Frank.' He grunted again, leaning forward and flicking a small piece of notepaper taped to the bench. I leaned in for a look: in the same spidery hand I had seen before Dr. Danco had written HONOR.

'Get the paramedics,' Doakes said.

I hurried over to where they were just closing the back doors of the ambulance. 'Do you have room for one more?' I asked. 'He won't take up a lot of space, but he'll need heavy sedation.'

'What kind of condition is he in?' the spike-haired one asked me.

It was a very good question for someone in his profession to ask, but the only answers that occurred to me seemed a little flippant, so I just said, 'I think you may want heavy sedation, too.'

They looked at me like they thought I was kidding and didn't really appreciate the seriousness of the situation. Then they looked at each other and shrugged.

'Okay, pal,' the older one said. 'We'll squeeze him in.' The spike-haired paramedic shook his head, but he turned and opened the back door of the ambulance again and began pulling out the gurney.

As they wheeled down the block to Danco's crashed van I climbed in the back of the ambulance to see how Debs was doing. Her eyes were closed and she was very pale, but she seemed to be breathing easier. She opened one eye and looked up at me. 'We're not moving,' she said.

'Dr. Danco crashed his van.'

She tensed and tried to sit up, both eyes wide open. 'You got him?'

'No, Debs. Just his passenger. I think he was about to deliver it, because it's all done.'

I had thought she was pale before, but she almost vanished now. 'Kyle,' she said.

'No,' I told her. 'Doakes says it's someone named Frank.'

'Are you sure?'

'Apparently positive. There's a tattoo on his neck. It's not Kyle, Sis.'

Deborah closed her eyes and drifted back down onto the cot as if she was a deflating balloon. 'Thank God,' she said.

'I hope you don't mind sharing your cab with Frank,' I said.

She shook her head. 'I don't mind,' she said, and then her eyes opened again. 'Dexter. No fucking around with Doakes. Help him find Kyle. Please?'

It must have been the drugs working on her, because I could count on one finger the number of times I had heard her ask anything so plaintively. 'All right, Debs. I'll do my best,' I said, and her eyes fluttered closed again.

'Thanks,' she said.

I got back to Danco's van just in time to see the older paramedic straighten up from where he had obviously been vomiting, and turn to talk to his partner, who was sitting on the curb mumbling to himself over the sounds that Frank was still making inside. 'Come on, Michael,' the older guy said. 'Come on, buddy.'

Michael didn't seem interested in moving, except for rocking back and forth as he repeated, 'Oh God. Oh Jesus. Oh God.' I decided he probably didn't need my encouragement, and went around to the driver's door of the van. It was sprung open and I peeked in.

Dr. Danco must have been in a hurry, because he had left behind a very pricey-looking scanner, the kind that police groupies and newshounds use to monitor emergency radio traffic. It was very comforting to know that Danco had been tracking us with this and not some kind of magic powers.

Other than that, the van was clean. There was no telltale matchbook, no slip of paper with an address or a cryptic word in Latin scribbled on the back. Nothing at all that could give us any kind of clue. There might turn out to be fingerprints, but since we already knew who had been driving that didn't seem very helpful.

I picked up the scanner and walked around to the rear of the van. Doakes was standing beside the open back door as the older paramedic finally got his partner onto his feet. I handed Doakes the scanner. 'It was in the front seat,' I said. 'He's been listening.'

Doakes just glanced at it and put it down inside the back door of the van. Since he didn't seem terribly chatty I asked, 'Do you have any ideas about what we should do next?'

He looked at me and didn't say anything and I looked back expectantly, and I suppose we could have stood like that until the pigeons began to nest on our heads, if it hadn't been for the paramedics. 'Okay, guys,' the senior one said, and we moved aside to let them get to Frank. The stocky paramedic seemed to be perfectly all right now, as if he was here to put a splint on a boy with a twisted ankle. His partner still looked quite unhappy, however, and even from six feet away I could hear his breathing.

I stood beside Doakes and watched them slide Frank onto the gurney and then wheel him away. When I looked back at Doakes he was staring at me again. Once more he gave me his very unpleasant smile. 'Down to you and me,' he said. 'And I don't know about you.' He leaned against the battered white van and crossed his arms. I heard the paramedics slam the ambulance door, and a moment later the siren started up. 'Just you and me,' Doakes said again, 'and no more referee.'

'Is this more of your simple country wisdom?' I said, because here I was, having sacrificed an entire left shoe and a very nice bowling shirt, to say nothing of my hobby, Deborah's collarbone, and a perfectly good motor-pool car – and there he stood without so much as a wrinkle in his shirt, making cryptically hostile remarks. Really, the man was too much.

'Don't trust you,' he said.

I thought it was a very good sign that Sergeant Doakes was opening up to me by sharing his doubts and feelings. Still, I felt like I should try to keep him focused. 'That doesn't matter. We're running out of time,' I said. 'With Frank finished and delivered, Danco will start on Kyle now.'

He cocked his head to one side and then shook it slowly. 'Don't matter about Kyle,' he said. 'Kyle knew what he was getting into. What matters is catching the Doctor.'

'Kyle matters to my sister,' I said. 'That's the only reason I'm here.'

Doakes nodded again. 'Pretty good,' he said. 'Could almost believe that.'

For some reason, it was then that I had an idea. I admit that Doakes was monumentally irritating – and it wasn't just because he had kept me from my important personal research, although that was clearly bad enough. But now he was even critiquing my acting, which was beyond the boundaries of all civilized behavior. So perhaps irritation was the mother of invention; it doesn't seem all that poetic, but there it is. In any case, a little door opened up in Dexter's dusty cranium and a small light came shining out; a genuine piece of mental activity. Of course, Doakes might not think much of it, unless I could help him to see what a good idea it actually was, so I gave it a shot. I felt a little bit like Bugs Bunny trying to talk Elmer Fudd into something lethal, but the man had it coming. 'Sergeant Doakes,' I said, 'Deborah is my only family, and it is not right for you to question my commitment. Particularly,' I said, and I had to fight the urge to buff my fingernails, Bugs-style, 'since so far you have not done doodley-squat.'

Whatever else he was, cold killer and all, Sergeant Doakes was apparently still capable of feeling emotion. Perhaps that was the big difference between us, the reason he tried to keep his white hat so firmly cemented to his head and fight against what should have been his own side. In any case, I could see a surge of anger flicker across his face, and deep down inside there was an almost audible growl from his interior shadow. 'Doodley-squat,' he said. 'That's good, too.'

'Doodley-squat,' I said firmly. 'Deborah and I have done all the legwork and taken all the risks, and you know it.'

For just a moment his jaw muscles popped straight out as if they were going to leap out of his face and strangle me, and the muted interior growl surged into a roar that echoed down to my Dark Passenger, which sat up and answered back, and we stood like that, our two giant shadows flexing and facing off invisibly in front of us.

Quite possibly, there might have been ripped flesh and pools of blood in the street if a squad car hadn't chosen that moment to screech to a halt beside us and interrupt. A young cop jumped out and Doakes reflexively took out his badge and held it toward them without looking away from me. He made a shooing motion with his other hand, and the cop backed off and stuck his head into the car to consult with his partner.

'All right,' Sergeant Doakes said to me, 'you got something in mind?'

It wasn't really perfect. Bugs Bunny would have made him think of it himself, but it was good enough. 'As a matter of fact,' I said, 'I do have an idea. But it's a little risky.'

'Uh-huh,' he said. 'Thought it might be.'

'If it's too much for you, come up with something else,' I said. 'But I think it's all we can do.'

I could see him thinking it over. He knew I was baiting him, but there was just enough truth to what I had said, and enough pride or anger in him that he didn't care.

'Let's have it,' he said at last.

'Oscar got away,' I said.

'Looks like it.'

'That only leaves one person we can be sure Dr. Danco might be interested in,' I said, and I pointed right at his chest. 'You.'

He didn't actually flinch, but something twitched on his forehead and he forgot to breathe for a few seconds. Then he nodded slowly and took a deep breath. 'Slick motherfucker,' he said.

'Yes, I am,' I admitted. 'But I'm right, too.'

Doakes picked up the scanner radio and moved it to one side so he could sit on the open back gate of the van. 'All right,' he said. 'Keep talking.'

'First, I'm betting he'll get another scanner,' I said, nodding at the one beside Doakes.

'Uh-huh.'

'So if we know he's listening, we can let him hear what we want him to hear. Which is,' I said with my very best smile, 'who you are, and where you are.'

'And who am I?' he said, and he didn't seem impressed by my smile.

'You are the guy who set him up to get taken by the Cubans,' I said.

He studied me for a moment, then shook his head. 'You really putting my pecker on the chopping block, huh?'

'Absolutely,' I said. 'But you're not worried, are you?'

'He got Kyle, no trouble.'

'You'll know he's coming,' I said. 'Kyle didn't. Besides, aren't you supposed to be just a little bit better than Kyle at this kind of thing?'

It was shameless, totally transparent, but he went for it. 'Yes, I am,' he said. 'You're a good ass-kisser, too.'

'No ass-kissing at all,' I said. 'Just the plain, simple truth.'

Doakes looked at the scanner beside him. Then he looked up and away over the freeway. The streetlights made an orange flare off a drop of sweat that rolled across his forehead and down into one eye. He wiped at it unconsciously, still staring away over I-95. He had been staring at me without blinking for so long that it was a little bit unsettling to be in his presence and have him look somewhere else. It was almost like being invisible.

'All right,' he said as he looked back at me at last, and now the orange light was in his eyes. 'Let's do it.'

CHAPTER 22

SERGEANT DOAKES DROVE ME BACK TO HEADQUARTERS. It was a strange and unsettling experience to sit so close to him, and we found very little to say to each other. I caught myself studying his profile out of the corner of my eye. What went on in there? How could he be what I knew he was without actually *doing* something about it? Holding back from one of my playdates was setting my teeth on edge, and yet Doakes apparently didn't have any such trouble. Perhaps he had gotten it all out of his system in El Salvador. Did it feel any different to do it with the official blessings of the government? Or was it simply easier, not having to worry about being caught?

I could not know, and I certainly could not see myself asking him. Just to underline the point, he came to a halt at a red light and turned to look at me. I pretended not to notice, staring straight ahead through the windshield, and he faced back around when the light changed to green.

We drove right to the motor pool and Doakes put me in the front seat of another Ford Taurus. 'Gimme fifteen minutes,' he said, nodding at the radio. 'Then call me.' Without another word, he got back into his car and drove away.

Left to my own devices, I pondered the last few surprise-filled hours. Deborah in the hospital, me in

205

league with Doakes – and my revelation about Cody during my near-death experience. Of course, I could be totally wrong about the boy. There might be some other explanation for his behavior at the mention of the missing pet, and the way he shoved the knife so eagerly into his fish could have been perfectly normal childish cruelty. But oddly enough, I found myself wanting it to be true. I wanted him to grow up to be like me – mostly, I realized, because I wanted to shape him and place his tiny feet onto the Harry Path.

Was this what the human reproductive urge was like, a pointless and powerful desire to replicate wonderful, irreplaceable me, even when the me in question was a monster who truly had no right to live among humans? That would certainly explain how a great many of the monumentally unpleasant cretins I encountered every day came to be. Unlike them, however, I was perfectly aware that the world would be a better place without me in it – I simply cared more about my own feelings in the matter than whatever the world might think. But now here I was eager to spawn more of me, like Dracula creating a new vampire to stand beside him in the dark. I knew it was wrong – but what fun it would be!

And what a total muttonhead I was being! Had my interval on Rita's sofa really turned my once-mighty intellect into such a quivering heap of sentimental mush? How could I be thinking such absurdities? Why wasn't I trying to devise a plan to escape marriage instead? No wonder I couldn't get away from Doakes's cloying surveillance – I had used up all my brain cells and was now running on empty.

I glanced at my watch. Fourteen minutes of time

wasted on absurd mental blather. It was close enough: I lifted the radio and called Doakes.

'Sergeant Doakes, what's your twenty?'

There was a pause, then a crackle. 'Uh, I'd rather not say just now.'

'Say again, Sergeant?'

'I have been tracking a perp, and I'm afraid he made me.'

'What kind of perp?'

There was a pause, as though Doakes was expecting me to do all the work and hadn't figured out what to say. 'Guy from my army days. He got captured in El Salvador, and he might think it was my fault.' Pause. 'The guy is dangerous,' he said.

'Do you want backup?'

'Not yet. I'm going to try to dodge him for now.'

'Ten-four,' I said, feeling a little thrill at getting to say it at last.

We repeated the basic message a few times more, just to be sure it would get through to Dr. Danco, and I got to say 'ten-four' each time. When we called it a night around 1:00 AM, I was exhilarated and fulfilled. Perhaps tomorrow I would try to work in 'That's a copy' and even 'Roger that.' At last, something to look forward to.

I found a squad car headed south and persuaded the cop driving to drop me at Rita's. I tiptoed over to my car, got in, and drove home.

When I got back to my little bunk and saw it in a state of terrible disarray, I remembered that Debs should have been here but was, instead, in the hospital. I would go see her tomorrow. In the meantime, I'd had a memorable but exhausting day;

chased into a pond by a serial limb-barber, surviving a car crash only to be nearly drowned, losing a perfectly good shoe, and on top of all that, as if that wasn't bad enough, forced to buddy up with Sergeant Doakes. Poor Drained Dexter. No wonder I was so tired. I fell into bed and went to sleep at once.

Early the next day Doakes pulled his car in beside mine in the parking lot at headquarters. He got out carrying a nylon gym bag, which he set down on the hood of my car. 'You brought your laundry?' I asked politely. Once again my lighthearted good cheer went right by him.

'If this works at all, either he gets me or I get him,' he said. He zipped open the bag. 'If I get him, it's over. If he gets me . . .' He took out a GPS receiver and placed it on the hood. 'If he gets me, you're my backup.' He showed me a few dazzling teeth. 'Think how good that makes me feel.' He took out a cell phone and placed it next to the GPS unit. 'This is my insurance.'

I looked at the two small items on the hood of my car. They did not seem particularly menacing to me, but perhaps I could throw one and then hit someone on the head with the other. 'No bazooka?' I asked.

'Don't need it. Just this,' he said. He reached into the gym bag one more time. 'And this,' he said, holding out a small steno notebook, flipped open to the first page. It seemed to have a string of numbers and letters on it and a cheap ballpoint was shoved through the spiral.

'The pen is mightier than the sword,' I said.

'This one is,' he said. 'Top line is a phone number. Second line is an access code.'

'What am I accessing?'

'You don't need to know,' he said. 'You just call it, punch in the code, and give 'em my cell phone number. They give you a GPS fix on my phone. You come get me.'

'It sounds simple,' I said, wondering if it really was.

'Even for you,' he said.

'Who will I be talking to?'

Doakes just shook his head. 'Somebody owes me a favor,' he said, and pulled a handheld police radio out of the bag. 'Now the easy part,' he said. He handed me the radio and got back into his car.

Now that we had clearly laid out the bait for Dr. Danco, step two was to get him to a specific place at the right time, and the happy coincidence of Vince Masuoka's party was too perfect to ignore. For the next few hours we drove around the city in our separate cars and repeated the same message back and forth a couple of times with subtle variations, just to be sure. We had also enlisted a couple of patrol units Doakes said just possibly might not fuck it up. I took that to be his understated wit, but the cops in question did not seem to get the joke and, although they did not actually tremble, they did seem to go a little overboard in anxiously assuring Sergeant Doakes that they would not, in fact, fuck it up. It was wonderful to be working with a man who could inspire such loyalty.

Our little team spent the rest of the day pumping the airwaves full of chatter about my engagement party, giving directions to Vince's house and reminding people of the time. And just after lunch, our coup de grâce. Sitting in my car in front of a Wendy's, I used the handheld radio and called Sergeant Doakes one last time for a carefully scripted conversation.

'Sergeant Doakes, this is Dexter, do you copy?'

'This is Doakes,' he said after a slight pause.

'It would mean a lot to me if you could come to my engagement party tonight.'

'I can't go anywhere,' he said. 'This guy is too dangerous.'

'Just come for one drink. In and out,' I wheedled.

'You saw what he did to Manny, and Manny was just a grunt. I'm the one gave this guy to some bad people. He gets his hands on me, what's he gonna do to me?'

'I'm getting married, Sarge,' I said. I liked the Marvel Comics flavor of calling him Sarge. 'That doesn't happen every day. And he's not going to try anything with all those cops around.'

There was a long dramatic pause in which I knew Doakes was counting to seven, just as we had written it down. Then the radio crackled again. 'All right,' he said. 'I'll come by around nine o'clock.'

'Thanks, Sarge,' I said, thrilled to be able to say it again, and just to complete my happiness, I added, 'This really means a lot to me. Ten-four.'

'Ten-four,' he said.

Somewhere in the city I hoped that our little radio drama was playing out to our target audience. As he scrubbed up for his surgery, would he pause, cock his head, and listen? As his scanner crackled with the beautiful mellow voice of Sergeant Doakes, perhaps he'd put down a bone saw, wipe his hands, and write the address on a scrap of paper. And then he would go happily back to work – on Kyle Chutsky? – with the inner peace of a man with a job to do and a full social calendar when he was done for the day.

Just to be absolutely sure, our squad-car friends would breathlessly repeat the message a few times, and without fucking it up; that Sergeant Doakes himself would be at the party tonight, live and in person, around nine o'clock.

And for my part, with my work done for a few hours, I headed for Jackson Memorial Hospital to look in on my favorite bird with a broken wing.

Deborah was wrapped in an upper-body cast, sitting in bed in a sixth-floor room with a lovely view of the freeway, and although I was sure they were giving her some kind of painkiller, she did not look at all blissful when I walked into her room. 'Goddamn it, Dexter,' she greeted me, 'tell them to let me the hell out of here. Or at least give me my clothes so I can leave.'

'I'm glad to see you're feeling better, sister dear,' I said. 'You'll be on your feet in no time.'

'I'll be on my feet the second they give me my goddamn clothes,' she said. 'What the hell is going on out there? What have you been doing?'

'Doakes and I have set a rather neat trap, and Doakes is the bait,' I said. 'If Dr. Danco bites, we'll have him tonight at my, um, party. Vince's party,' I added, and I realized I wanted to distance myself from the whole idea of being engaged and it was a silly way to do it, but I felt better anyway – which apparently brought no comfort to Debs.

'Your engagement party,' she said, and then snarled. 'Shit. You got Doakes to set himself up for you.' And I admit it sounded kind of elegant when she said it, but I didn't want her thinking such things; unhappy people heal slower.

'No, Deborah, seriously,' I said in my best soothing voice. 'We're doing this to catch Dr. Danco.'

She glared at me for a long time and then, amazingly, she sniffled and fought back a tear. 'I have to trust you,' she said. 'But I hate this. All I can think about is what he's doing to Kyle.'

'This will work, Debs. We'll get Kyle back.' And because she was, after all, my sister, I did not add, 'or most of him anyway.'

'Christ, I hate being stuck here,' she said. 'You need me there for backup.'

'We can handle this, Sis,' I said. 'There will be a dozen cops at the party, all armed and dangerous. And I'll be there, too,' I said, feeling just a little miffed that she so undervalued my presence.

But she continued to do so. 'Yeah. And if Doakes gets Danco, we get Kyle back. If Danco gets Doakes, you're off the hook. Real slick, Dexter. You win either way.'

'That had never occurred to me,' I lied. 'My only thought is to serve the greater good. Besides, Doakes is supposed to be very experienced at this sort of thing. And he knows Danco.'

'Goddamn it, Dex, this is killing me. What if – ' She broke off and bit her lip. 'This better work,' she said. 'He's had Kyle too long.'

'This will work, Deborah,' I said. But neither one of us really believed me.

The doctors quite firmly insisted on keeping Deborah for twenty-four hours, for observation. And so with a hearty hi-ho to my sister, I galloped off into the sunset, and from there to my apartment for a shower and change of clothes. What to wear? I could think of no guidelines on what we were wearing this season to a party forced on you to celebrate an unwanted engagement that might turn into a violent confrontation with a vengeful maniac. Clearly brown shoes were out, but beyond that nothing really seemed de rigueur. After careful consideration I let simple good taste guide me, and selected a lime green Hawaiian shirt covered with red electric guitars and pink hot rods. Simple but elegant. A pair of khaki pants and some running shoes, and I was ready for the ball.

But there was still an hour left before I had to be there, and I found my thoughts turning again to Cody. Was I right about him? If so, how could he deal with his awakening Passenger on his own? He needed my guidance, and I found that I was eager to give it to him.

I left my apartment and drove south, instead of north to Vince's house. In fifteen minutes I was knocking at Rita's door and staring across the street at the empty spot formerly occupied by Sergeant Doakes in his maroon Taurus. Tonight he was no doubt at home preparing, girding his loins for the coming conflict and polishing his bullets. Would he try to kill Dr. Danco, secure in the knowledge that he had legal permission to do so? How long had it been since he killed something? Did he miss it? Did the Need come roaring over him like a hurricane, blowing away all the reason and restraints?

The door opened. Rita beamed and lunged at me, wrapping me in a hug and kissing me on the face. 'Hey, handsome,' she said. 'Come on in.'

I hugged back briefly for form's sake and then disengaged myself. 'I can't stay very long,' I said.

She beamed bigger. 'I know,' she said. 'Vince called and told me. He was so cute about the whole thing. He promised he would keep an eye on you so you wouldn't do anything too crazy. Come inside,' she said, and dragged me in by the arm. When she closed the door she turned to me, suddenly serious. 'Listen Dexter. I want you to know that I am not the jealous type and I trust you. You just go and have fun.'

'I will, thank you,' I said, although I doubted that I would. And I wondered what Vince had said to her to make her think that the party would be some kind of dangerous pit of temptation and sin. For that matter, it might well be. Since Vince was largely synthetic, he could be somewhat unpredictable in social situations, as shown by his bizarre duels of sexual innuendo with my sister.

'It was sweet of you to stop here before the party,' Rita said, leading me to the couch where I had spent so much of my recent life. 'The kids wanted to know why they couldn't go.'

'I'll talk to them,' I said, eager to see Cody and try to discover if I had been right.

Rita smiled, as if thrilled to learn that I would actually talk to Cody and Astor. 'They're out back,' she said. 'I'll go get them.'

'No, stay here,' I said. 'I'll go out.'

Cody and Astor were in the yard with Nick, the surly clot from next door who had wanted to see Astor naked. They looked up as I slid the door open, and Nick turned away and scurried back to his own yard. Astor ran over to me and gave me a hug, and Cody trailed behind, watching, no emotion at all on his face. 'Hi,' he said, in his quiet voice.

'Greetings and salutations, young citizens,' I said. 'Shall we put on our formal togas? Caesar calls us to the senate.'

Astor cocked her head to one side and looked at me as if she had just seen me eat a raw cat. Cody merely said, 'What,' very quietly.

'Dexter,' Astor said, '*why* can't we go to the party with you?'

'In the first place,' I told her, 'it's a school night. And in the second place, I am very much afraid this is a grown-up party.'

'Does that mean there will be naked girls there?' she asked.

'What kind of a person do you think I am?' I said, scowling fiercely. 'Do you really think I would *ever* go to a party with no naked girls?'

'Eeeeeewwwww,' she said, and Cody whispered, 'Ha.'

'But more important, there will also be stupid dancing and ugly shirts, and these are not good for you to see. You would lose all your respect for grown-ups.'

'What respect?' Cody said, and I shook him by the hand.

'Well said,' I told him. 'Now go to your room.'

Astor finally giggled. 'But we want to go to the party,' she said.

'I'm afraid not,' I said. 'But I brought you a piece of treasure so you won't run away.' I handed her a roll of Necco wafers, our secret currency. She would split it evenly with Cody later, out of sight of all prying eyes.

'Now then, young persons,' I said. They looked up at me expectantly. But at that point I was stuck, all aquiver with eagerness to know the answer but not at all sure where or even how to start asking. I could not very well say, 'By the way, Cody, I was wondering if you like to kill things?' That, of course, was exactly what I wanted to know, but it didn't really seem like the kind of thing you could say to a child – especially Cody, who was generally about as talkative as a coconut.

His sister, Astor, though, often seemed to speak for him. The pressures of spending their early childhood together with a violent ogre for a father had created a symbiotic relationship so close that when he drank soda she would burp. Whatever might be going on inside Cody, Astor would be able to express it.

'Can I ask something very serious?' I said, and they exchanged a look that contained an entire conversation, but said nothing to anyone else. Then they nodded to me, almost as if their heads were mounted together on a Foosball rod.

'The neighbor's dog,' I said.

'Told you,' Cody said.

'He was always knocking over the garbage,' Astor said. 'And pooping in our yard. And Nicky tried to make him bite us.'

'So Cody took care of him?' I asked.

'He's the boy,' said Astor. 'He likes to do that stuff. I just watch. Are you going to tell Mom?'

There it was. *He likes to do that stuff.* I looked at the two of them, watching me with no more worry than if they had just said they liked vanilla ice cream better than strawberry. 'I won't tell your mom,' I said. 'But you can't tell anybody else in the world, not ever. Just the three of us, nobody else, understand?'

'Okay,' Astor said, with a glance at her brother. 'But why, Dexter?'

'Most people won't understand,' I said. 'Not even your mom.'

'You do,' said Cody in his husky near-whisper.

'Yes,' I said. 'And I can help.' I took a deep breath and felt an echo rolling through my bones, down across the years from Harry so long ago to me right now, under the same Florida nightscape Harry and I had stood under when he said the same thing to me. 'We have to get you squared away,' I said, and Cody looked at me with large blinkless eyes and nodded.

'Okay,' he said.

CHAPTER 23

VINCE MASUOKA HAD A SMALL HOUSE IN NORTH Miami, at the end of a dead-end street off N.E. 125th Street. It was painted pale yellow with pastel purple trim, which really made me question my taste in associates. There were a few very well-barbered bushes in the front yard and a cactus garden by the front door, and he had a row of those solar-powered lamps lighting the cobblestone walkway to his front door.

I had been there once before, a little more than a year ago, when Vince had decided for some reason to have a costume party. I had taken Rita, since the whole purpose of having a disguise is to be seen wearing it. She had gone as Peter Pan, and I was Zorro, of course; the Dark Avenger with a ready blade. Vince had answered the door in a body-hugging satin gown with a basket of fruit on his head.

'J. Edgar Hoover?' I asked him.

'You're very close. Carmen Miranda,' he had said before leading us in to a fountain of lethal fruit punch. I had taken one sip and decided to stick with the sodas, but of course that had been before my conversion to a beer-swilling red-blooded male. There had been a nonstop soundtrack of monotonous techno-pop music turned up to a volume designed to induce voluntary self-performed brain surgery, and the party had gotten exceedingly loud and hilarious.

218

As far as I knew, Vince had not entertained since then, at least not on that scale. Still, the memory apparently lingered, and Vince had no trouble in gathering an enthusiastic crowd to join in my humiliation with only twenty-four-hours' notice. True to his word, there were dirty movies playing all over the house on a number of video monitors he had set up, even out back on his patio. And, of course, the fruit-punch fountain was back.

Because the rumors of that first party were still fresh on the grapevine, the place was packed with rowdy people, mostly male, who attacked the punch like they had heard there was a prize for the first one to achieve permanent brain damage. I even knew a few of the partiers. Angel Batista-no-relation was there from work, along with Camilla Figg and a handful of other forensic lab geeks, and a few cops I knew, including the four who had not fucked it up for Sergeant Doakes. The rest of the crowd seemed to be pulled off South Beach at random, chosen for their ability to make a loud, high-pitched WHOO! sound when the music changed or the video monitor showed something particularly undignified.

It didn't take long at all for the party to settle into something we would all regret for a very long time. By a quarter of nine I was the only one left who could still stand upright unassisted. Most of the cops had camped out by the fountain in a grim clot of rapidly bending elbows. Angel-no-relation was lying under the table sound asleep with a smile on his face. His pants were gone and someone had shaved a bare streak down the center of his head.

Things being as they were, I thought this would be

an ideal time to slip outside undetected to see if Sergeant Doakes had arrived yet. As it turned out, however, I was wrong. I had taken no more than two steps toward the door when a great weight came down on me from behind. I spun around quickly to find that Camilla Figg was attempting to drape herself across my back. 'Hi,' she said with a very bright and somewhat slurred smile.

'Hello,' I said cheerfully. 'Can I get you a drink?'

She frowned at me. 'Don't need drink. Jus wanna say hello.' She frowned harder. 'Jeez Christ you're cute,' she said. 'Always wand to tell you that.'

Well, the poor thing was obviously drunk, but even so – Cute? Me? I suppose too much alcohol can blur the sight, but come on – what could possibly be cute about someone who would rather cut you open than shake your hand? And in any case, I was already way over my limit for women with one, Rita. As far as I could recall, Camilla and I had rarely said more than three words to each other. She had never before mentioned my alleged cuteness. She had seemed to avoid me, in fact, preferring to blush and look away rather than say a simple good morning. And now she was practically raping me. Did that make sense?

In any case, I had no time to waste on deciphering human behavior. 'Thank you very much,' I said as I tried to undrape Camilla without causing any serious injuries to either of us. She had locked her hands around my neck and I pried at them, but she clung like a barnacle. 'I think you need some fresh air, Camilla,' I said, hoping that she might take the hint and wander away out back. Instead she lunged closer, mashing her face against mine as I frantically backpedaled away.

'I'll take my fresh air right here,' she said. She squeezed her lips into a pouty kissy-face and pushed me back until I bumped into a chair and nearly fell over.

'Ah – would you like to sit down?' I asked hopefully.

'No,' she said, pulling me downward toward her face with what felt like at least twice her actual weight, 'I would like to screw.'

'Ah, well,' I stammered, overcome by the absolute shocking effrontery and absurdity of it – were all human women crazy? Not that the men were any better. The party around me looked like it had been arranged by Hieronymus Bosch, with Camilla ready to drag me behind the fountain where no doubt a gang with bird beaks was waiting to help her ravish me. But it hit me that I now had the perfect excuse to avoid ravishment. 'I am getting married, you know.' As difficult as it was to admit, it was only fair that it come in handy once in a while.

'Bassurd,' Camilla said. 'Beautiful bassurd.' She slumped suddenly and her arms flopped off my neck. I barely managed to catch her and keep her from falling to the floor.

'Probably so,' I said. 'But in any case I think you need to sit down for a few minutes.' I tried to ease her into the chair, but it was like pouring honey onto a knife blade, and she flowed off onto the floor.

'Beautiful bassurd,' she said, and closed her eyes.

It's always nice to learn that you are well regarded by your co-workers, but my romantic interlude had used up several minutes and I very much needed to get out front and check in with Sergeant Doakes. And so leaving Camilla to slumber sweetly amid her dewy dreams of love, I headed for the front door once again.

And once again I was waylaid, this time by a savage attack on my upper arm. Vince himself grabbed my bicep and pulled me away from the door and back into surrealism. 'Hey!' he yodeled. 'Hey, party boy! Where ya going?'

'I think I left my keys in my car,' I said, trying to disengage from his death grip. But he just yanked at me harder.

'No, no, no,' he said, pulling me toward the fountain. 'It's your party, you're not going anywhere.'

'It's a wonderful party, Vince,' I said. 'But I really need to – '

'Drink,' he said, splashing a cup into the fountain and pushing it at me so it slopped onto my shirt. 'That's what you need. Banzai!' He held his own cup up in the air and then drained it. Happily for all concerned, the drink sent him into a coughing fit, and I managed to slip away as he doubled over and struggled for air.

I made it all the way out the front door and partway down the walk before he appeared at the door. 'Hey!' he yelled at me. 'You can't leave yet, the strippers are coming!'

'I'll be right back,' I called. 'Fix me another drink!'

'Right!' he said with his phony smile. 'Ha! Banzai!' And he went back in to the party with a cheery wave. I turned to look for Doakes.

He had been parked right across the street from wherever I was for so long that I should have spotted him immediately, but I didn't. When I finally saw the familiar maroon Taurus, I realized what a clever thing he had done. He was parked up the street under a large tree, which blocked any light from the streetlights. It was the kind of thing a man trying to hide might do, but at the same time it would allow Dr. Danco to feel confident that he could get close without being seen.

I walked over to the car and as I approached the window slid down. 'He's not here yet,' Doakes said.

'You're supposed to come in for a drink,' I said.

'I don't drink.'

'You obviously don't go to parties, either, or you would know that you can't do them properly sitting across the street in your car.'

Sergeant Doakes didn't say anything, but the window rolled up and then the door opened and he stepped out. 'What're you gonna do if he comes now?' he asked me.

'Count on my charm to save me,' I said. 'Now come on in while there's still someone conscious in there.'

We crossed the street together, not actually holding hands, but it seemed so odd under the circumstances that we might as well have. Halfway across a car turned the corner and came down the street toward us. I wanted to run and dive into a row of oleanders, but was very proud of my icy control when instead I merely glanced at the oncoming car. It cruised slowly along, and Sergeant Doakes and I were all the way across the street by the time it got to us.

Doakes turned to look at the car, and I did, too. A row of five sullen teen faces looked out at us. One of them turned his head and said something to the others, and they laughed. The car rolled on by.

'We better get inside,' I said. 'They looked dangerous.'

Doakes didn't respond. He watched the car turn around at the end of the street and then continued on his way to Vince's front door. I followed along behind, catching up with him just in time to open the front door for him.

I had only been outside for a few minutes, but the body count had grown impressively. Two of the cops beside the fountain were stretched out on the floor, and one of the South Beach refugees was throwing up into a Tupperware container that had held Jell-O salad a few minutes ago. The music was pounding louder than ever, and from the kitchen I heard Vince yelling, 'Banzai!' joined by a ragged chorus of other voices. 'Abandon all hope,' I said to Sergeant Doakes, and he mumbled something that sounded like, 'Sick motherfuckers.' He shook his head and went in.

Doakes did not take a drink and he didn't dance, either. He found a corner of the room with no unconscious body in it and just stood there, looking like a cut-rate Grim Reaper at a frat party. I wondered if I should help him get into the spirit of the thing. Perhaps I could send Camilla Figg over to seduce him.

I watched the good sergeant stand in his corner and look around him, and I wondered what he was thinking. It was a lovely metaphor: Doakes standing silent and alone in a corner while all around him human life raged riotously on. I probably would have felt a wellspring of sympathy for him bubbling up, if only I could feel. He seemed completely unaffected by the whole thing, not even reacting when two of the South Beach gang ran past him naked. His eyes fell on the nearest monitor, which was portraying some rather startling and original images involving animals.

Doakes looked at it without interest or emotion of any kind; just a look, then his gaze moved on to the cops on the floor, Angel under the table, and Vince leading a conga line in from the kitchen. His gaze traveled all the way over to me and he looked at me with the exact same lack of expression. He crossed the room and stood in front of me.

'How long we got to stay?' he asked.

I gave him my very best smile. 'It is a bit much, isn't it? All this happiness and fun – it must make you nervous.'

'Makes me want to wash my hands,' he said. 'I'll wait outside.'

'Is that really a good idea?' I asked.

He tilted his head at Vince's conga line, which was collapsing in a heap of spastic hilarity. 'Is that?' he said. And of course he had a point, although in terms of sheer lethal pain and terror a conga line on the floor couldn't really compete with Dr. Danco. Still, I suppose one has to consider human dignity, if it truly exists somewhere. At the moment, looking around the room, that didn't seem possible.

The front door swung open. Both Doakes and I turned to face it, all our reflexes up on tiptoe, and it was a good thing we were ready for danger because otherwise we might have been ambushed by two half-naked women carrying a boom box. 'Hello?' they called out, and were rewarded with a ragged high-pitched roar of 'WHOOOO!' from the conga line on the floor. Vince struggled out from under the pile of bodies and swayed to his feet. 'Hey!' he shouted. 'Hey everybody! Strippers are here! Banzai!' There was an even louder 'WHOOOO!' and one of the cops on the floor struggled to his knees, swaying gently and staring as he mouthed the word, 'Strippers . . .'

Doakes looked around the room and back at me. 'I'll be outside,' he said, and turned for the door.

'Doakes,' I said, thinking it really wasn't a good idea. But I got no more than one step after him when once again I was savagely ambushed.

'Gotcha!' Vince roared out, holding me in a clumsy bear hug.

'Vince, let me go,' I said.

'No way!' he chortled. 'Hey, everybody! Help me out with the blushing bridegroom!' There was a surge of ex–conga liners from the floor and the last standing cop by the fountain and I was suddenly at the center of a mini–mosh pit, the press of bodies heaving me toward the chair where Camilla Figg had passed out and rolled onto the floor. I struggled to get away, but it was no use. There were too many of them, too filled with Vince's rocket juice. I could do nothing but watch as Sergeant Doakes, with a last molten-stone glare, went through the front door and out into the night.

They levered me into the chair and stood around me in a tight half-circle and it was obvious that I was going nowhere. I hoped Doakes was as good as he thought he was, because he was clearly on his own for a while.

The music stopped, and I heard a familiar sound that made the hairs on my arms stand up straight: it was the ratchet of duct tape spooling off the roll, my own favorite prelude to a Concerto for Knife Blade. Someone held my arms and Vince wrapped three big loops of tape around me, fastening me to the chair. It was not tight enough to hold me, but it would certainly slow me enough to allow the crowd to keep me in the chair.

'All righty then!' Vince called out, and one of the strippers turned on her boom box and the show began. The first stripper, a sullen-looking black woman, began to undulate in front of me while removing a few unnecessary items of clothing. When she was almost naked, she sat on my lap and licked my ear while wiggling her butt. Then she forced my head between her breasts, arched her back, and leaped backward, and the other stripper, a woman with Asian features and blond hair, came forward and repeated the whole process. When she had wiggled around on my lap for a few moments, she was joined by the first stripper, and the two of them sat together, one on each side of me. Then they leaned forward so that their breasts rubbed my face, and began to kiss each other.

At this point, dear Vince brought them each a large glass of his murderous fruit punch, and they drank it off, still wiggling rhythmically. One of them muttered, 'Whoo. Good punch.' I couldn't tell which one of them said it, but they both seemed to agree. The two women began to writhe a great deal more now and the crowd around me began to howl like it was full moon at a rabies convention. Of course, my view was somewhat obscured by four very large and unnaturally hard breasts – two in each shade – but at least it sounded like everyone except me was having a great deal of fun.

Sometimes you have to wonder if there is some kind of malign force with a sick sense of humor running our universe. I knew enough about human males to know that most of them would happily trade their excess body parts to be where I was. And yet, all I could think of was that I would be equally pleased to trade a body part or two to get out of this chair and away from the naked squirming women. Of course, I would have preferred it to be somebody else's body part, but I would cheerfully collect it.

But there was no justice; the two strippers sat there on my lap, bouncing to the music and sweating all over my beautiful rayon shirt and each other, while around us the party raged on. After what seemed like an endless spell in purgatory, broken only by Vince bringing the strippers two more drinks, the two roiling women finally moved off my lap and danced around the circling crowd. They touched faces, sipped from the partyers' drinks, and grabbed at an occasional crotch. I used the distraction to free my hands and remove the duct tape, and it was only then that I noticed that no one was paying any attention at all to Dimpled Dexter, the theoretical Man of the Hour. One quick look around showed me why: everyone in the room was standing in a slack-jawed circle watching the two strippers as they danced, completely naked now, glistening with sweat and spilled drinks. Vince looked like a cartoon the way he stood there with his eyes almost bulged out of his head, but he was in good company. Everyone who was still conscious was in a similar pose, staring without breathing, swaying slightly from side to side. I could have barreled through the room blasting away on a flaming tuba and no one would have paid me any attention.

I stood up, walked carefully around behind the crowd, and slipped out the front door. I had thought that Sergeant Doakes would wait somewhere near the house, but he was nowhere to be seen. I walked across the street and looked in his car. It was empty, too. I looked up and down the street and it was the same. There was no sign of him.

Doakes was gone.

CHAPTER 24

THERE ARE MANY ASPECTS OF HUMAN EXISTENCE that I will never understand, and I don't just mean intellectually. I mean that I lack the ability to empathize, as well as the capacity to feel emotion. To me it doesn't seem like much of a loss, but it does put a great many areas of ordinary human experience completely outside my comprehension.

However, there is one almost overwhelmingly common human experience I feel powerfully, and that is temptation. And as I looked at the empty street outside Vince Masuoka's house and realized that somehow Dr. Danco had taken Doakes, I felt it wash over me in dizzying, nearly suffocating waves. *I was free.* The thought surged around me and pummeled me with its elegant and completely justified simplicity. It would be the easiest thing in the world just to walk away. Let Doakes have his reunion with the Doctor, report it in the morning, and pretend that I'd had too much to drink – my engagement party, after all! – and I wasn't really sure what had happened to the good sergeant. And who would contradict me? Certainly no one inside at the party could say with anything approaching realistic certainty that I was not watching the peep show with them the whole time.

Doakes would be gone. Whisked away forever into a final haze of lopped off limbs and madness, never to lighten my dark doorway again. Liberty for Dexter, free to be me, and all I had to do was absolutely nothing. Even I could handle that.

So why not walk away? For that matter, why not take a slightly longer stroll, down to Coconut Grove, where a certain children's photographer had been waiting for my attentions much too long? So simple, so safe – why, indeed, not? A perfect night for dark delight with a downbeat, the moon nearly full and that small missing edge lending the whole thing a casual, informal air. The urgent whispers agreed, rising in a hissed insistent chorus.

It was all there. Time and target and most of a moon and even an alibi, and the pressure had been growing for so long now that I could close my eyes and let it happen all by itself, walk through the whole happy thing on autopilot. And then the sweet release again, the afterglow of buttery muscles with all the knots drained out, the happy coasting into my first complete sleep of far too long now. And in the morning, rested and relieved, I would tell Deborah . . .

Oh. Deborah. There was that, wasn't there?

I would tell Deborah that I had taken the sudden opportunity of a no-Doakes zone and gone dashing into the darkness with a Need and a Knife as the last few fingers of her boyfriend trickled away into a trash heap? Somehow, even with my inner cheerleaders insisting that it would be all right, I didn't think she would go for it. It had the feel of something final in my relationship with my sister, a small lapse in judgment, perhaps, but one she would find a bit hard to forgive, and even though I am not capable of feeling actual love, I did want to keep Debs relatively happy with me.

And so once again I was left with virtuous patience and a feeling of long-suffering rectitude. Dour Dutiful Dexter. *It will come,* I told my other self. *Sooner or later, it will come. Has to come; it will not wait forever, but this must come first.* And there was some grumbling, of course, because it had not come in far too long, but I soothed the growls, rattled the bars with false good cheer one time, and pulled out my cell phone.

I dialed the number Doakes had given me. After a moment there was a tone, and then nothing, just a faint hiss. I punched in the long access code, heard a click, and then a neutral female voice said, 'Number.' I gave the voice Doakes's cell number. There was a pause, and then it read me some coordinates; I hurriedly scribbled them down on the pad. The voice paused, and then added, 'Moving due west, 65 miles per hour.' The line went dead.

I never claimed to be an expert navigator, but I do have a small GPS unit that I use on my boat. It comes in handy for marking good fishing spots. So I managed to put in the coordinates without bumping my head or causing an explosion. The unit Doakes had given me was a step up from mine and had a map on the screen. The coordinates on the map translated to Interstate 75, heading for Alligator Alley, the corridor to the west coast of Florida.

I was mildly surprised. Most of the territory between Miami and Naples is Everglades, swamp broken up by small patches of semidry land. It was filled with snakes, alligators, and Indian casinos, which did not seem at all like the kind of place to relax and enjoy a peaceful dismemberment. But the GPS could not lie, and supposedly neither could the voice on the phone. If the coordinates were wrong, it was Doakes's doing, and he was lost anyway. I had no choice. I felt a little guilty about leaving the party without thanking my host, but I got into my car and headed for I-75.

I was up on the interstate in just a few minutes, then quickly north to I-75. As you head west on 75 the city gradually thins away. Then there is one final furious explosion of strip malls and houses just before the toll booth for Alligator Alley. At the booth I pulled over and called the number again. The same neutral female voice gave me a set of coordinates and the line went dead. I took it to mean that they were no longer moving.

According to the map, Sergeant Doakes and Dr. Danco were now settling comfortably into the middle of an unmarked watery wilderness about forty miles ahead of me. I didn't know about Danco, but I didn't think Doakes would float very well. Perhaps the GPS could lie after all. Still, I had to do something, so I pulled back onto the road, paid my toll, and continued westward.

At a spot parallel to the location on the GPS, a small access road branched off to the right. It was nearly invisible in the dark, especially since I was traveling at seventy miles per hour. But as I saw it whiz past I braked to a stop on the shoulder of the road and backed up to peer at it. It was a one-lane dirt road that led nowhere, up over a rickety bridge and then straight as an arrow into the darkness of the Everglades. In the headlights of the passing cars I could only see about fifty yards down the road, and there was nothing to see. A patch of knee-high weeds grew up in the center of the road between the two deeply rutted tire tracks. A clump of short trees hung over the road at the edge of darkness, and that was it.

I thought about getting out and looking for some kind of clue, until I realized how silly that was. Did I think I was Tonto, faithful Indian guide? I couldn't look at a bent twig and tell how many white men had been past in the last hour. Perhaps Dexter's dutiful but uninspired brain pictured him as Sherlock Holmes, able to examine the wheel ruts and deduce that a left-handed hunchback with red hair and a limp had gone down the road carrying a Cuban cigar and a ukelele. I would find no clues, not that it mattered. The sad truth was, this was either it or I was all done for the night, and Sergeant Doakes was done for considerably longer.

Just to be absolutely sure – or at any rate, absolutely free of guilt – I called Doakes's top secret telephone number again. The voice gave me the same coordinates and hung up; wherever they were, they were still there, down this dark and dirty little road.

I was apparently out of choices. Duty called, and Dexter must answer. I turned the wheel hard and started down the road.

According to the GPS, I had about five and a half miles to travel before I got to whatever was waiting for me. I put my headlights on low and drove slowly, watching the road carefully. This gave me plenty of time to think, which is not always a good thing. I thought about what might be there at the end of the road, and what I would do when I got there. And although it was a rather bad time for this to occur to me, I realized that even if I found Dr. Danco at the end of this road I had no idea what I was going to do about it. 'Come get me,' Doakes had said, and it sounded simple enough until you were driving into the Everglades on a dark night with no weapon more threatening than a steno pad. And Dr. Danco had apparently not had much trouble with any of the others he had taken, in spite of the fact that they were rough, well-armed customers. How could poor, helpless Docile Dexter hope to thwart him when the Mighty Doakes had gone down so fast?

And what would I do if he got me? I did not think I would make a very good yodeling potato. I was not sure if I could go crazy, since most authorities would most likely say that I already was. Would I snap anyway and go burbling out of my brain to the land of the eternal scream? Or because of what I am, would I remain aware of what was happening to me? Me, precious me, strapped to a table and offering a critique of the dismemberment technique? The answer would certainly tell me a great deal about what I was, but I decided that I didn't really want to know the answer that badly. The very thought was almost enough to make me feel real emotion, and not the kind that one is grateful for.

The night had closed in around me, and not in a good way. Dexter is a city boy, used to the bright lights that leave dark shadows. The farther along this road I went, the darker it seemed to get, and the darker it got the more this whole thing began to seem like a hopeless, suicidal trip. This situation clearly called for a platoon of Marines, not an occasionally homicidal forensic lab geek. Who did I really think I was? Sir Dexter the Valiant, galloping to the rescue? What could

I possibly hope to do? For that matter, what could anyone do except pray?

I don't pray, of course. What would something like me pray to, and why should It listen to me? And if I found Something, whatever It was, how could It keep from laughing at me, or flinging a lightning bolt down my throat? It would have been very comforting to be able to look to some kind of higher power, but of course, I only knew one higher power. And even though it was strong and swift and clever, and very good at stalking silently through the nightscape, would even the Dark Passenger be enough?

According to the GPS unit I was within a quarter of a mile of Sergeant Doakes, or at least his cell phone, when I came to a gate. It was one of those wide gates made of aluminum that they use on dairy farms to keep the cows in. But this was no dairy farm. A sign that hung on the gate said,

BLALOCK GATOR FARM
Trespassers Will Be Eaten

This seemed like a very good place for a gator farm, which did not necessarily make it the kind of place I wanted to be. I am ashamed to admit that even though I have lived my entire life in Miami, I know very little about gator farms. Did the animals roam freely through watery pastures, or were they penned in somehow? It seemed like a very important question at the moment. Could alligators see in the dark? And how hungry were they, generally? All good questions, and very relevant.

I switched off my headlights, stopped the car, and

got out. In the sudden silence I could hear the engine ticking, the keening of mosquitoes, and, in the distance, music was playing on a tinny speaker. It sounded like Cuban music. Possibly Tito Puente.

The Doctor was in.

I approached the gate. The road on the far side still ran straight, up to an old wooden bridge and then into a grove of trees. Through the branches I could see a light. I did not see any alligators basking in the moonlight.

Well, Dexter, here we are. And what would you like to do tonight? At the moment, Rita's couch didn't seem like such a bad place to be. Especially compared to standing here in the nighttime wild. On the far side of this gate were a maniacal vivisectionist, hordes of ravenous reptiles, and a man I was supposed to rescue even though he wanted to kill me. And in this corner, wearing dark trunks, the Mighty Dexter.

I certainly seemed to be asking this an awful lot lately, but why was it always me? I mean, really. Me, braving all this to rescue Sergeant Doakes of all people? Hello? Isn't there something wrong with this picture? Like the fact that I am in it?

Nevertheless, I was here, and might as well go through with it. I climbed over the gate and headed toward the light.

The normal night sounds started to return a few at a time. At least I assumed they were normal for out here in the savage primeval forest. There were clicks and hums and buzzes from our insect friends, and a mournful sort of shriek that I very much hoped was only some kind of owl; a small one, please. Something rattled the shrubbery off to my right and then went completely silent. And happily for me, instead of getting nervous or scared like a human being, I found myself slipping into nightstalker mode. Sounds shifted down, movement around me slowed, and all my senses seemed to come slightly more alive. The darkness bleached out a little lighter; details sprang into focus from the night around me, and a slow cold careful silent chuckle began to grow just under the surface of my awareness. Was poor misunderstood Dexter feeling out of his element and over his head? Then let the Passenger take the wheel. He would know what to do, and he would do it.

And why, after all, not? At the end of this driveway and over the bridge, Dr. Danco was waiting for us. I had been wanting to meet him, and now I would. Harry would approve of anything I did to this one. Even Doakes would have to admit that Danco was fair game – he would probably thank me for it. It was dizzying; this time I had permission. And even better, it had poetry to it. For so very long Doakes had kept my genie trapped in its bottle. There would be a certain justice if his rescue were to let it out again. And I would rescue him, certainly, of course I would. Afterward . . .

But first.

I crossed the wooden bridge. Halfway over a board creaked and I froze for a moment. The night sounds did not change, and from up ahead I heard Tito Puente say, 'Aaaaaahh-YUH!' before returning to his melody. I moved on.

On the far side of the bridge the road widened into a parking area. To the left was a chain-link fence and straight ahead was a small, one-story building with a light shining in the window. It was old and battered and needed paint, but perhaps Dr. Danco wasn't as thoughtful of appearances as he should have been. Off to the right a chickee hut moldered quietly beside a canal, chunks of its palm-frond roof dangling like tattered old clothes. An airboat was tied to a dilapidated dock jutting out into the canal.

I slid into the shadows cast by a row of trees and felt a predator's cool poise take control of my senses. I circled carefully around the parking area, to the left, along the chain-link fence. Something grunted at me and then splashed into the water, but it was on the other side of the fence so I ignored it and moved on. The Dark Passenger was driving and did not stop for such things.

The fence ended in a right-angle turn away from the house. There was one last stretch of emptiness, no more than fifty feet, and one last stand of trees. I moved to the last tree for a good long look at the house, but as I paused and placed my hand on the trunk something crashed and fluttered in the branches above me and a horribly loud bugling shriek split the night. I jumped back as whatever it was smashed down through the leaves of the tree and onto the ground.

Still making a sound like an insane over-amplified trumpet, the thing faced me. It was a large bird, bigger than a turkey, and it was apparent from the way he hissed and hooted that he was angry at me. It strutted a step forward, whisking a massive tail across the ground, and I realized that it was a peacock. Animals do not like me, but this one seemed to have formed an extreme and violent hatred. I suppose it did not understand that I was much bigger and more dangerous. It seemed intent on either eating me or driving me away, and since I needed the hideous caterwauling din to stop as quickly as possible I obliged him with a dignified retreat and hurried back along the fence to the shadows by the bridge. Once I was safely tucked into a quiet pool of darkness I turned to look at the house.

The music had stopped, and the light was out.

I stood frozen in my shadow for several minutes. Nothing happened, except that the peacock quit its bugling and, with a final mean-spirited mutter in my direction, fluttered back up into his tree. And then the night sounds came back again, the clicks and whines of the insects and another snort and splash from the alligators. But no more Tito Puente. I knew that Dr. Danco was watching and listening just as I was, that each of us was waiting for the other to make some move, but I could wait longer. He had no idea what might be out there in the dark – for all he could tell it might be either a SWAT team or the Delta Rho Glee Club – and I knew that there was only him. I knew where he was, and he could not know if there was someone on the roof or even if he was surrounded. And so he would have to do something first, and there were just two choices. Either he had to attack, or –

At the far end of the house there came the sudden roar of an engine and as I tensed involuntarily the airboat leaped away from the dock. The engine revved higher and the boat raced off down the canal. In less than a minute it was gone, around a bend and away into the night, and with it went Dr. Danco.

CHAPTER 25

FOR A FEW MINUTES I JUST STOOD AND WATCHED the house, partly because I was being cautious. I had not actually seen the driver of the airboat, and it was possible that the Doctor was still lurking inside, waiting to see what would happen. And to be honest, I did not wish to be savaged by any more gaudy predatory chickens, either.

But after several minutes when nothing at all happened, I knew I had to go into the house and take a look. And so, circling widely around the tree where the evil bird roosted, I approached the house.

It was dark inside, but not silent. As I stood outside next to the battered screen door that faced the parking area, I heard a kind of quiet thrashing coming from somewhere inside, followed after a moment by a rhythmic grunting and an occasional whimper. It did not seem like the kind of noise someone would make if they were hiding in a lethal ambush. Instead, it was very much the kind of sound somebody might make if they were tied up and trying to escape. Had Dr. Danco fled so quickly that he had left Sergeant Doakes behind?

Once again I found the entire cellar of my brain flooded with ecstatic temptation. Sergeant Doakes, my nemesis, tied up inside, gift-wrapped and delivered to me in the perfect setting. All the tools and supplies I could want, no one around for miles – and when I was done I only had to say, 'Sorry, I got there too late. Look what that awful Dr. Danco did to poor old Sergeant Doakes.' The idea was intoxicating, and I believe I actually swayed a little as I tasted it. Of course it was just a thought, and I would certainly never do anything of the kind, would I? I mean, would I really? Dexter? Hello? Why are you salivating, dear boy?

Certainly not, not me. Why, I was a moral beacon in the spiritual desert of South Florida. Most of the time. I was upright, scrubbed clean, and mounted on a Dark Charger. Sir Dexter the Chaste to the rescue. Or at any rate, probably to the rescue. I mean, all things considered. I pulled open the screen door and went in.

Immediately inside the door I flattened against the wall, just to be cautious, and felt for a light switch. I found one right where it should be and flipped it up.

Like Danco's first den of iniquity, this one was sparsely furnished. Once again, the main feature of the place was a large table in the center of the room. A mirror hung on the opposite wall. Off to the right a doorway without a door led to what looked like the kitchen, and on the left a closed door, probably a bedroom or bathroom. Directly across from where I stood was another screen door leading outside, presumably the way Dr. Danco had made his escape.

And on the far side of the table, now thrashing more furiously than ever, was something dressed in a pale orange coverall. It looked relatively human, even from across the room. 'Over here, oh please, help me, help me,' it said, and I crossed the room and knelt beside it.

His arms and legs were bound with duct tape, naturally, the choice of every experienced, discriminating monster. As I cut the tape I examined him, listening but not really hearing his constant blubbering of, 'Oh thank God, oh please, oh God, get me loose, buddy, hurry hurry for God's sake. Oh Christ, what took you so long, Jesus, thank you, I knew you'd come,' or words to that effect. His skull was completely shaved, even the eyebrows. But there was no mistaking the rugged manly chin and the scars festooning his face. It was Kyle Chutsky.

Most of him, anyway.

As the tape came off and Chutsky was able to wiggle up to a sitting position, it became apparent that he was missing his left arm up to the elbow and his right leg up to the knee. The stumps were wrapped with clean white gauze, nothing leaking through; again, very nice work, although I did not think Chutsky would appreciate the care Danco had used in taking his arm and leg. And how much of Chutsky's mind was also missing was not yet clear, although his constant wet yammering did nothing to convince me that he was ready to sit at the controls of a passenger jet.

'Oh, God, buddy,' he said. 'Oh Jesus. Oh thank God, you came,' and he leaned his head onto my shoulder and wept. Since I had some recent experience with this, I knew just what to do. I patted him on the back and said, 'There there.' It was even more awkward than when I had done it with Deborah, since the stump of his left arm kept thumping against me and that made it much harder to fake sympathy.

But Chutsky's crying jag lasted only a few moments, and when he finally pulled away from me, struggling to stay in an upright position, my beautiful

Hawaiian shirt was soaked. He gave a huge snuffle, a little too late for my shirt. 'Where's Debbie?' he said.

'She broke her collarbone,' I told him. 'She's in the hospital.'

'Oh,' he said, and he snuffled again, a long wet sound that seemed to echo somewhere inside him. Then he glanced quickly behind him and tried to struggle to his feet. 'We better get out of here. He might come back.'

It hadn't occurred to me that Danco might come back, but it was true. It's a time-honored predator's trick to run off and then circle back to see who's sniffing your spoor. If Dr. Danco did that, he would find a couple of fairly easy targets. 'All right,' I said to Chutsky. 'Let me have a quick look around.'

He snaked a hand out – his right hand, of course – and grabbed my arm. 'Please,' he said. 'Don't leave me alone.'

'I'll just be a second,' I said and tried to pull away. But he tightened his grip, still surprisingly strong considering what he had gone through.

'Please,' he repeated. 'At least leave me your gun.'

'I don't have a gun,' I said, and his eyes got much bigger.

'Oh, God, what the hell were you thinking? Christ, we've got to get out of here.' He sounded close to panic, as though any second now he would begin to cry again.

'All right,' I said. 'Let's get you up on your, ah, foot.' I hoped he didn't catch my glitch; I didn't mean to sound insensitive, but this whole missing-limbs thing was going to require a bit of retooling in the area of vocabulary. But Chutsky said nothing, just held out his arm. I helped him up, and he leaned against the table. 'Just give me a few seconds to check the other rooms,' I said. He looked at me with moist, begging eyes, but he didn't say anything and I hurried off through the little house.

In the main room, where Chutsky was, there was nothing to be seen beyond Dr. Danco's working equipment. He had some very nice cutting instruments, and after carefully considering the ethical implications, I took one of the nicest with me, a beautiful blade designed for cutting through the stringiest flesh. There were several rows of drugs; the names meant very little to me, except for a few bottles of barbiturates. I didn't find any clues at all, no crumpled matchbook covers with phone numbers written in them, no dry-cleaning slips, nothing.

The kitchen was practically a duplicate of the kitchen at the first house. There was a small and battered refrigerator, a hot plate, a card table with one folding chair, and that was it. Half a box of doughnuts sat on the counter, with a very large roach munching on one of them. He looked at me as if he was willing to fight for the doughnut, so I left him to it.

I came back in to the main room to find Chutsky still leaning on the table. 'Hurry up,' he said. 'For Christ's sake let's go.'

'One more room,' I said. I crossed the room and opened the door opposite the kitchen. As I had expected, it was a bedroom. There was a cot in one corner, and on the cot lay a pile of clothing and a cell phone. The shirt looked familiar, and I had a thought about where it might have come from. I pulled out my own phone and dialed Sergeant Doakes's number. The phone on top of the clothing began to ring.

'Oh, well,' I said. I pushed disconnect and went to get Chutsky.

He was right where I had left him, although he looked like he would have run away if he could have. 'Come on, for Christ's sake, hurry up,' he said. 'Jesus, I can almost feel his breath on my neck.' He twisted his head to the back door and then over to the kitchen and, as I reached to support him, he turned and his eyes snapped onto the mirror that hung on the wall.

For a long moment he stared at his reflection and then he slumped as if all the bones had been pulled out of him. 'Jesus,' he said, and he started to weep again. 'Oh, Jesus.'

'Come on,' I said. 'Let's get moving.'

Chutsky shuddered and shook his head. 'I couldn't even move, just lying there listening to what he was doing to Frank. He sounded so happy – "What's your guess? No? All right, then – an arm." And then the sound of the saw, and – '

'Chutsky,' I said.

'And then when he got me up there and he said, "Seven," and "What's your guess." And then – '

It's always interesting to hear about someone else's technique, of course, but Chutsky seemed like he was about to lose whatever control he had left, and I could not afford to let him snuffle all over the other side of my shirt. So I stepped close and grabbed him by the good arm. 'Chutsky. Come on. Let's get out of here,' I said.

He looked at me like he didn't know where he was, eyes as wide as they could go, and then turned back to the mirror. 'Oh Jesus,' he said. Then he took a deep and ragged breath and stood up as if he was responding to an imaginary bugle. 'Not so bad,' he said. 'I'm alive.'

'Yes, you are,' I said. 'And if we can get moving we might both stay that way.'

'Right,' he said. He turned his head away from the mirror decisively and put his good arm around my shoulder. 'Let's go.'

Chutsky had obviously not had a great deal of experience at walking with only one leg, but he huffed and clumped along, leaning heavily on me between each hopping step. Even with the missing parts, he was still a big man, and it was hard work for me. Just before the bridge he paused for a moment and looked through the chain-link fence. 'He threw my leg in there,' he said, 'to the alligators. He made sure I was watching. He held it up so I could see it and then he threw it in and the water started to boil like . . .' I could hear a rising note of hysteria in his voice, but he heard it, too, and stopped, inhaled shakily, and said, somewhat roughly, 'All right. Let's get out of here.'

We made it back to the gate with no more side trips down memory lane, and Chutsky leaned on a fence post while I got the gate open. Then I hopped him around to the passenger seat, climbed in behind the wheel, and started the car. As the headlights flicked on, Chutsky leaned back in his seat and closed his eyes. 'Thanks, buddy,' he said. 'I owe you big-time. Thank you.'

'You're welcome,' I said. I turned the car around and headed back toward Alligator Alley. I thought Chutsky had fallen asleep, but halfway along the little dirt road he began to talk.

'I'm glad your sister wasn't here,' he said. 'To see me

like this. It's – Listen, I really have to pull myself together before – ' He stopped abruptly and didn't say anything for half a minute. We bumped along the dark road in silence. The quiet was a pleasant change. I wondered where Doakes was and what he was doing. Or perhaps, what was being done to him. For that matter, I wondered where Reiker was and how soon I could take him somewhere else. Someplace quiet, where I could contemplate and work in peace. I wondered what the rent might be on the Blalock Gator Farm.

'Might be a good idea if I don't bother her anymore,' Chutsky said suddenly, and it took me a moment to realize he was still talking about Deborah. 'She's not going to want anything to do with me the way I am now, and I don't need anybody's pity.'

'Nothing to worry about,' I said. 'Deborah is completely without pity.'

'You tell her I'm fine, and I went back to Washington,' he said. 'It's better that way.'

'It might be better for you,' I said. 'But she'll kill me.'

'You don't understand,' he said.

'No, *you* don't understand. She told me to get you back. She's made up her mind and I don't dare disobey. She hits very hard.'

He was silent for a while. Then I heard him sigh heavily. 'I just don't know if I can do this,' he said.

'I could take you back to the gator farm,' I said cheerfully.

He didn't say anything after that, and I pulled onto Alligator Alley, made the first U-turn, and headed back toward the orange glow of light on the horizon that was Miami.

CHAPTER 26

WE RODE IN SILENCE ALL THE WAY BACK TO THE first real clump of civilization, a housing development and a row of strip malls on the right, a few miles past the toll booth. Then Chutsky sat up and stared out at the lights and the buildings. 'I have to use a phone,' he said.

'You can use my phone, if you'll pay the roaming charges,' I said.

'I need a land line,' he said. 'A pay phone.'

'You're out of touch with the times,' I said. 'A pay phone might be a little hard to find. Nobody uses them anymore.'

'Take this exit here,' he said, and although it was not getting me any closer to my well-earned good night's sleep, I drove down the off-ramp. Within a mile we found a mini-mart that still had a pay phone stuck to the wall beside the front door. I helped Chutsky hop over to the phone and he leaned up against the shield around it and lifted the receiver. He glanced at me and said, 'Wait over there,' which seemed a little bit bossy for somebody who couldn't even walk unassisted, but I went back to my car and sat on the hood while Chutsky chatted.

An ancient Buick chugged into the parking spot next to me. A group of short, dark-skinned men in dirty clothes got out and walked toward the store.

They stared at Chutsky standing there on one leg with his head so very shaved, but they were too polite to say anything. They went in and the glass door whooshed behind them and I felt the long day rolling over me; I was tired, my neck muscles felt stiff, and I hadn't gotten to kill anything. I felt very cranky, and I wanted to go home and go to bed.

I wondered where Dr. Danco had taken Doakes. It didn't really seem important, just idle curiosity. But as I thought about the fact that he had indeed taken him somewhere and would soon begin doing rather permanent things to the sergeant, I realized that this was the first good news I'd had in a long time, and I felt a warm glow spread through me. I was free. Doakes was gone. One small piece at a time he was leaving my life and releasing me from the involuntary servitude of Rita's couch. I could live again.

'Hey, buddy,' Chutsky called. He waved the stump of his left arm at me and I stood up and walked over to him. 'All right,' he said. 'Let's get going.'

'Of course,' I said. 'Going where?'

He looked off in the distance and I could see the muscles along the side of his jaw tighten. The security lights of the mini-mart's parking lot lit up his coveralls and gleamed off his head. It's amazing how different a face looks if you shave off the eyebrows. There's something freakish to it, like the makeup in a low-budget science-fiction movie, and so even though Chutsky should have looked tough and decisive as he stared at the horizon and clenched his jaw, he instead looked like he was waiting for a blood-curdling command from Ming the Merciless. But he just said, 'Take me back to my hotel, buddy. I got work to do.'

'What about a hospital?' I asked, thinking that he couldn't be expected to cut a walking stick from a sturdy yew tree and stump on down the trail. But he shook his head.

'I'm okay,' he said. 'I'll be okay.'

I looked pointedly at the two patches of white gauze where his arm and leg used to be and raised an eyebrow. After all, the wounds were still fresh enough to be bandaged, and at the very least Chutsky had to be feeling somewhat weak.

He looked down at his two stumps, and he did seem to slump just a little and become slightly smaller for a moment. 'I'll be fine,' he said, and he straightened up a bit. 'Let's get going.' And he seemed so tired and sad that I didn't have the heart to say anything except, 'All right.'

He hopped back to the passenger door of my car, leaning on my shoulder, and as I helped ease him into the seat the passengers of the old Buick trooped out carrying beer and pork rinds. The driver smiled and nodded at me. I smiled back and closed the door. 'Crocodilios,' I said, nodding at Chutsky.

'Ah,' the driver said back. 'Lo siento.' He got behind the wheel of his car, and I walked around to get into mine.

Chutsky had nothing at all to say for most of the drive. Right after the interchange onto I-95, however, he began to tremble badly. 'Oh fuck,' he said. I looked over at him. 'The drugs,' he said. 'Wearing off.' His teeth began to chatter and he snapped them shut. His breath hissed out and I could see sweat begin to form on his bald face.

'Would you like to reconsider the hospital?' I asked.

'Do you have anything to drink?' he asked, a rather abrupt change of subject, I thought.

'I think there's a bottle of water in the backseat,' I said helpfully.

'Drink,' he repeated. 'Some vodka, or whiskey.'

'I don't generally keep any in the car,' I said.

'Fuck,' he said. 'Just get me to my hotel.'

I did that. For reasons known only to Chutsky, he was staying at the Mutiny in Coconut Grove. It had been one of the first luxury high-rise hotels in the area and had once been frequented by models, directors, drug runners, and other celebrities. It was still very nice, but it had lost a little bit of its cachet as the once-rustic Grove became overrun with luxury high-rises. Perhaps Chutsky had known it in its heyday and stayed there now for sentimental reasons. You really had to be deeply suspicious of sentimentality in a man who had worn a pinkie ring.

We came down off 95 onto Dixie Highway, and I turned left on Unity and rolled on down to Bayshore. The Mutiny was a little ways ahead on the right, and I pulled up in front of the hotel. 'Just drop me here,' Chutsky said.

I stared at him. Perhaps the drugs had affected his mind. 'Don't you want me to help you up to your room?'

'I'll be fine,' he said. That may have been his new mantra, but he didn't look fine. He was sweating heavily now and I could not imagine how he thought he would get up to his room. But I am not the kind of person who would ever intrude with unwanted help, so I simply said, 'All right,' and watched as he opened the door and got out. He held on to the roof of the car and stood unsteadily on his one leg for a minute before the bell captain saw him swaying there. The captain frowned at this apparition with the orange jumpsuit and the gleaming skull. 'Hey, Benny,' Chutsky said. 'Gimme a hand, buddy.'

'Mr. Chutsky?' he said dubiously, and then his jaw dropped as he noticed the missing parts. 'Oh, Lord,' he said. He clapped his hands three times and a bellboy ran out.

Chutsky looked back at me. 'I'll be fine,' he said.

And really, when you're not wanted there's not much you can do except leave, which is what I did. The last I saw of Chutsky he was leaning on the bell captain as the bellboy pushed a wheelchair toward them out the front door of the hotel.

It was still a little bit shy of midnight as I drove down Main Highway and headed for home, which was hard to believe considering all that had happened tonight. Vince's party seemed like several weeks ago, and yet he probably hadn't even unplugged his fruit-punch fountain yet. Between my Trial by Stripper and rescuing Chutsky from the gator farm, I had earned my rest tonight, and I admit that I was thinking of little else except crawling into my bed and pulling the covers over my head.

But of course, there's no rest for the wicked, which I certainly am. My cell phone rang as I turned left on Douglas. Very few people call me, especially this late at night. I glanced at the phone; it was Deborah.

'Greetings, sister dear,' I said.

'You asshole, you said you'd call!' she said.

'It seemed a little late,' I said.

'Did you really think I could fucking *SLEEP?!*' she

yelled, loud enough to cause pain to people in passing cars. 'What happened?'

'I got Chutsky back,' I said. 'But Dr. Danco got away. With Doakes.'

'Where is he?'

'I don't know, Debs, he got away in an airboat and – '

'Kyle, you idiot. Where is Kyle? Is he all right?'

'I dropped him at the Mutiny. He's, um . . . He's almost all right,' I said.

'What the fuck does that mean?!?' she screamed at me, and I had to switch my phone to the other ear.

'Deborah, he's going to be okay. He's just – he lost half of his left arm and half the right leg. And all his hair,' I said. She was quiet for several seconds.

'Bring me some clothes,' she said at last.

'He's feeling very uncertain, Debs. I don't think he wants – '

'Clothes, Dexter. Now,' she said, and she hung up.

As I said, no rest for the wicked. I sighed heavily at the injustice of it all, but I obeyed. I was almost back to my apartment, and Deborah had left some things there. So I ran in and, although I paused to look longingly at my bed, I gathered a change of clothing for her and headed for the hospital.

Deborah was sitting on the edge of her bed tapping her feet impatiently when I came in. She held her hospital gown closed with the hand that protruded from her cast, and clutched her gun and badge with the other. She looked like Avenging Fury after an accident.

'Jesus Christ,' she said, 'where the hell have you been? Help me get dressed.' She dropped her gown and stood up.

254

I pulled a polo shirt over her head, working it awkwardly around the cast. We just barely had the shirt in place when a stout woman in a nurse's uniform hurried into the room. 'What you think you're doing?' she said in a thick Bahamian accent.

'Leaving,' Deborah said.

'Get back in that bed or I will call doctor,' the nurse said.

'Call him,' Deborah said, now hopping on one foot as she struggled into her pants.

'No you don't,' the nurse said. 'You get back in the bed.'

Deborah held up her shield. 'This is a police emergency,' she said. 'If you impede me I am authorized to arrest you for obstruction of justice.'

The nurse thought she was going to say something very severe, but she opened her mouth, looked at the shield, looked at Deborah, and changed her mind. 'I will have to tell doctor,' she said.

'Whatever,' Deborah said. 'Dexter, help me close my pants.' The nurse watched disapprovingly for another few seconds, then turned and whisked away down the hall.

'Really, Debs,' I said. 'Obstruction of justice?'

'Let's go,' she said, and marched out the door. I trailed dutifully behind.

Deborah was alternately tense and angry on the drive back over to the Mutiny. She would chew on her lower lip, and then snarl at me to hurry up, and then as we came close to the hotel, she got very quiet. She finally looked out her window and said, 'What's he like, Dex? How bad is it?'

'It's a very bad haircut, Debs. It makes him look

pretty weird. But the other stuff . . . He seems to be adjusting. He just doesn't want you to feel sorry for him.' She looked at me, again chewing her lip. 'That's what he said,' I told her. 'He wanted to go back to Washington rather than put up with your pity.'

'He doesn't want to be a burden,' she said. 'I know him. He has to pay his own way.' She looked back out the window again. 'I can't even imagine what it was like. For a man like Kyle to lie there so helpless as – ' She shook her head slowly, and a single tear rolled down her cheek.

Truthfully, I could imagine very well what it had been like, and I had done so many times already. What I was having difficulty with was this new side of Deborah. She had cried at her mother's funeral, and at her father's, but not since then, as far as I knew. And now here she was practically flooding the car over what I had come to regard as an infatuation with someone who was a little bit of an oaf. Even worse, he was now a disabled oaf, which should mean that a logical person would move on and find somebody else with all the proper pieces still attached. But Deborah seemed even more concerned with Chutsky now that he was permanently damaged. Could this be love after all? Deborah in love? It didn't seem possible. I knew that theoretically she was capable of it, of course, but – I mean, after all, she was my sister.

It was pointless to wonder. I knew nothing at all about love and I never would. It didn't seem like such a terrible lack to me, although it does make it difficult to understand popular music.

Since there was nothing else I could possibly say about it, I changed the subject. 'Should I call Captain

Matthews and tell him that Doakes is gone?' I said.

Deborah wiped a tear off her cheek with one fingertip and shook her head. 'That's for Kyle to decide,' she said.

'Yes, of course, but Deborah, under the circumstances – '

She slammed a fist onto her leg, which seemed pointless as well as painful. 'GodDAMN it, Dexter, I won't lose him!'

Every now and then I feel like I am only receiving one track of a stereo recording, and this was one such time. I had no idea what – well, to be honest, I didn't even have an idea what to have an idea about. What did she mean? What did it have to do with what I had said, and why had she reacted so violently? And how can so many fat women think they look good in a belly shirt?

I suppose some of my confusion must have showed on my face, because Deborah unclenched her fist and took a deep breath. 'Kyle is going to need to stay focused, keep working. He needs to be in charge, or this will finish him.'

'How can you know that?'

She shook her head. 'He's always been the best at what he does. That's his whole – it's who he is. If he gets to thinking about what Danco did to him – ' She bit her lip and another tear rolled down her cheek. 'He has to stay who he is, Dexter. Or I'll lose him.'

'All right,' I said.

'I can't lose him, Dexter,' she said again.

There was a different doorman on duty at the Mutiny, but he seemed to recognize Deborah and simply nodded as he held the door open for us. We walked silently to the elevator and rode up to the twelfth floor.

I have lived in Coconut Grove my entire life, so I knew very well from gushing newspaper accounts that Chutsky's room was done in British Colonial. I never understood why, but the hotel had decided that British Colonial was the perfect setting to convey the ambience of Coconut Grove, although as far as I knew there had never been a British colony here. So the entire hotel was done in British Colonial. But I find it hard to believe that either the interior decorator or any Colonial British had ever pictured something like Chutsky flopped onto the king size bed of the penthouse suite Deborah led me to.

His hair had not grown back in the last hour, but he had at least changed out of the orange coverall and into a white terry-cloth robe and he was lying there in the middle of the bed shaved, shaking, and sweating heavily with a half-empty bottle of Skyy Vodka lying beside him. Deborah didn't even slow down at the door. She charged right over to the bed and sat beside him, taking his only hand in her only hand. Love among the ruins.

'Debbie?' he said in a quavery old-man voice.

'I'm here now,' she said. 'Go to sleep.'

'I guess I'm not as good as I thought I was,' he said.

'Sleep,' she said, holding his hand and settling down next to him.

I left them like that.

CHAPTER 27

I SLEPT LATE THE NEXT DAY. AFTER ALL, HADN'T I earned it? And although I arrived at work around ten o'clock, I was still there well before Vince, Camilla, or Angel-no-relation, who had apparently all called in deathly ill. One hour and forty-five minutes later Vince finally came in, looking green and very old. 'Vince!' I said with great good cheer and he flinched and leaned against the wall with his eyes closed. 'I want to thank you for an epic party.'

'Thank me quietly,' he croaked.

'Thank you,' I whispered.

'You're welcome,' he whispered back, and staggered softly away to his cubicle.

It was an unusually quiet day, by which I mean that, besides the lack of new cases, the forensics area was silent as a tomb, with the occasional pale-green ghost floating by suffering silently. Luckily there was also very little work to do. By five o'clock I had caught up on my paperwork and arranged all my pencils. Rita had called at lunchtime to ask me to come for dinner. I think she might have wanted to make sure I had not been kidnapped by a stripper, so I agreed to come after work. I did not hear from Debs, but I didn't really need to. I was quite sure she was with Chutsky in his penthouse. But I was a little bit concerned, since Dr. Danco knew where to find them and might come looking for his missing project. On the other hand, he had Sergeant Doakes to play with, which should keep him busy and happy for several days.

Still, just to be safe, I called Deborah's cell phone number. She answered on the fourth ring. 'What,' she said.

'You do remember that Dr. Danco had no trouble getting in there the first time,' I said.

'*I* wasn't here the first time,' she said. And she sounded so very fierce that I had to hope she wouldn't shoot someone from room service.

'All right,' I said. 'Just keep your eyes open.'

'Don't worry,' she said. I heard Chutsky muttering something cranky in the background, and Deborah said, 'I have to go. I'll call you later.' She hung up.

Evening rush hour was in full swing as I headed south to Rita's house, and I found myself humming cheerfully as a red-faced man in a pickup truck cut me off and gave me the finger. It was not just the ordinary feeling of belonging I got from being surrounded by the homicidal Miami traffic, either; I felt like a great burden had been removed from my shoulders. And, of course, it had been. I could go to Rita's and there would be no maroon Taurus parked across the street. I could go back to my apartment, free of my clinging shadow. And even more important, I could take the Dark Passenger out for a spin and we would be alone together for some badly needed quality time. Sergeant Doakes was gone, out of my life – and soon, presumably, out of his own life, too.

I felt absolutely giddy as I wheeled down South Dixie and made the turn to Rita's house. I was free – and free of obligation, too, since one really had to believe that Chutsky and Deborah would stay put to recuperate for a while. As for Dr. Danco – it is true that I had felt a certain twinge of interest in meeting him, and even now I would gladly take a few moments out of my busy social schedule for some real quality bonding time with him. But I was quite sure that Chutsky's mysterious Washington agency would send someone else to deal with him, and they would certainly not want me hovering around and offering advice. With that ruled out, and with Doakes out of the picture, I was back to plan A and free to assist Reiker into early retirement. Whoever would now have to deal with the problem of Dr. Danco, it would not be Delightfully Discharged Dexter.

I was so happy that I kissed Rita when she answered the door, even though no one was watching. And after dinner, while Rita cleaned up, I went out into the backyard once again, playing kick the can with the neighborhood children. This time, though, there was a special edge to it with Cody and Astor, our own small secret adding a touch more zest. It was almost fun to watch them stalking the other children, my own little predators in training.

After half an hour of stalking and pouncing, however, it became apparent that we were severely outnumbered by even stealthier predators – mosquitoes, several billion of the disgusting little vampires, all ravenously hungry. And so, weak from loss of blood, Cody, Astor, and I staggered back into the house and reconvened around the dining table for a session of hangman.

'I'll go first,' Astor announced. 'It's my turn anyway.'

'Mine,' said Cody, frowning.

'Nuh-uh. Anyway, I got one,' she told him. 'Five letters.'

'C,' said Cody.

'No! Head! Ha!' she howled in triumph, and drew the little round head.

'You should ask the vowels first,' I said to Cody.

'What,' he said softly.

'A, E, I, O, U, and sometimes Y,' Astor told him. 'Everybody knows that.'

'Is there an E?' I asked her, and some of the wind went out of her sails.

'Yes,' Astor said, sulkily, and she wrote the E on the middle blank line.

'Ha,' said Cody.

We played for almost an hour before their bedtime. All too soon my magical evening drew to a close and I was once again on the couch with Rita. But this time, free as I was from spying eyes, it was an easy matter for me to disengage myself from her tentacles and head for home, and my own little bed, with well-meaning excuses of having partied too hard at Vince's and a big day of work tomorrow. And then I was off, all alone in the night, just my echo, my shadow, and me. It was two nights until the full moon, and I would make this one well worth my wait. This full moon I would spend not with Miller Lite but with Reiker Photography, Inc. In two nights I would turn loose the Passenger at last, slide into my true self, and fling the sweat-stained costume of Dearly Devoted Dexter into the garbage heap.

Of course I needed to find proof first, but somehow I was quite confident that I would. After all, I had a whole day for that, and when the Dark Passenger and I work together everything seems to fall right into place.

And filled with such cheerful thoughts of dark delights I motored back to my comfy apartment, and climbed into bed to sleep the deep and dreamless sleep of the just.

The next morning my offensively cheerful mood continued. When I stopped for doughnuts on the way to work I gave in to impulse and bought a full dozen, including several of the cream-filled ones with chocolate icing, a truly extravagant gesture that was not lost on Vince, who had finally recovered. 'Oh, my,' he said with raised eyebrows. 'You have done well, O mighty hunter.'

'The gods of the forest have smiled upon us,' I said. 'Cream-filled or raspberry jelly?'

'Cream-filled, of course,' he said.

The day passed quickly, with only one trip out to a homicide scene, a routine dismemberment with garden equipment. It was strictly amateur work; the idiot had tried to use an electric hedge clipper and succeeded only in making a great deal of extra work for me, before finishing off his wife with the pruning shears. A truly nasty mess, and it served him right that they caught him at the airport. A well-done dismemberment is *neat*, above all, or so I always say. None of this puddled blood and caked flesh on the walls. It shows a real lack of class.

I finished up at the scene just in time to get back to my little cubbyhole off the forensics lab and leave my notes on my desk. I would type them up and finish the report on Monday, no hurry. Neither the killer nor the victim was going anywhere.

And so there I was, out the door to the parking lot and into my car, free to roam the land as I pleased. No one to follow me or feed me beer or force me to do things I would rather avoid. No one to shine the unwanted light into Dexter's shadows. I could be me again, Dexter Unchained, and the thought was far more intoxicating than all Rita's beer and sympathy. It had been too long since I felt this way, and I promised myself I would never again take it for granted.

A car was on fire at the corner of Douglas and Grand, and a small but enthusiastic crowd had gathered to watch. I shared their good cheer as I eased through the traffic jam caused by the emergency vehicles and headed for home.

At home I sent out for a pizza and made some careful notes on Reiker; where to look for proof, what sort of thing would be enough – a pair of red cowboy boots would certainly be a good start. I was very nearly certain that he was the one; pedophile predators tend to find ways to combine business and pleasure, and child photography was a perfect example. But 'very nearly' was not certain enough. And so I organized my thoughts into a neat little file – nothing incriminating, of course, and it would all be carefully destroyed before showtime. By Monday morning there would be no hint at all of what I had done except a new glass slide in the box on my shelf. I spent a happy hour planning and eating a large pizza with anchovies and then, as the nearly full moon began to mutter through the window, I got restless. I could feel the icy fingers of moonlight stroking me, tickling at my spine, urging me into the night to stretch the predator's muscles that had been dormant for too long.

And why not? It would do no harm to slide out into the chuckling evening and steal a look or two. To stalk, to watch unseen, to cat-foot down Reiker's game trails and sniff the wind – it would be prudent as well as fun. Dark Scout Dexter must Be Prepared. Besides, it was Friday night. Reiker might very well leave the house for some social activity – a visit to the toy store, for instance. If he was out, I could slip into his house and look around.

And so I dressed in my best dark nightstalker clothes and took the short drive from my apartment, up Main Highway and through the Grove to Tigertail Avenue and down to the modest house where Reiker lived. It was in a neighborhood of small concrete-block houses and his seemed no different from all the others, set back from the road just far enough for a short driveway. His car was parked there, a little red Kia, which gave me a surge of hope. Red, like the boots; it was his color, a sign that I was on track.

I drove by the house twice. On my second pass the dome light in his car was on and I was just in time to catch a glimpse of his face as he climbed into the car. It was not a very impressive face: thin, nearly chinless, and partly hidden by long bangs and large-frame glasses. I could not see what he was wearing on his feet, but from what I could see of the rest of him he might well wear cowboy boots to make himself seem a little taller. He got into the car and closed the door, and I went on by and around the block.

When I came by again, his car was gone. I parked a few blocks away on a small side street and went back, slowly slipping into my night skin as I walked. The lights were all out at a neighbor's house and I cut through the yard. There was a small guesthouse behind Reiker's place, and the Dark Passenger whispered in my inner ear, *studio*. It was indeed a perfect place for a photographer to set up, and a studio was exactly the right kind of place to find incriminating photographs. Since the Passenger is seldom wrong about these things, I picked the lock and went in.

The windows were all boarded over on the inside, but in the dimness from the open door I could see the outline of darkroom equipment. The Passenger had been right. I closed the door and flipped up the light switch. A murky red light flooded the room, just enough to see by. There were the usual trays and bottles of chemicals over by a small sink, and to the left of that a very nice computer workstation with digital equipment. A four-drawer filing cabinet stood against the far wall and I decided to start there.

After ten minutes of flipping through pictures and negatives, I had found nothing more incriminating than a few dozen photos of naked babies posed on a white fur rug, pictures that would generally be regarded as 'cute' even by people who think Pat Robertson is too liberal. There were no hidden compartments in the filing cabinet as far as I could tell, and no other obvious place to hide pictures.

Time was short; I could not take the chance that Reiker had simply gone to the store to buy a quart of milk. He might come back at any minute and decide to poke through his files and gaze fondly at the dozens of dear little pixies he had captured on film. I moved to the computer area.

Next to the monitor there was a tall CD rack and I

went through the disks one at a time. After a handful of program disks and others hand-lettered GREENFIELD or LOPEZ, I found it.

'It' was a bright pink jewel case. Across the front of the case in very neat letters it said, NAMBLA 9/04.

It may well be that NAMBLA is a rare Hispanic name. But it also stands for North American Man/Boy Love Association, a warm and fuzzy support group that helps pedophiles maintain a positive self-image by assuring them that what they do is perfectly natural. Well, of course it is – so are cannibalism and rape, but really. One mustn't.

I took the CD with me, turned out the light, and slid back into the night.

Back at my apartment it took only a few minutes to discover that the disk was a sales tool, presumably carried to a NAMBLA gathering of some kind and offered around to a select list of discriminating ogres. The pictures on it were arranged in what are called 'thumbnail galleries,' miniature series of shots almost like the picture decks that Victorian dirty old men used to flip through. Each picture had been strategically blurred so you could imagine but not quite see the details.

And oh, yes: several of the shots were professionally cropped and edited versions of the ones I had discovered on MacGregor's boat. So while I had not actually found the red cowboy boots, I had found quite enough to satisfy the Harry Code. Reiker had made the A-list. With a song in my heart and a smile on my lips, I trundled off to bed, thinking happy thoughts about what Reiker and I would be doing tomorrow night.

The next morning, Saturday, I got up a little late and went for a run through my neighborhood. After a shower and a hearty breakfast I went shopping for a few essentials – a new roll of duct tape, a razor-sharp fillet knife, just the basic necessities. And because the Dark Passenger was flexing and stretching to wakefulness, I stopped at a steak house for a late lunch. I ate a sixteen-ounce New York strip, well done of course, so there was absolutely no blood. Then I drove by Reiker's one more time to see the place again in daylight. Reiker himself was mowing his lawn. I slowed for a casual look; alas, he was wearing old sneakers, not red boots. He was shirtless and on top of scrawny, he looked flabby and pale. No matter: I would put a little color into him soon enough.

It was a very satisfying and productive day, my Day Before. And I was sitting quietly back in my apartment wrapped in my virtuous thoughts when the telephone rang.

'Good afternoon,' I said into the receiver.

'Can you get over here?' Deborah said. 'We have some work to finish up.'

'What sort of work?'

'Don't be a jerk,' she said. 'Come on over,' and she hung up. This was more than a little bit irritating. In the first place, I didn't know of any kind of unfinished work, and in the second, I was not aware of being a jerk – a monster, yes, certainly, but on the whole a very pleasant and well-mannered monster. And to top it all off, the way she hung up like that, simply assuming I had heard and would tremble and obey. The nerve of her. Sister or not, vicious arm punch or no, I trembled for no one.

I did, however, obey. The short drive to the Mutiny took longer than usual, this being Saturday afternoon, a time when the streets in the Grove flood with aimless people. I wove slowly through the crowd, wishing for once that I could simply pin the gas pedal to the floorboard and smash into the wandering horde. Deborah had spoiled my perfect mood.

She didn't make it any better when I knocked on the penthouse door at the Mutiny and she opened it with her on-duty-in-a-crisis face, the one that made her look like a bad-tempered fish. 'Get in here,' she said.

'Yes master,' I said.

Chutsky was sitting on the sofa. He still didn't look British Colonial – maybe it was the lack of eyebrows – but he did at least look like he had decided to live, so apparently Deborah's rebuilding project was going well. There was a metal crutch leaning against the wall beside him, and he was sipping coffee. A platter of Danish sat on the end table next to him. 'Hey, buddy,' he called out, waving his stump. 'Grab a chair.'

I took a British Colonial chair and sat, after snagging a couple of Danish as well. Chutsky looked at me like he was going to object, but really, it was the very least they could do for me. After all, I had waded through flesh-eating alligators and an attack peacock to rescue him, and now here I was giving up my Saturday for who-knows-what kind of awful chore. I deserved an entire cake.

'All right,' Chutsky said. 'We have to figure where Henker is hiding, and we have to do it fast.'

'Who?' I asked. 'You mean Dr. Danco?'

'That's his name, yeah. Henker,' he said. 'Martin Henker.'

'And we have to *find* him?' I asked, filled with a sense of ominous foreboding. I mean, why were they looking at me and saying 'we'?

Chutsky gave a small snort as if he thought I was joking and he got it. 'Yeah, that's right,' he said. 'So where are you thinking he might be, buddy?'

'Actually, I'm not thinking about it at all,' I said.

'Dexter,' Deborah said with a warning tone in her voice.

Chutsky frowned. It was a very strange expression without eyebrows. 'What do you mean?' he said.

'I mean, I don't see why it's my problem anymore. I don't see why I or even *we* have to find him. He got what he wanted – won't he just finish up and go home?'

'Is he kidding?' Chutsky asked Deborah, and if he'd only had eyebrows they would have been raised.

'He doesn't like Doakes,' Deborah said.

'Yeah, but listen, Doakes is one of our guys,' Chutsky said to me.

'Not one of mine,' I said.

Chutsky shook his head. 'All right, that's your problem,' he said. 'But we still have to find this guy. There's a political side to this whole thing, and it's deep doo-doo if we don't collar him.'

'Okay,' I said. 'But why is it my problem?' And it seemed like a very reasonable question to me, although to see his reaction you would have thought I wanted to fire bomb an elementary school.

'Jesus Christ,' he said, and he shook his head in mock admiration. 'You really are a piece of work, buddy.'

'Dexter,' Deborah said. 'Look at us.' I did look, at

Deb in her cast and Chutsky with his twin stumps. To be honest, they did not look terribly fierce. 'We need your help,' she said.

'But Debs, really.'

'Please, Dexter,' she said, knowing full well that I found it very hard to refuse her when she used that word.

'Debs, come on,' I said. 'You need an action hero, somebody who can kick down the door and storm in with guns blazing. I'm just a mild-mannered forensics geek.'

She crossed the room and stood in front of me, inches away. 'I know what you are, Dexter,' she said softly. 'Remember? And I know you can do this.' She put her hand on my shoulder and lowered her voice even farther, almost whispering. 'Kyle *needs* this, Dex. Needs to catch Danco. Or he'll never feel like a man again. That's important to me. Please, Dexter?'

And after all, what can you do when the big guns come out? Except summon your reserves of goodwill and wave the white flag gracefully.

'All right, Debs,' I said.

Freedom is such a fragile, fleeting thing, isn't it?

CHAPTER 28

HOWEVER RELUCTANT I HAD BEEN, I HAD GIVEN my word to help, and so poor Dutiful Dexter instantly attacked the problem with all the resourceful cunning of his powerful brain. But the sad truth was that my brain seemed to be off-line; no matter how diligently I typed in clues, nothing dropped into the out-box.

Of course it was possible that I needed more fuel to function at the highest possible level, so I wheedled Deborah into sending down for more Danish. While she was on the phone with room service Chutsky focused a sweaty, slightly glazed smile on me and said, 'Let's get to it, okay, buddy?' Since he asked so nicely – and after all, I had to do something while I waited for the Danish – I agreed.

The loss of his two limbs had removed some kind of psychic lock from Chutsky. In spite of being just a little bit shaky, he was far more open and friendly, and actually seemed eager to share information in a way that would have been unthinkable to the Chutsky with four complete limbs and a pair of expensive sunglasses. And so out of what was really no more than an urge to be tidy and know as many details as possible, I took advantage of his new good cheer by getting the names of the El Salvador team from him.

He sat with a yellow legal pad balanced precariously on his knee, holding it still with his wrist while he scrawled the names with his right, and only, hand. 'Manny Borges you know about,' he said.

'The first victim,' I said.

'Uh-huh,' Chutsky said without looking up. He wrote the name and then drew a line through it. 'And then there was Frank Aubrey?' He frowned and actually stuck the tip of his tongue out of the corner of his mouth as he wrote and then crossed out. 'He missed Oscar Acosta. God knows where he is now.' He wrote the name anyway and put a question mark beside it. 'Wendell Ingraham. Lives on North Shore Drive, out on Miami Beach.' The pad slipped to the floor as he wrote the name, and he grabbed at it as it fell, missing badly. He stared at the pad where it lay for a moment, then leaned over and retrieved it. A drop of sweat rolled off his hairless head and onto the floor. 'Fucking drugs,' he said. 'Got me a little woozy.'

'Wendell Ingraham,' I said.

'Right. Right.' He scribbled the rest of the name and without pausing went on with, 'Andy Lyle. Sells cars now, up in Davie.' And in a furious burst of energy he went right on and triumphantly scrawled the last name. 'Two other guys dead, one guy still in the field, that's it, the whole team.'

'Don't any of these guys know Danco is in town?'

He shook his head. Another drop of sweat flew off and narrowly missed me. 'We're keeping a pretty tight lid on this thing. Need-to-know only.'

'They don't need to know that somebody wants to convert them to squealing pillows?'

'No, they don't,' he said, clamping his jaw and looking like he was going to say something tough again; perhaps he would offer to flush them. But he

273

glanced up at me and thought better of it.

'Can we at least check and see which one is missing?' I asked, without any real hope.

Chutsky started shaking his head before I even finished speaking. Two more drops of sweat flew off, left, right. 'No. Uh-uh, no way. These guys always have an ear to the ground. Somebody starts asking around about them, they'll know. And I can't risk having them run. Like Oscar did.'

'Then how do we find Dr. Danco?'

'That's what you're going to figure out,' he said.

'What about the house by Mount Trashmore?' I asked hopefully. 'The one you checked out with the clipboard.'

'Debbie had a patrol car drive by. Family has moved in. No,' he said, 'we're putting all our chips on you, buddy. You'll think of something.'

Debs rejoined us before I could think of anything meaningful to say to that, but in truth, I was too surprised at Chutsky's official attitude toward his former comrades. Wouldn't it have been the nice thing to do, to give his old friends a running start or at least a heads-up? I certainly don't pretend to be a paragon of civilized virtue, but if a deranged surgeon was after Vince Masuoka, for instance, I like to think I might find a way to drop a hint into casual conversation by the coffee machine. Pass that sugar, please. By the way – there's a medical maniac after you who wants to lop off all your limbs. Would you like the creamer?

But apparently that wasn't the way the game was played by the guys with the big manly chins, or at least not by their representative Kyle Chutsky. No matter; I had a list of names, at least, which was a place to start, although nothing else. I had no idea where to begin turning my starting point into some kind of actual helpful information, and Kyle did not seem to be doing quite as well with creativity as he had done with sharing. Deborah was little help. She was totally wrapped up in fluffing Kyle's pillow, mopping his fevered brow, and making sure he took his pills, a matronly kind of behavior that I would have thought impossible for her, but there it was.

It became apparent that little real work would be accomplished here in the hotel penthouse. The only thing I could suggest was that I return to my computer and see what I could turn up. And so after prying two final Danish out of Kyle's remaining hand I headed for home and my trusty computer. There were no guarantees that I would come up with anything, but I was committed to trying. I would give it my best effort, poke around at the problem for a few hours and hope that someone might wrap a secret message around a rock and throw it through my window. Perhaps if the rock hit me on the head, it would jar loose some kind of idea.

My apartment was just as I'd left it, which was comforting. The bed was even made, since Deborah was no longer in residence. I soon had my computer humming and began to search. I checked the real estate database first, but there were no new purchases that fit the pattern of the others. Still, it was obvious that Dr. Danco had to be somewhere. We had run him out of his prepared hidey-holes and yet I was quite sure that he would not wait to begin on Doakes and whoever else from Chutsky's list might have caught his attention.

How did he decide the order of his victims anyway?

By seniority? By how much they pissed him off? Or was it random? If I knew that, it was at least possible that I could find him. He had to go somewhere, and his operations were not the sort of thing one would do in a hotel room. So where would he go?

It was not a rock crashing through the window and bouncing off my head after all, but a very small idea began to trickle onto the floor of Dexter's brain. Danco had to go somewhere to work on Doakes, obviously, and he couldn't wait to set up another safe house. Wherever he went had to be in the Miami area, close to his victims, and he could not afford to risk all the variables of grabbing a place at random. A seemingly empty house might suddenly be overrun by prospective buyers, and if he snatched an occupied place he could not know when Cousin Enrico might drop in for a visit. So – why not simply use the home of his next victim? He had to believe that Chutsky, the only one who knew the list until now, was out of action for a while and would not pursue him. By moving in on the next name on the list he could amputate two limbs with one scalpel, as it were, by using his next victim's house to finish Doakes and then make a leisurely start on the happy homeowner.

It made a certain amount of sense and was a more definite starting point than the list of names. But even if I was right, which of the men would be next?

The thunder rumbled outside. I looked again at the list of names and sighed. Why wasn't I somewhere else? Even playing hangman with Cody and Astor would be a big improvement over this kind of frustrating drudgery. I had to keep after Cody to find the vowels first. Then the rest of the word would start to swim into focus. And when he mastered that, I could start to teach him other, more interesting things. Very strange to have child instruction to look forward to, but I was actually kind of eager to begin. A shame he had already taken care of the neighbor's dog – it would have been a perfect place to start learning security as well as technique. The little scamp had so much to learn. All the old Harry lessons, passed on to a new generation.

And as I thought of helping Cody along, I realized that the price tag was accepting my engagement to Rita. Could I really go through with it? Fling away my carefree bachelor ways and settle into a life of domestic bliss? Oddly enough, I thought I might be able to pull it off. Certainly the kids were worth a little bit of sacrifice, and making Rita a permanent disguise would actually lower my profile. Happily married men are not as likely to do the kind of thing I live for.

Maybe I could go through with it. We would see. But of course, this was procrastination. It was getting me no closer to my evening out with Reiker, and no closer to finding Danco. I called my scattered senses back and looked at the list of names: Borges and Aubrey done. Acosta, Ingraham, and Lyle still to go. Still unaware that they had an appointment with Dr. Danco. Two down, three more to go, not including Doakes, who must be feeling the blade now, with Tito Puente playing his dance music in the background and the Doctor leaning over with his so-bright scalpel and leading the sergeant through his dance of dismemberment. Dance with me, Doakes. Baila conmigo, amigo, as Tito Puente would put it. A little bit harder to dance with no legs, of course, but well worth the effort.

And in the meantime, here I was dancing in circles just as surely as if the good Doctor had removed one of my legs.

All right: let's assume Dr. Danco was at the house of his current victim, not counting Doakes. Of course, I didn't know who that might be. So where did that leave me? When scientific inquiry was eliminated, that left lucky guess. Elementary, dear Dexter. Eeny meeny miney mo –

My finger landed on the notepad on Ingraham's name. Well then, that was definite, wasn't it? Sure it was. And I was King Olaf of Norway.

I got up and walked to the window where I had so many times peered out at Sergeant Doakes parked across the street in his maroon Taurus. He wasn't there. Soon he wouldn't actually be anywhere unless I found him. He wanted me dead or in prison, and I would be happier if he simply disappeared – one small piece at a time, or all at once, it made no difference. And yet here I was working overtime, pushing Dexter's mighty mental machinery through its awesome paces, in order to rescue him – so he could kill or imprison me. Is it any wonder I find the whole idea of life overrated?

Perhaps stirred by the irony, the almost-perfect moon snickered through the trees. And the longer I stared out, the more I felt the weight of that wicked old moon, sputtering softly just under the horizon and already puffing hot and cold at my spine, urging me into action, until I found myself picking up my car keys and heading for the door. After all, why not just go check it out? It would take no more than an hour, and I wouldn't have to explain my thinking to Debs and Chutsky.

I realized that the idea seemed appealing to me partly because it was quick and easy and if it paid off it would return me to my hard-won liberty in time for tomorrow night's playdate with Reiker – and even more, I was beginning to develop a small hankering for an appetizer. Why not warm up a little on Dr. Danco? Who could fault me for doing unto him what he oh-so-readily did unto others? If I had to save Doakes in order to get Danco, well, no one ever said life was perfect.

And so there I was, headed north on Dixie Highway and then up onto I-95, taking it all the way to the 79th Street Causeway and then straight over to the Normandy Shores area of Miami Beach, where Ingraham lived. It was night by the time I turned down the street and drove slowly past. A dark green van was parked in the driveway, very similar to the white one Danco had crashed only a few days ago. It was parked next to a newish Mercedes, and looked very much out of place in this tony neighborhood. Well, then, I thought. The Dark Passenger began to mutter words of encouragement but I kept going through the bend in the road past the house and on to a vacant lot before I stopped. Just around the corner I pulled over.

The green van did not belong there, judging by the type of neighborhood this was. Of course, it could be that Ingraham was having some plastering work done and the workers had decided to stay until the job was done. But I didn't think so, and neither did the Dark Passenger. I took out my cell phone to call Deborah.

'I may have found something,' I told her when she answered.

'What took you so long?' she said.

'I think Dr. Danco is working out of Ingraham's house on Miami Beach,' I said.

There was a short pause in which I could almost see her frown. 'Why do you think that?'

The idea of explaining to her that my guess was only a guess was not terribly appealing, so I just said, 'It's a long story, Sis. But I think I'm right.'

'You think,' she said. 'But you're not sure.'

'I will be in a few minutes,' I said. 'I'm parked around the corner from the house, and there's a van parked in front that looks a little out of place in this neighborhood.'

'Stay put,' she said. 'I'll call you back.' She hung up and left me looking at the house. It was an awkward angle to watch from and I could not really look without developing a severe knot in my neck. So I turned the car around and faced down the street toward the bend where the house sat sneering at me and as I did – there it was. Poking its bloated head through the trees, guttering bleary beams of light down onto the rancid landscape. That moon, that always laughing lighthouse of a moon. There it was.

I could feel the cold fingers of moonlight poking at me, prodding and teasing and urging me on to some foolish and wonderful something, and it had been so very long since I had listened that the sounds came twice as loud as ever, washing over my head and down my spine and in truth, what harm could it do to be absolutely sure before Deborah called back? Not to do anything stupid, of course, but just to ease out of the car and down the street past the house, just a casual stroll in the moonlight along a quiet street of houses. And if by chance the opportunity arose to play a few small games with the Doctor –

It was mildly upsetting to notice that my breath was slightly shaky as I climbed out of my car. Shame on you, Dexter. Where's that famous icy control? Perhaps it had slipped from being under wraps too long, and perhaps it was just that the same hiatus had made me a little too eager, but this would never do. I took a long, deep breath to steady myself and headed up the street, just a casual monster out for an evening stroll past an impromptu vivisection clinic. Hello, neighbor, beautiful night to remove a leg, isn't it?

With each step closer to the house I felt That Something growing taller and harder inside me, and at the same time the old cold fingers clamping down to hold it in place. I was fire and ice, alive with moonlight and death, and as I came even with the house the whispers inside began to well up as I heard the faint sounds from the house, a chorus of rhythm and saxophones that sounded very much like Tito Puente and I did not need the rising whispers to tell me that I was right, this was indeed the place where the Doctor had set up his clinic.

He was here, and he was at work.

And now, what did I do about that? Of course the wise thing to do would be to stroll back to my car and wait for Deborah's call – but was this really a night for wisdom, with that lyrically sneering moon so low in the sky and ice pouring through my veins and urging me onward?

And so when I had walked on past the house, I slipped into the shadows around the house next door and slid carefully through the backyard until I could see the back of Ingraham's house. There was a very bright light showing in the back window and I stalked into the yard in the shadow of a tree, closer and closer. A few more cat-footed steps and I could almost see in the window. I moved a little closer, just outside the line that light cast on the ground.

From where I now stood I could at last see in the window, upward at a slight angle, inside, to the ceiling of the room. And there was the mirror Danco seemed so fond of using, showing me half the table –

– and slightly more than half of Sergeant Doakes.

He was strapped securely in place, motionless, even his newly shaved head clamped tight to the table. I could not see too many details, but from what I could see, both his hands were gone at the wrist. The hands first? Very interesting, a totally different approach from the one he had used on Chutsky. How did Dr. Danco decide what was right for each individual patient?

I found myself increasingly intrigued by the man and his work; there was a quirky sense of humor in motion here and as silly as it is, I wanted to know just a little bit more about how it worked. I moved half a step closer.

The music paused and I paused with it, and then as the mambo beat picked up again I heard a metallic cough behind me and felt something flick my shoulder, stinging and tingling, and I turned around to see a small man with large, thick glasses looking at me. He was holding in his hand what looked like a paintball gun, and I just had time to feel indignant that it was aimed at me before somebody removed all the bones from my legs and I melted down into the dew-smeared moonlit grass where it was all dark and full of dreams.

CHAPTER 29

I WAS CUTTING HAPPILY AWAY AT A VERY BAD person who I had taped securely and strapped to a table but somehow the knife was made of rubber and only wobbled from side to side. I reached up and grabbed a giant bone saw instead and laid it into the alligator on the table, but the real joy would not come to me and instead there was pain and I saw that I was slicing away at my own arms. My wrists burned and bucked but I could not stop cutting and then I hit an artery and the awful red spewed out everywhere and blinded me with a scarlet mist and then I was falling, falling forever through the darkness of dim empty me where the awful shapes twisted and yammered and pulled at me until I fell through and hit the dreadful red puddle there on the floor beside where two hollow moons glared down at me and demanded: Open your eyes, you are awake –

And it all came back into focus on the two hollow moons that were actually the pair of thick lenses set in large black frames and wedged onto the face of a small, wiry man with a mustache who was bending over me with a syringe in his hand.

Dr. Danco, I presume?

I didn't think I had said it out loud, but he nodded and said, 'Yes, they called me that. And who are you?' His accent was slightly strained, as if he had to think a little too hard about each word. There was a trace of Cuban to it, but not like Spanish was his native tongue. For some reason his voice made me very unhappy, as if it had an odor of Dexter Repellant to it. But deep inside my lizard brain an old dinosaur lifted its head and roared back and so I did not cringe away from him as I had at first wanted to. I tried to shake my head, but found that very hard to do for some reason.

'Don't try to move yet,' he said. 'It won't work. But don't worry, you'll be able to see everything I do to your friend on the table. And soon enough it will be your turn. You can see yourself, then, in the mirror.' He blinked at me, and a light touch of whimsy came into his voice. 'It's a wonderful thing about mirrors. Did you know that if someone is standing outside the house looking into a mirror, you can see them from inside the house?'

He sounded like an elementary-school teacher explaining a joke to a student he was fond of, but who might be too dumb to get it. And I felt just dumb enough for that to make sense, because I had walked right into this with no thought deeper than, *Gee, that's interesting*. My own moon-driven impatience and curiosity had made me careless and he had seen me peeping in. Still, he was gloating, and that was annoying, so I felt compelled to say something, however feeble.

'Why yes, I knew that,' I said. 'And did you know that this house has a front door, too? And no peacocks on guard this time.'

He blinked. 'Should I be alarmed?' he said.

'Well, you never know who might come barging in uninvited.'

Dr. Danco moved the left corner of his mouth upward perhaps a quarter of an inch. 'Well,' he said, 'if your friend on the operating table is a fair sample, I think I may be all right, don't you?' And I had to admit that he had a point. The first-team players had not been impressive; what did he have to fear from the bench? If only I wasn't still a little dopey from whatever drugs he had used on me, I'm quite sure I would have said something far more clever, but in truth I was still in a little bit of a chemical fog.

'I do hope I'm not supposed to believe that help is on the way?' he said.

I was wondering the same thing, but it didn't seem entirely smart to say so. 'Believe what you like,' I said instead, hoping that was ambiguous enough to give him pause, and cursing the slowness of my normally swift mental powers.

'All right then,' he said. 'I believe you came here alone. Although I am curious about why.'

'I wanted to study your technique,' I said.

'Oh, good,' he said. 'I'll be happy to show you – firsthand.' He flickered his tiny little smile at me again and added, 'And then feet.' He waited for a moment, probably to see if I would laugh at his hilarious pun. I felt very sorry to disappoint him, but perhaps later it might seem funnier, if I got out of this alive.

Danco patted my arm and leaned in just a bit. 'We'll have to have your name, you know. No fun without it.'

I pictured him speaking to me by name as I lay strapped to the table, and it was not a cheerful image.

'Will you tell me your name?' he asked.

'Rumplestiltskin,' I said.

He stared at me, his eyes huge behind the thick

lenses. Then he reached down to my hip pocket and worked my wallet out. He flipped it open and found my driver's license. 'Oh. So YOU'RE Dexter. Congratulations on your engagement.' He dropped my wallet beside me and patted my cheek. 'Watch and learn, because all too soon I will be doing the same things to you.'

'How wonderful for you,' I said.

Danco frowned at me. 'You really should be more frightened,' he said. 'Why aren't you?' He pursed his lips. 'Interesting. I'll increase the dosage next time.' And he stood up and moved away.

I lay in a dark corner next to a bucket and a broom and watched him bustle about the kitchen. He made himself a cup of instant Cuban coffee and stirred in a huge amount of sugar. Then he moved back to the center of the room and stared down at the table, sipping thoughtfully.

'Nahma,' the thing on the table that had once been Sergeant Doakes pleaded. 'Nahana. Nahma.' Of course his tongue had been removed – obvious symbology for the person Danco believed had squealed on him.

'Yes, I know,' Dr. Danco said. 'But you haven't guessed a single one yet.' He almost seemed to be smiling as he said that, although his face did not look like it was formed to make any expression beyond thoughtful interest. But it was enough to set Doakes off into a fit of yammering and trying to thrash his way out of his bonds. It didn't work very well, and didn't seem to concern Dr. Danco, who moved away sipping his coffee and humming along off-key to Tito Puente. As Doakes flopped about I could see that his right foot was gone, as well as his hands and tongue. Chutsky had said his entire lower leg had been removed all at once. The Doctor was obviously making this one last a little longer. And when it was my turn – how would he decide what to take and when?

Piece by small dim piece my brain was clearing itself of fog. I wondered how long I had been unconscious. It didn't seem like the kind of thing I could discuss with the Doctor.

The dosage, he had said. He had been holding a syringe as I woke up, been surprised that I was not more frightened – Of course. What a wonderful idea, to inject his patients with some kind of psychotropic drug to increase their sense of helpless terror. I wished I knew how to do that. Why hadn't I gotten medical training? But, of course, it was a little late to worry about that. And in any case, it sounded very much like the dosage was adjusted just right for Doakes.

'Well, Albert,' said the Doctor to the sergeant, in a very pleasant and conversational voice, slurping his coffee, 'what's your guess?'

'Nahana! Nah!'

'I don't think that's right,' said the Doctor. 'Although perhaps if you had a tongue, it might have been. Well, in any case,' he said, and he bent to the edge of the table and made a small mark on a piece of paper, almost like he was crossing something out. 'It is rather a long word,' he said. 'Nine letters. Still, you have to take the good with the bad, don't you?' And he put down his pencil and picked up a saw, and as Doakes bucked wildly against his bonds the Doctor sawed off Doakes's left foot, just above the ankle. He did it very quickly and neatly, placing the severed foot beside Doakes's head as he reached over to his array of instruments and picked up what looked a large soldering iron. He applied this to the new wound and a wet hiss of steam billowed up as he cauterized the stump for minimal blood flow. 'There now,' he said. Doakes made a strangled noise and went limp as the smell of seared flesh drifted through the room. With any luck at all he would be unconscious for a while.

And I, happily, was a little more conscious all the time. As the chemicals from the Doctor's dart gun seeped out of my brain, a sort of muddy light began to trickle in.

Ah, memory. Isn't it a lovely thing? Even when we are in the middle of the worst of times, we have our memories to cheer us. I, for example, lay there helpless, able only to watch as dreadful things happened to Sergeant Doakes, knowing that soon it would be my turn. But even so, I had my memories.

And what I remembered now was something Chutsky had said when I rescued him. 'When he got me up there,' he had said, 'he said, "Seven," and "What's your guess?" ' At the time I had thought it a rather strange thing to say, and wondered if Chutsky had imagined it as a side effect of the drugs.

But I had just heard the Doctor say the same things to Doakes: 'What's your guess?' followed by, 'Nine letters.' And then he had made a mark on the piece of paper taped to the table.

Just as there had been a piece of paper taped near each victim we had found, each time with a single word on it, the letters crossed out one at a time. HONOR. LOYALTY. Irony, of course: Danco reminding his former comrades of the virtues they had forsaken by turning him over to the Cubans. And poor

Burdett, the man from Washington whom we found in the shell of the house in Miami Shores. He had been worth no real mental effort. Just a quick five letters, POGUE. And his arms, legs, and head had been quickly cut off and separated from his body. P-O-G-U-E. Arm, leg, leg, arm, head.

Was it really possible? I knew that my Dark Passenger had a sense of humor, but it was quite a bit darker than this – this was playful, whimsical, and even silly.

Much like the Choose Life license plate had been. And like everything else I had observed about the Doctor's behavior.

It seemed so completely unlikely, but –

Doctor Danco was playing a little game as he sliced and diced. Perhaps he had played it with others in those long years inside the Cuban prison at the Isle of Pines, and maybe it had come to seem like just the right thing to serve his whimsical revenge. Because it certainly seemed like he was playing it now – with Chutsky, and with Doakes and the others. It was quite absurd, but it was also the only thing that made sense.

Doctor Danco was playing hangman.

'Well,' he said, squatting beside me again. 'How do you think your friend is doing?'

'I think you have him stumped,' I said.

He cocked his head to one side and his small, dry tongue flicked out and over his lips as he stared at me, his eyes large and unblinking through his thick glasses. 'Bravo,' he said, and he patted my arm again. 'I don't think you really believe this will happen to you,' he said. 'Perhaps a ten will persuade you.'

'Does it have an E in it?' I asked, and he rocked back

slightly as if some offensive odor had drifted up to him from my socks.

'Well,' he said, still without blinking, and then something that may have been related to a smile twitched at the corner of his mouth. 'Yes, there are two E's. But of course, you guessed out of turn, so . . .' He shrugged, a tiny gesture.

'You could count it as a wrong guess – for Sergeant Doakes,' I suggested, quite helpfully, I thought.

He nodded. 'You don't like him. I see,' he said, and he frowned a little. 'Even so, you really should be more afraid.'

'Afraid of what?' I said. Sheer bravado, of course, but how often does one get a chance to banter with an authentic villain? And the shot seemed to go home; Danco stared at me for a long moment before he finally gave his head a very slight shake.

'Well, Dexter,' he said, 'I can see we're going to have our work cut out for us.' And he gave me his tiny, almost invisible smile. 'Among other things,' he added, and a cheerful black shadow reared up behind him as he spoke, thundering a happy challenge to my Dark Passenger, which slid forward and bellowed back. For a moment we faced off like that, and then he finally blinked, just once, and stood up. He walked back over to the table where Doakes slumbered so peacefully, and I sank back in my homey little corner and wondered what sort of miracle the Great Dexterini might come up with for this, his greatest escape.

Of course, I knew that Deborah and Chutsky were on their way, but I found that more worrisome than anything else. Chutsky would insist on restoring his damaged manhood by charging in on his crutch waving a gun in his only hand, and even if he allowed Deborah to back him up, she was wearing a large cast that made movement difficult. Hardly a rescue team to inspire confidence. No, I had to believe that my little corner of the kitchen was simply going to become crowded, and with all three of us taped and doped there would be no help coming for any of us.

And truthfully, in spite of my brief spatter of heroic dialogue, I was still somewhat woozy from whatever had been in Danco's sleepy dart. So I was doped, tightly bound, and all alone. But there's always some positive to every situation, if you just look hard enough, and after trying to think of one for a moment, I realized that I had to admit that so far I had not been attacked by rabid rats.

Tito Puente swung into a new tune, something a bit softer, and I grew more philosophical. We all have to go sometime. Even so, this would not make my list of top ten preferred ways to perish. Falling asleep and not waking up was number one on my list, and it got rapidly more distasteful after that.

What would I see when I died? I can't really bring myself to believe in the soul, or Heaven and Hell, or any of that solemn nonsense. After all, if human beings have souls, wouldn't I have one, too? And I can assure you, I don't. Being what I am, how could I? Unthinkable. It's hard enough just to be me. To be me with a soul and a conscience and the threat of some kind of afterlife would be impossible.

But to think of wonderful, one-of-a-kind me going away forever and never coming back – very sad. Tragic, really. Perhaps I should consider reincarnation. No control there, of course. I could come back as a dung beetle, or even worse, come back as another monster like me. There was certainly nobody who would grieve over me, especially if Debs went out at the same time. Selfishly, I hoped I would go first. Just get it over with. This whole charade had gone on long enough. Time to end it. Perhaps it was just as well.

Tito started a new song, very romantic, singing something about 'Te amo,' and now that I thought of it, it might very well be that Rita would grieve over me, the idiot. And Cody and Astor, in their damaged way, would surely miss me. Somehow I had been picking up an entire train of emotional attachments lately. How could this keep happening to me? And hadn't I been thinking much the same thoughts far too recently, as I hung upside down underwater in Deborah's flipped car? Why was I spending so much time dying lately, and not getting it right? As I knew only too well, there really wasn't much to it.

I heard Danco rattling around on a tray of tools and turned my head to look. It was still very difficult to move, but it seemed to be getting a little easier and I managed to get him into focus. He had a large syringe in his hand and approached Sergeant Doakes with the instrument held up as if he wanted it to be seen and admired. 'Time to wake up, Albert,' he said cheerfully and jammed the needle into Doakes's arm. For a moment, nothing happened; then Doakes twitched awake and gave out a gratifying series of groans and yammers, and Dr. Danco stood there watching him and enjoying the moment, syringe once again held aloft.

There was a thud of some kind from the front of the house and Danco spun around and grabbed for his paintball gun just as the large and bald form of Kyle Chutsky filled the door to the room. As I had feared, he was leaning on his crutch and holding a gun in what even I could tell was a sweaty and unsteady hand. 'Son of a bitch,' he said, and Dr. Danco shot him with the paintball gun once, twice. Chutsky stared at him, slack-jawed, and Danco lowered his weapon as Chutsky began to slide to the floor.

And right behind Chutsky, invisible until he slumped to the floor, was my dear sister, Deborah, the most beautiful thing I had ever seen, next to the Glock pistol she held in her steady right fist. She did not pause to sweat or call Danco names. She simply tightened down her jaw muscles and fired two quick shots that took Dr. Danco in the middle of the chest and lifted him off his feet to spill backward over the frantically squealing Doakes.

Everything was very quiet and motionless for a long moment, except for the relentless Tito Puente. Then Danco slipped off the table, and Debs knelt beside Chutsky and felt for a pulse. She eased him down to a more comfy position, kissed his forehead, and finally turned to me. 'Dex,' she said. 'Are you all right?'

'I'll be fine, Sis,' I said, feeling somewhat light-headed, 'if you'll just turn off that horrible music.'

She crossed to the battered boom box and yanked the plug from the wall, looking down at Sergeant Doakes in the sudden huge silence and trying not to show too much on her face. 'We'll get you out of here now, Doakes,' she said. 'It's going to be all right.' She put a hand on his shoulder as he blubbered, and then turned suddenly away and came over to me with the tears starting down her face. 'Jesus,' she whispered as she cut me loose. 'Doakes is a mess.'

But as she ripped the last of the tape off my wrists it was hard for me to feel any distress about Doakes, because I was free at last, all the way free, of the tape and the Doctor and doing favors and yes, it looked like I might finally be free of Sergeant Doakes, too.

I stood up, which was not as easy as it sounds. I stretched my poor cramped limbs as Debs pulled out her radio to summon our friends on the Miami Beach police force. I walked over to the operating table. It was a little thing, but my curiosity had gotten the best of me. I reached down and grabbed the piece of paper taped to the edge of the table.

In those familiar, spidery block letters, Danco had written, 'TREACHERY.' Five of the letters were crossed out.

I looked at Doakes. He looked back at me, wide-eyed and broadcasting a hate that he would never be able to speak.

So you see, sometimes there really are happy endings.

EPILOGUE

IT IS A VERY BEAUTIFUL THING TO WATCH THE SUN come up over the water in the stillness of South Florida's subtropical morning. It is far more beautiful when that great yellow full moon hangs so low on the opposite horizon, slowly paling to silver before it slides below the waves of the open ocean and lets the sun take over the sky. And it is even more beautiful still to watch all this out of sight of land, from the deck of a twenty-six-foot cabin cruiser as you stretch the last knots from your neck and arms, tired but fulfilled and oh-so-very happy at last, from a night of work that had waited just a bit too long.

Soon I would step into my own little boat, towing behind us now, and I would throw off the tow line and head back in the direction the moon had gone, motoring sleepily home to a brand-new life as a soon-to-be-married man. And the *Osprey*, the twenty-six-foot borrowed cabin cruiser, would motor slowly in the opposite direction, toward Bimini, out into the Gulf Stream, the great blue bottomless river that runs through the ocean so conveniently near Miami. The *Osprey* would not make it to Bimini, would not even make it across the Gulf Stream. Long before I closed my happy eyes in my little bed, its engines would stall, flooded with water, and then the boat would slowly fill with water, too, rocking sluggishly in the waves before it slid under, down into the endless crystal clear depths of the Gulf Stream.

And perhaps somewhere far below the surface it would finally settle onto the bottom among the rocks and giant fish and sunken ships, and it was whimsically wonderful to think that somewhere nearby was a neatly bound package swaying gently in the current as the crabs nibbled it down to the bones. I had used four anchors on Reiker after wrapping the pieces with rope and chain, and the neat, bloodless bundle with two awful red boots firmly chained to the bottom had sunk quickly out of sight, all of it except one tiny drop of rapidly drying blood on the glass slide in my pocket. The slide would go in the box on my shelf, right behind MacGregor's, and Reiker would feed the crabs and life would at last go on again, with its happy rhythms of pretending and then pouncing.

And a few years from now I would bring Cody along and show him all the wonders that unfold in a Night of the Knife. He was far too young now, but he would start small, learn to plan, and move slowly upward. Harry had taught me that, and now I would teach it to Cody. And someday, perhaps he would follow in my shadowy footsteps and become a new Dark Avenger, carrying the Harry Plan forward against a new generation of monsters. Life, as I said, goes on.

I sighed, happy and content and ready for all of it. So beautiful. The moon was gone now and the sun had begun to burn away the cool of the morning. It was time to go home.

I stepped into my own boat, started the engine, and cast off the tow line. Then I turned my boat around and followed the moon home to bed.